She switched off the bedside lamp and tried to turn off her brain.

Her cell chirped.

For a long time she lay there, warring with herself about checking it.

Another persistent chirp.

Damn it. She rolled over and snatched up her phone, yanking it loose from the charger.

New text message.

She put on her glasses, slid her fingertip across the screen, and the text message appeared: Private number.

It was him.

Good night, Agent Harris.

Jess bolted to a sitting position. How could he know to send that message at this exact moment?

The drapes were pulled. Her car was in the garage.

Another chirp. Then another.

Five pretty girls.

I hope you'll be able to help those girls better than you did the last ones…

Praise for Debra Webb and OBSESSION

"Compelling main characters and chilling villains elevate Debra Webb's Faces of Evil series into the realm of high-intensity thrillers that readers won't be able to resist."

—CJ Lyons, *New York Times* bestselling author

"Just when you think Debra Webb can't get any better, she does. OBSESSION is her best work yet. This gritty, edge-of-your-seat, white-knuckle thriller is peopled with tough, credible characters and a brilliant plot that will keep you guessing until the very end. Move over Jack Reacher—Jess Harris is comin' to town."

—Cindy Gerard, *New York Times* bestselling author

"Debra Webb has done it again with OBSESSION—which may well be her best book yet—a top-notch thriller that will keep you riveted to the page and wanting more. Webb is a writer's writer, who delivers the kinds of books we all wish we had written."

—Robert Gregory Browne, author of *Trial Junkies*

"With her extraordinary thriller, OBSESSION, Debra Webb joins the ranks of Stephen King (*Misery*) and Thomas Harris (*The Silence of the Lambs*). This gifted author turns the search for missing persons into a novel that is chilling, unusual, and impossible to put down."

—Peggy Webb, author of *The Tender Mercy of Roses* (as Anna Michaels)

"OBSESSION is certain to please Debra Webb's existing fans and gain her a legion of new ones. An engaging, edgy thriller that's a one-sit read—with the lights on!"

—Vicki Hinze, author of *Beyond the Misty Shore*

"Breathtaking romantic suspense that grabs the reader from the beginning and doesn't let up. Riveting."

—Allison Brennan, *New York Times* bestselling author

"Webb keeps the suspense teasingly taut, dropping clues and red herrings one after another on her way to a chilling conclusion."

—*Publishers Weekly*

"Bestselling author Debra Webb intrigues and tantalizes her readers from the first word."

—SingleTitles.com

"Masterful edge-of-your seat suspense."

—ARomanceReview.com

"Romantic suspense at its best!"

—Erica Spindler, *New York Times* bestselling author

"Fast-paced, action-packed suspense, the way romantic suspense is supposed to be. Webb crafts a tight plot, a kick-butt heroine, a sexy hero with a past and a mystery as dark as the black water at night."

—*RT Book Reviews*

Also by Debra Webb

The Faces of Evil Series

Impulse

Power

OBSESSION

FACES OF EVIL

DEBRA WEBB

FOREVER

NEW YORK BOSTON

Forever
Hachette Book Group
237 Park Avenue
New York, NY 10017

www.HachetteBookGroup.com

Printed in the United States of America

First Edition: March 2013
10 9 8 7 6 5 4 3 2 1
OPM

Forever is an imprint of Grand Central Publishing.

Acknowledgments

A special thank you to Dr. Michael Stone, forensics psychiatrist and author, whose research and analysis of evil inspired me to focus more closely on motive and the real person behind the evil when creating the villains in this series.

A huge thank you to true friends and talented authors Regan Black, Cindy Gerard, Vicki Hinze, CJ Lyons, Toni Magee-Causey, Peggy Webb, and Robert Browne. You gave me the strength and the courage to persevere.

The face of "evil" is always the face of total need.

—William S. Burroughs II

OBSESSION

Birmingham, Alabama
Wednesday, July 14, 1:03 p.m.

Special Agent Jess Harris's career was in the toilet along with the breakfast she'd wolfed down and then lost in a truck stop bathroom the other side of Nashville.

God, this wasn't supposed to happen.

Jess couldn't breathe. She told herself to either get out of thc car or power down a window, but her body refused to obey a single, simple command.

The scorching ninety-five degrees baking the city's asphalt and concrete had invaded the interior of the car about two seconds after she parked and shut off the engine. That appeared to be of little consequence to whatever reason she still possessed considering that ten minutes later her fingers were still locked around the steering wheel as if the final hours of her two-day drive had triggered the onset of rigor mortis.

She was *home*. Two weeks' worth of long overdue

leave was at her disposal. Her mail was on hold at the post office back in Stafford, Virginia, where absolutely no one would miss her. Still, she hesitated in taking the next step. Changing her mind and driving away was out of the question no matter how desperately she wanted to do exactly that.

Her word was all she had left at this point. The sheer enormity of her current circumstances should have her laughing hysterically but the muscles of her throat had constricted in equal parts disbelief and terror.

Screw this up and there's nothing left.

With a deep breath for courage, she relaxed her death grip, grabbed her bag, and climbed out. A horn honked a warning and she flattened against the dusty fender of her decade-old Audi. Cars and trucks whizzed by, determined to make the Eighteenth Street and First Avenue intersection before the traffic light changed. Exhaust fumes lingered in the humid air, mingling with the heat and the noise of downtown.

She barely recognized the heart of Birmingham. Renovated shops from a bygone era and newer, gleaming buildings stood side by side, their facades softened by carefully placed trees and shrubbery. An elegant park complete with a spectacular fountain welcomed strolling shoppers and relaxing picnickers. Great strides had been taken to transform the gritty streets of the city once recognized as the infamous center of the civil rights movement to a genteel version of a proud Southern town.

What the hell was she doing here?

For twenty-two years she had worked harder than a prized pupil of Henry Higgins himself to alter her speech patterns and to swipe the last damned trace of the South from her voice. A master's degree in psychology from Boston College and seventeen years of relentless dedication to build an admirable career distinguished her résumé.

And for what? To come running back with her tail tucked between her legs and her head hanging low enough to the ground to smell the ugly truth.

Nothing had changed.

All the spritzing fountains and meticulously manicured storefronts couldn't hide the fact that this was still Birmingham—the place she'd put in her rearview mirror at eighteen—and the four-hundred-dollar red suit and matching high heels she wore would not conceal her plunge from grace.

He had called and she had promised to come and have a look at his case. It was the first time he'd asked her for anything since they parted ways after college. That he extended any sort of invitation astonished her and provided a much needed self-esteem boost. No one from her hometown had a clue about her current career debacle or the disaster zone that was her personal life. If she had her way, they would never know. The million-dollar question, however, remained: What did she do after this?

The wind from a passing car flapped her skirt around her legs, reminding her that this curbside parking slot was not exactly the place to conduct a cerebral overview of *This Is Your Life*.

Game face in place, her shoulders squared with determination, she strode to the Birmingham Police Department's main entrance. Another bout of hesitation slowed her but she kicked it aside, opened the door, and presented a smile for the security guard. "Good morning."

"Good morning to you, too, ma'am," said the guard, Elroy Carter according to the name tag pinned to his shirt. "I'll need your ID. You can place your bag here." He indicated the table next to him.

Jess handed over her official credentials and placed her bag as directed for inspection. Since she'd stopped bothering with earrings years ago and the gold band she still wore for reasons that continued to escape her didn't set off any alarms except in her head, she walked through the metal detector and waited on the other side for her bag.

"Enjoy your visit to the Magic City, Agent Harris." Another broad smile brightened the big man's face.

Probably retired Birmingham PD, undeniably Southern through and through. He obviously took pride in his work, past and present, and likely carried a wallet full of photos of his grandchildren. The only trait that wouldn't be readily discernible by way of a passing inspection was whether he was an Auburn or an Alabama fan. By September that, too, would be as clear as the rich color of his brown eyes. In Alabama, college football season turned even the closest of friends into fierce rivals.

"Thank you, Mr. Carter."

Extending a please, welcome, and thank you remained a stalwart Southern tradition. On the etiquette scale, the idea of passing a stranger without at least smiling ranked right below blasphemy. Keeping up with your neighbor's or coworker's business wasn't viewed as meddling. Not at all. It was the right thing to do. Concern was, of course, the motive.

Jess would give it twenty-four hours max before speculation about her business became the subject of watercooler talk. Then the sympathetic glances would begin.

Along with the reassuring smiles and the total pretense that everything was fine.

Fine. Fine. Fine.

As much as she wanted to avoid her dirty laundry being aired, the odds of complete circumvention fell along the lines of being hit by falling satellite debris twice in the same day. Once the news hit the AP there would be no stopping or even slowing the media frenzy.

Her life was a mess. She doubted any aspect of her existence would ever be *fine* again. But that was irrelevant at the moment. She was here to advise on a case—one that wouldn't wait for her to gather up the pieces of her life or for her to lick her wounds.

Jess set those worries aside, steeled herself, and headed for the bank of elevators that would take her to the fourth floor. *To him.*

None of the faces she encountered looked familiar. Not the guard who'd processed her in or either of his colleagues monitoring the lobby and not the woman who joined her in the elevator car to make the trip to Birmingham Police Department's administrative offices.

Once the doors glided closed, the woman attempted a covert inspection, taking note of Jess's Mary Jane pumps with their four-inch heels, the swath of skin separating the hem of her pencil skirt from the tops of her knees and the leather bag that had been her gift to herself on her fortieth birthday. When eye contact inevitably happened, a faint smile flashed, a superficial pleasantry intended to disguise the sizing-up of competition. *If she only knew.*

The car bumped to a stop. The other woman exited first and strolled down the long corridor on the right. Jess's destination waited straight ahead. The office of the chief of police. At the door she conducted a final inventory of her appearance in the glass, straightened her belted jacket, and plucked a blond hair from her lapel. She looked . . . the same. Didn't she? Her hand fell to her side.

Did she look like a failure? Like the woman who had just provided a heinous killer with a get-out-of-jail-free card and who'd lost her husband to geography?

Deep breath. She reached for the door sporting the name Daniel T. Burnett and passed the point of no return.

"Good afternoon, Agent Harris." The young woman, Tara Morgan according to the nameplate on her desk, smiled. "Welcome to Birmingham."

Since Jess hadn't introduced herself, she assumed that the chief had ensured his office personnel, certainly his receptionist, would recognize his anticipated visitor. "Thank you. I'm here to see Chief Burnett."

"Yes, ma'am. If you'd like to have a seat, I'll let the chief know you've arrived."

At last, Tara politely left off. Jess was late by twelve minutes, most of which had been spent fortifying her resolve and gathering her composure to face the final buffeting winds of the emotional hurricane that had descended upon her life. The receptionist offered water or a soft drink. Jess declined. Getting anything, even water, past the massive lump lodged firmly in her throat was unlikely. Keeping it down, an unmitigated no-go.

Jess used the intervening time to evaluate the changes Birmingham's newest chief had made since taking over the office of top cop. From the marble-floored entry to the classic beige carpet and walls, the tranquil lobby looked less like the anteroom to the chief of police and more like the waiting area of a prestigious surgeon's office. Though she hadn't been in this office since career day back in high school, the decorating and furnishings were far too fresh to have seen more than a couple of years' wear.

Law enforcement and political journals rested in a crisp stack atop the table flanked by two plush, upholstered chairs. The fabric resembled a European tapestry and carried the distinct flavor of his mother's taste. It wasn't enough she'd influenced the decorating scheme of the palatial homes belonging to select members of Birmingham's elite simply by hosting a grand soiree and inviting the city's who's who list. Katherine Burnett set the gold standard for keeping up with the Joneses.

Jess wondered if the fine citizens of Birmingham approved of such wasteful use of their tax dollars. Knowing Katherine, she had paid for the renovation herself and spelled it all out on the front page of the Lifestyle section of the *Birmingham News*.

Just another example of how nothing changed around here. Ever. Jess deposited her bag on a chair and stretched her travel-cramped muscles. Eight grueling hours on the road on Tuesday and four this morning had taken its toll. She was exhausted. A flight would have provided far more efficient transportation, but she preferred to have her car while she was here. Made the potential for escape much more feasible.

Actually she'd needed time to think.

"You made it."

Whether it was the sound of his voice or the idea that he looked better now, in spite of current circumstances, than he had on Christmas Eve ten years ago, she suddenly felt very fragile and unquestionably old. His dark hair was still thick without even a hint of gray. The elegant navy suit he wore brought out the blue in his eyes. But it was his face, leaner than before but no less handsome, that conveyed the most damage to her brittle psyche.

The weight of the past seventy-two hours crashed down on her in one big knee-weakening wallop. The floor shifted beneath her feet and the urge to run into his strong arms or to simply burst into tears made a fleeting but powerful appearance.

But she wasn't that kid anymore. And they...they were little more than strangers.

She managed a stiff nod. "I did."

Funny how they both avoided calling each other by name. Not funny at all was the idea that five seconds in his presence had the two little words she'd uttered sounding as Southern as the day she'd hit the road after high school graduation.

She cleared her throat. "And I'm ready to get to work. First, I'd like some time to review the files."

"Of course." He offered his hand, then drew it back and gestured awkwardly as if belatedly realizing that touching was not a good idea. "Shall we go to my office?"

"Absolutely." She draped her bag over her shoulder and moved toward him, each step a supreme test of her self-control. Things that hadn't been said and should have battled with the numerous other troubles clashing in her head for priority. *This wasn't the time.*

"Coming all this way to help us figure this out means a great deal to me."

Still skirting her name. Jess pushed aside the confusion or frustration, maybe both, and the weariness and matched his stride as he led the way. "I can't make any promises but I'll do what I can."

He hadn't given her many details over the phone; that he had called at all was proof enough of the gravity of the situation.

He introduced her to his personal secretary, then ushered her into his office and closed the door. Like the lobby, his spacious office smacked of Katherine's touch. Jess placed her bag on the floor next to a chair at the small conference table and surveyed the four case files waiting in grim formation for her inspection. Clipped to the front of each jacket was a photo of a missing girl.

This was why she had come all this way. However much his call gratified her ego, piecing together this puzzle was her ultimate goal. She leaned forward to study the attractive faces. Four young women in the space of two and a half weeks had disappeared, the latest just three days ago. No common threads other than age, no suggestion of foul play, not a hint of evidence left behind. Macy York, Callie Fanning, Reanne Parsons, and Andrea Denton had simply vanished.

"These two are Jefferson County residents." He tapped the first and second photos; Macy and Callie were both blondes. "This one's Tuscaloosa." Reanne, a redhead. "The latest is from Mountain Brook, my jurisdiction." The fourth girl, Andrea, was a brunette and his attention idled there an extra moment or two.

Jess lowered herself into a chair. She opened the files, one by one, and reviewed the meager contents. Interviews with family and friends. Photos and reports from the scenes. All but one of the missing, Reanne, were college students.

"No contact with the families? No sightings?"

She looked up, the need to assess his facial expressions

as he answered a force of habit. His full attention rested on the files for a time before settling on her. The weight of the public service position he held had scored lines at the corners of his eyes and mouth. Lines that hadn't been there ten years ago. Funny how those same sorts of lines just made her look old, but on him they lent an air of distinction.

He shook his head in response to her question.

"No credit card or cell phone trails?" she went on. "No good-bye or suicide notes? No ransom demands?"

"Nothing."

With a fluidity and ease that spoke of confidence as well as physical strength and fitness, he propped one hip on the edge of the table and studied her, those familiar blue eyes searching hers as blatantly as she had assessed his seconds ago. "Sheriff Roy Griggs—you may remember him—and Chief Bruce Patterson in Tuscaloosa are doing all they can, but there's nowhere to go. The bureau won't budge on the issue of age of consent. All four of these girls are nineteen or older, and with the lack of evidence to indicate foul play there's nothing to investigate, in their opinion. File the report, add the photos to the various databases, and wait. That's what they can do."

According to the law, the bureau was correct. Unless there was evidence of foul play or vulnerability to a crime, there was no action the bureau or any law enforcement agency could take. He knew this but his cop instincts or his emotions, she hadn't concluded which yet, wouldn't let it go at that. And she did remember Griggs. He had served as Jefferson County sheriff for the past three decades.

"But you think there's a connection that suggests this is not only criminal but perhaps serial." This wasn't a question. He'd told her as much on the phone, but she needed to hear his conclusion again and to see what his face and eyes had to show about his words.

His call, just hearing his voice, had resurrected memories and feelings she'd thought long dead and buried. They hadn't spoken since the summer after college graduation until ten years ago when they bumped into each other at the Publix in Hoover. Of all the grocery stores in the Birmingham area how they'd ended up at the same one on the first holiday she'd spent with her family in years still befuddled her. He had been newly divorced from his second wife. Jess had been celebrating a promotion. A volatile combination when merged with the holiday mania and the nostalgia of their explosive history. The last-minute dessert she had hoped to grab at the market before dinner with her sister's family had never made it to the table.

Jess hadn't heard from him since. Not that she could fault his after-frantic-sex lack of propriety; she'd made no attempt at contact either. There had been no random shopping ventures since on her rare visits to Birmingham.

"There has to be a connection." He surveyed the happy, carefree faces in the photos again. "Same age group. All attractive. Smart. No records, criminal or otherwise. Their entire futures—bright futures—ahead of them. And no one in their circle of family or friends saw a disappearing act coming." He tapped the fourth girl's photo. "I know Andrea Denton personally. There's no way she would just vanish like this. No way."

Two things registered distinctly as he made this passionate declaration. One, he wasn't wearing a wedding band. Two, he didn't just know number four personally. He knew her intimately on some level.

"Someone took her," he insisted. "Someone took them all." His expression softened a fraction. "I know your profiling reputation. If anyone can help us find these girls, it's you."

A genuine smile tugged at the frown Jess had been wearing most waking hours for days now. She had absolutely nothing to smile about but somehow the compliment coming from him roused the reaction. "That might be a bit of a stretch, Chief." Sitting here with him staring down at her so intently felt entirely too familiar . . . too personal. She stood, leveling the playing field. "And even the best can't create something out of nothing and, unfortunately, that's exactly what you appear to have so far."

"All I'm asking is that you try. These girls," he gestured to the files, "deserve whatever we can do."

He'd get no argument from her there. "You know the statistics." If they had in fact been abducted, the chances of finding one or more alive at this stage were minimal at best. The only good thing she could see was that they didn't have a body. *Yet.*

"I do." He dipped his head in a weary, somber move, emphasizing the grave tone of his voice.

Eventually she would learn the part he was leaving out. No one wanted to admit there was nothing to be done when anyone went missing, particularly a child or young adult. But this urgency and unwavering insistence that foul play was involved went beyond basic human compassion and the desire to get the job done. She could feel his anxiety and worry vibrating with escalating intensity.

"Will your counterparts cooperate?" Kicking a hornet's nest when it came to jurisdiction would compound her already complicated situation. That she could do without. Once the news hit the public domain, there would be trouble enough.

"They'll cooperate. You have my word."

Jess had known Daniel Burnett her whole life. He believed there was more here than met the eye in these seemingly random disappearances. Unless emotion was somehow slanting his assessment, his instincts rarely missed the mark. More than twenty years ago he had known she was going to part ways with him well before she had recognized that unexpected path herself, and he had known she was his for the taking that cold, blustery evening in that damned Publix. She would lay odds on his instincts every time.

She just hadn't ever been able to count on him when it came to choosing her over his own personal and career goals. As ancient as that history was, the hole it left in her heart had never completely healed. Even knowing that hard truth, she held her breath, waiting for what came next.

"I need your help, Jess."

Jess. The smooth, deep nuances of his voice whispered over her skin and just like that it was ten years ago all over again.

Only this time, she would make certain they didn't end up in bed together.

2

Andrea Denton squeezed her eyes shut and tried to fight the effects of the drug. She didn't know what the white pill she'd been forced to swallow was but she knew it was bad. The other girls were like zombies. Andrea would be too if she didn't fight harder. She couldn't let that happen.

Stumbling and staggering like a drunk person, she paced back and forth in the darkness. The other two girls huddled in the corner, too afraid to move.

Andrea's stomach churned with the urge to puke again but she held it back. She'd eaten handful after handful of dirt, clawing it from the packed floor and shoving it into her mouth. She'd lost count of the number. Maybe it was stupid and she'd probably swallowed rat poop and no telling what else, but whenever any of her friends got this messed up they ate everything in sight and danced or walked or jumped around to try and wear off the effects of the alcohol or the drugs they'd partied with.

Doing something was better than doing nothing.

She kept walking. Once or twice she bumped into

the metal bunk beds. The beds were shoved against the back wall. The springs stretched and creaked whenever they were forced to lie down. That and the oatmeal were her only ways to measure time. Oatmeal before bedtime. Bedtime being at night made sense. Then oatmeal again when they were roused from bed, in the morning she assumed. Her brain hurt when she tried to remember how long she'd been here. Three plastic bowls of soggy, unsweetened oatmeal.

Looking for a way to escape, she had felt her way around the whole room. She'd almost had a heart attack when a rat ran over her hands. She shuddered. But she'd kept searching. There was a door but it was steel and there was no knob or lock on this side. A case of bottled water—she'd chugged as much as she could stand—sat in one corner, and a stinky pot with a lid for a toilet was in the other.

After her first day she'd had to use it. When she lifted the lid, a stench had hit her in the face and made her puke. She tried not to use it until she couldn't hold it anymore. The walls were mostly dirt and brick. Except for where the door was. That wall felt different. Wood or something. Smelled like a basement to her. Like the one in her great-uncle's house. He'd always told Andrea it was haunted to make sure she didn't sneak down there. Eventually she had and she'd discovered his nasty magazines and stash of weed. Creepy old bastard.

When those bad people brought her here, the bag over her head had prevented her from seeing anything. Maybe this was a cave, but she didn't think so. A cave would have stone floors. Probably. This place smelled like a basement.

As strong as the musty, damp odor in the air was, it

didn't cover up the smell of human waste where some of the others had peed their pants or worse. Andrea figured the effects of the drug and the fear caused them not to be able to make it to the pot. That happened sometimes to people when they died too. She shuddered. Didn't want to think about dying.

Where was she? Why had these crazy people taken her and the others? For money? The trembling started again, first in her legs, then in her arms.

Maybe they were planning something really bad. Like in the movies when they tortured their victims or cut them into pieces.

She had to get out of here.

Walk. Just walk. *You'll figure something out.* Her mother would be upset. Maybe her dad, too. And Dan. Tears burned her eyes as Andrea hugged herself. He had warned her about stuff like this. And she'd listened. She was smart. Always watchful. She never drank too much like some of her friends.

But she hadn't expected the evil Dan had warned her about to come in the form of a nice lady who clipped coupons. Andrea had seen her plenty of times at the super Walmart nearest her house. She carried one of those ridiculously massive binders with coupons stuffed into the pockets of the plastic pages inside. She had told Andrea about taking the coupons from the newspapers others tossed away. Stupidly, Andrea had suggested she check the recycle bins in neighborhoods like her own.

After that, every week on recycle day Andrea had been giving the woman whatever coupons had been jammed into the Wednesday and Sunday papers. They even laughed about that crazy coupon reality show. A bitter taste welled in her throat. She shouldn't have trusted a stranger, even one who looked like she could be anyone's mother.

A thump overhead made her freeze. Her heart thudded hard. Were they coming back?

Andrea couldn't breathe...couldn't think. The silence screamed in her ears as she listened harder than she had ever listened in her life. Her heart pounded faster and faster, made her chest ache.

Please don't let them come back!

Last time they had taken a girl. Andrea tried to remember her name. Mason or Macy. She'd been gone for what felt like hours.

Even though Andrea couldn't see shit, she lifted her gaze to the ceiling. She hadn't heard any shouting or crying from up there. Maybe they wouldn't hurt the other girl. Maybe this was a mistake...a joke. Some crazy sorority prank. If some of those crazy bitches had set this up Andrea would beat their effing asses.

Another *thwack* overhead made her jump. The girls huddled in the corner started to moan and sob. Their misery grew louder and louder with every shuddering breath that filled their lungs.

"Be quiet!" Andrea whispered. "They'll hear you!"

But the girls didn't stop. She put her hands over her ears to block the sounds. She didn't want to hear them. She didn't want to be here. This wasn't supposed to happen to a girl as smart and careful as her.

A door slammed.

The moans and sobs hushed as if a switch had been flipped.

Heavy footfalls echoed in the darkness.

They were coming!

Adrenaline fired through Andrea's veins, clearing the fog from her brain but doing nothing for her frozen limbs.

Run! There was nowhere to run.

Hide! There was nowhere to hide.

Fight! She was too weak to fight.

Warm pee trickled down her thighs.

Jefferson County Sheriff's Department, 5:00 p.m.

Dan watched as Jess placed the photos on the case board, then sketched a timeline. Beneath each photo she wrote the relevant information. Name. Address. The names of family and close friends. Then the date, time, and location of disappearance.

Exhaustion tugged at his ability to concentrate. The past three days he'd worked night and day and he had nothing to show for it.

He stared at the photos and another wave of regret and urgency washed over him. How could his and two other departments have slogged through every aspect of these girls' lives and have nothing?

Jess faced the group assembled at the conference table and adjusted her glasses.

When had she started wearing glasses? He squeezed his eyes shut for a moment and fought the wave of melancholy. The idea that she was really here still amazed him.

Startled him on some level. He'd fully expected her to flat-out refuse his request. But she hadn't done that. She'd dropped everything and come to his rescue.

After that night ten years ago—the memory was permanently seared into his brain—he wouldn't have blamed her for turning him down.

For nearly two decades he'd kept up with her career. Jessie Harris had climbed the ranks at the bureau like a fire scaling a mountainside in the driest part of August. According to his liaison at the local bureau office, she was one of the sharpest profilers on staff at Quantico. She possessed an innate ability to nail an unknown subject's motive with uncanny accuracy.

He'd stopped asking about her a couple of years ago. Hell, it was way past time he'd gotten on with his life. Two doomed marriages were two too many. He'd met Annette and decided it was time to move on and start a real family.

Only that hadn't happened. Annette had gone back to her ex and that was that. He caught himself before he shook his head. This case was far too important for distraction. Escape, he realized. His mind needed the escape. As tempting as it was, that was a luxury he couldn't afford.

"Gentlemen," Jess said, drawing his attention back to her. She paused. "And Detective Wells," she added with a quick nod to the one female member on this task force besides herself. "I've provided my preliminary profile for your review. It's on the table." She gestured to the neat stack of stapled documents in the center of the conference table.

Each cover sheet carried the BPD logo, not the bureau's. Made sense. Jess was here in an unofficial capacity. Dan wondered how her husband felt about her rushing to the aid of her former lover. The wedding band she wore was simple, not a piece of jewelry that would draw the eye. Yet he had spotted that delicate gold band the instant he saw her standing in his waiting room.

Focus, Dan.

The stack was passed around, the final copy of her profile landing in his hands. He flipped over the cover sheet and stopped. Turned another page and then another. Each was the same. "The pages are blank." What the devil was she doing?

Patterson, Griggs, and the two detectives, like Dan, stared from the unmarked white pages to the woman standing before them.

She waited, hands on hips, until the muttered remarks had ceased. Then she gestured to the packets they held and announced, "This is the profile I developed based on the findings you've provided."

Dan opened his mouth to demand an explanation but she silenced him with an uplifted palm.

"If you"—she sent an accusing look at him—"called me down here to do your job for you, then you've vastly overestimated your charm and my patience."

"What in blazes is the meaning of this?" Griggs demanded.

Roy Griggs had done police work too long to be yanked around by anyone, Quantico's hotshot profiler included. Dan couldn't believe Jess would pull a stunt like this without some point she felt genuinely compelled to make. There had to be a point. *And it better be good.*

Jess acknowledged the senior cop, in terms of service, with a nod. "If you'll give me about two minutes, I'll gladly tell you."

Dan relaxed. His lips twitched with the urge to smile. There wasn't a damned thing humorous about this case. It was her. He'd almost forgotten how she loved to get under the skin of authority—any authority. More than two decades in the Northeast hadn't changed her much. Her manner of dress was more sophisticated but beneath that stylish veneer she was still the same old Jess, he would wager. When the lady had a point to make, she intended for the room to listen. Didn't matter who was in the room.

"There are two potential explanations for the disappearance of these young women." She directed everyone's attention to the photos on the board. "One is"—she crossed her arms over her chest and stared straight at her attentive, however annoyed, audience—"that they left of their own accord and they don't want to be found. They're certainly all of the legal age to make that decision and the only cause to consider vulnerability in these disappearances is the statements of the families who say the actions are out of character. Frankly, their statements are of little consequence, in my opinion. After all, what parent is going to say otherwise?"

"Not possible," Chief Patterson objected. "We've been through that scenario already and it's off the table, Agent Harris." He sent a livid glare in Dan's direction. "I don't know why you're behind the curve here, but I know the Parsons family nearly as well as I know my own."

"Macy and Callie are honor students," Griggs added his two cents. "They're good, smart girls. They wouldn't do this to themselves or to their families."

"I suppose you also know those families nearly as well as you know your own," Jess suggested. "Like Chief Patterson knows the Parsons."

The tension thickened, forcing the air out of the room. Any inkling of humor he'd felt at her tactics evaporated. Sweat lined Dan's brow. Jess needed to get to the point. If her intention was to piss off everyone at the table first, she was well on her way.

"Damn straight I do," Griggs mouthed off.

"Burnett?" Patterson demanded. "What kind of dog-and-pony show is this?"

"Jess, maybe—"

Her hand went up to silence Dan a second time. "All right then," she said calmly. "Let's explore the other possibility."

Dan gritted his teeth to keep his mouth shut. Her pointed censure had signed him up for that same PO'd club his colleagues had already joined. She was the only one still calm and wherever she was going with this presentation remained frustratingly unclear. These people—*he*—needed help. Not a block of instruction in identifying intent or motive.

"It appears we all agree that there is only one feasible explanation. These girls"—she indicated the photos again—"were taken against their will by someone who means them harm, since there have been no ransom demands. We could be looking at a human trafficking ring, a sexual predator, or just a plain old psychopath."

A quiet, heavy with agony, coagulated in the air, making a decent breath impossible.

"If that is, indeed, the case," Jess continued, "you"—she pointed to Griggs—"you"—then Patterson—"and you"—her attention rested finally on Dan—"are missing relevant details in your investigations."

Disgruntled glances were exchanged but no one

argued. She was right. It was difficult to argue with that. Guilt added another layer to the burden already straddling Dan's shoulders and knotting in his gut.

"Every single one of you has been in this game long enough to understand the one fact that makes all the difference in this case and all others." She paused, made eye contact with each member of the task force. "When a person commits an act against another person, violent or otherwise, that act is always driven by motive. Always. Whether the act was impulse or calculated, a motive exists. There are no exceptions. Whoever took these girls, whether one unknown subject or four, had a motive."

Jess moved to the table and leaned down to flatten her palms on the shiny, manufactured-wood surface. "We have to find that motive. Otherwise we won't be looking for four young women." She pointed to the photos on the board. "We'll be looking for four bodies."

That heavy silence continued to reign for one, two, three more beats.

"Did you come all this way just to tell us what we don't know, *Special* Agent Harris?" Griggs spoke up, breaking the spell she had cast. "Or are we going to talk about what we do know?"

Jess straightened, eyed him with blatant skepticism. "I read the interviews with family and friends. I studied the photos of the homes and the places where the girls were last seen. Pardon my frankness, Sheriff Griggs, but what you do know is irrelevant to this case, as far as I can see. It's all that you don't know that makes the difference."

Face beet red, cheeks puffed with outrage, Griggs visibly braced for retaliation but Jess beat him to the punch. "These girls didn't vanish without someone somewhere seeing or hearing something. It may be the smallest detail. So small that it seems insignificant to the person who knows it. So commonplace, it goes unnoticed. But it's there and we need to find it. If all four of these girls were taken by the same unsub, then there's a connection we've missed. This one seemingly insignificant thing they have in common could be the key we need for a break in this case."

"Agent Harris," Detective Wells said, "we haven't found even one person these girls have in common. Not a friend or minister or employer. Nothing." Wells shook her head. "None of the associates or intimates has a record or history of trouble or violence. If we're looking for a serial perpetrator, wouldn't there be some of those details you're talking about in his background? Some suggestion of unacceptable or questionable behavior?"

Wells made detective last year and she had quickly shown she was one of the best Birmingham PD employed. Despite twenty years in law enforcement, Dan found himself on the edge of his seat in anticipation of Jess's answer to the detective's provocative query.

"Study your serial offenders, Detective. Whether they're killers or rapists or plain old Peeping Toms, the experts often disagree as to whether they were born that way or evolved as a result of environmental factors. But the one thing those same experts all agree on is that these offenders have a single trait in common. Not one was a serial anything until he committed that first act. As far as evil goes"—she shrugged one shoulder—"I've spent a dozen years studying the subject and there's one thing *I* know for sure." Her expression grew distant, breakable somehow. She blinked and seemed to push whatever had distracted her aside. "If you want to know what evil looks like, look in the mirror."

She leaned down, flattened her hands on the table once more, and went face-to-face with Wells. "Any one of us is capable of evil, Detective. We all have a line. It's not crossing it that separates us from the Ed Geins and Charles Mansons of the world."

"With all due respect, Agent Harris," Patterson piped up.

Jess drew to her full height, squared her shoulders, and turned to him.

"I'm sure we all appreciate the lecture on motive and overlooked details, but I, for one, would like to get to the part where we do something besides talk about what we don't have and don't know."

"You read my mind, Chief Patterson." Jess strode back to the board and directed their attention to the information she'd posted there. "We go back to the source. To the people who know these girls best. Their family and friends. And we find what we're missing. We don't stop until we do."

"What about involving the media?" Griggs ventured. "The girls' photos have been running on all the local channels and in the papers. It's time we stepped up that venue, wouldn't you say?"

Dan bit back the acid response he wanted to give to that one. With the families' pleas for help, the thousands of fliers distributed, and the news updates there had been near continuous coverage in the media and the community. Obviously, this unsub wasn't feeling neglected by the media. "What else do you want to do, Griggs? Rewards have been offered. Pleas for information. This guy *ain't* taking the bait."

"No offense, Burnett," Griggs fired back, "but I'd like to hear what the agent has to say about the subject."

Fury roiled in Dan's gut, twisting those infernal knots. The man was old school. Dan had to bear that in mind. It would take them all working together to get the job done.

"The media can be an ally, that's a given." Jess rubbed at her forehead.

She had to be exhausted from the drive. She'd turned down his offer of lunch after her arrival. Her whole life she'd been thin, but, in his opinion, she was too thin. Too pale. Not that she would care what he thought. And he damned sure wouldn't mention it.

"After nearly three weeks," Jess said in answer to Griggs's suggestion, "I would conclude that attention isn't what this unsub is looking for based on the simple fact that he hasn't responded. If he wanted more attention, you would certainly know it by now."

"We go back through the steps," Patterson offered.

Jess nodded. "We go back through the steps until we find something on which to build a profile. Or until the unsub gives us something."

"This profile business is just fancy talk," Griggs countered. "What difference will your idea of who he is and what his motives are make? In my experience, you beat the bushes and shake things up until he makes a move."

Jess took the slight in stride. "We will beat the bushes, Sheriff. And we'll shake things up. And you have my word that when I have sufficient details to put together my profile, we will find him. That's a promise."

"I'll set up the interviews with the families," Wells offered. "We won't be able to start until morning."

"Why can't we start now?" Patience had never been one of Jess's virtues.

"There's a prayer service tonight for the missing girls.

The families and friends are supposed to be there. I assume," Wells added with a glance at Dan, "that setting would not be conducive to interviews."

Dan had forgotten to mention the prayer service to Jess. "We have a dozen undercover officers and another ten in uniform covering the service."

In fact, he and everyone seated at this table had to be on site in just over an hour. Damn, he was losing his edge in addition to the perspective he felt confident was already compromised.

"That'll do for tonight." Jess hesitated. "Wells, we'll work together. You introduce me to the families and significant friends. There is something to be gained from merely observing the persons of interest in a case."

"It would be a privilege, ma'am."

Wells was obviously impressed by Jess. Patterson and Griggs, on the other hand, exchanged another of those skeptical looks.

"Gentlemen," Jess said, commanding their attention once more, "I'd like you to watch all significant persons closely tonight. Take note of who's missing, of anything at all that seems off. We'll share notes at seven tomorrow morning."

With that Jess picked up her bag and walked out of the conference room.

"Is she running the investigation now?" Griggs demanded.

"Dan," Patterson said before blowing out a lungful of frustration, "this is not what I expected. Are you sure she's as good as you've been told?"

Dan didn't know what he'd expected. He had worked with the bureau before and most often they spent their time with him speaking in polite tones and offering reassurances. They worked their magic behind the walls of their slick federal building and returned with what they wanted to share compiled in a neatly organized and labeled folder. Jess hadn't sugar coated one damned thing. And he was glad. They were against a wall here. There was no room for platitudes.

"We need her, that much I can say without reservation. As far as the other, I'm running this investigation," he reminded all present. That decision had been unanimous a week ago when Griggs and Patterson insisted Dan take the lead. He stood. "I'll see you at the prayer service."

He didn't hang around to hear them vent their complaints. He went in search of Jess.

The corridor and lobby outside the conference room were empty, the offices all locked up for the night. That left only one other place to look.

He tapped on the ladies' room door. "Jess, you okay?"

"Just a minute!"

The response was muffled by the door but it sounded like... she was crying. "I'm coming in."

"Don't you dare—"

"Too late." Just like he thought, she was swabbing her eyes with a wad of cheap toilet paper. "Hey," he offered, "don't let these good old boys get to you."

He wanted to pat her on the back or hug her or something. But that wouldn't be a good move, at least not for him. The last time he'd touched her he hadn't wanted to let go. He doubted the final embers of that old connection had died beyond rekindling even now.

She made a face. "You think I'm crying over those old geezers?" She winced and a pained sound escaped her as she dropped her head in her hands. "What is wrong with me? Geezers? Really?" She shook her head and swiped at her eyes again. "I just need a few minutes alone. That's all."

Not trusting his self-control, he shoved his hands into his trouser pockets. A woman in tears never failed to rouse his protective instincts. He'd had this same problem with Andrea. And back in high school and college with Jess, not that she cried often. Jesus Christ, this was a mess. His gut clenched. Andrea had to be okay and he had to find her. Anything else was unacceptable.

Smart or not, he had somehow pinned his hopes on Jess. Maybe he just wanted to believe she could swoop in here and save Andrea and the others. Maybe he needed saving, too.

The water running hauled his attention back to Jess. On the counter next to the sink was a small gold band. *Her wedding band.* She exhaled a big breath and he lifted his gaze to hers. "I'm fine," she said. "Just tired, that's all."

She picked up the band and slid it onto her left ring finger. She'd gotten married a couple of years back. Her sister had put an announcement in the *Birmingham News.* He'd stopped keeping tabs on her after that. Thinking of her as married just felt wrong somehow.

You had your chance, buddy.

Ancient history. Jess had done him a huge favor coming here. He wasn't about to say or do anything to make her regret that decision. If she could help him find those girls, he would owe her big-time.

"We have time to grab a bite before the service." She needed to eat. And he needed a way to comfort her that didn't involve touching or delving into personal areas of discussion.

"I'd like to change." She tugged at her jacket and smoothed a hand over her hair. "Freshen up."

The striking red looked good on her, but then anything would. Her hair still hung in long, thick honey-blond waves. Those wide, rich brown eyes had always gotten to him. As kids he had been mesmerized by the vivid contrast. Another good reason to get her to a restaurant as quickly as possible. He needed the diversion.

She faced him, all signs of whatever demons she'd battled gone except for the faint redness around her eyes. "I can eat later. I need a hotel."

"No hotel." He opened the door for her to precede him into the corridor and came face-to-face with Detective Wells.

She blinked. "Sorry." Frowning, she checked the door, then looked from Jess to him. "I can... use the men's room."

"We're done," Jess announced as she barged out, forcing him aside.

Dan opened his mouth but Detective Wells waved him off. "No problem." She sidled past him and hurried to one of the stalls.

The click of the stall door locking snapped him into action. He launched out the door and quickened his pace to catch up with Jess. He would explain the incident to Wells later. He had no desire to hazard a guess at the conclusion she had no doubt reached.

"The Holiday Inn will work," Jess commented as she strode back to the conference room. "Unless you made a reservation someplace else."

Lucky for him the others had cleared out of the room already. She wasn't going to readily agree with his decision and under no circumstances did he want the others to get wind of any discord between him and Jess. "No hotel." He braced for her argument. He wasn't giving in.

She paused in the dismantling of the case board. "Are you telling me that there isn't a room to be had in this city? What kind of convention is it this time? Mary Kay or Tupperware? Surely I can find something within a half hour's drive." She shook her head and continued with tucking the photos and other material into her enormous purse.

It was actually more like a piece of luggage than a purse. What the devil did she carry in there? She looked at him expectantly when he failed to respond in a timely manner.

"What kind of friend would I be if I stuck you in a hotel?" He scoffed at the idea, mostly to conceal the new rush of uncertainty at his hasty decision. Maybe a hotel would have been the smart way to go. "My folks are in Vegas for their anniversary and I know they would want you to make yourself at home at their place." He'd gotten out the whole spiel and she hadn't tried interrupting once. He wasn't sure if that was good or bad.

The longer she stood there staring at him, the stronger the taste of shoe heel got. Evidently he had stuck his foot fully into his mouth with the offer. Did their history as lovers preclude any possibility of being friends?

As if the offer had suddenly penetrated her thoughts she shrugged. "That works." She hauled her bag onto her shoulder, then frowned. "Does your mother know I'll be staying at *her* house?"

The question was delivered with aplomb, but like the profiles she created the motive was all too clear. Twenty years and Jess still hated his mother. "My mother wouldn't have it any other way." *If she knew.*

Suspicion narrowed Jess's gaze. "You don't live there, do you?"

He smiled, felt more like a flinch. At least he knew where he rated on her opinion poll. "No." He motioned to the door, "Let's go, Agent Harris."

Mountain Brook Methodist Church, 8:15 p.m.

That's Reanne Parsons's mother." Detective Wells directed Jess's attention to a petite woman in a white blouse and pink skirt. "Her father didn't come."

Jess studied the woman deep in conversation with Chief Patterson near the podium that had been set up for the occasion. Mrs. Parsons stood small and frail, nothing like the tall, athletic build of her daughter Reanne. The red hair was lighter, almost a strawberry blond. She wore it high atop her head in an old fashioned beehive 'do. The hem of her skirt fell well below her knees and the sleeves of her blouse were long, no matter that the temperature outside still hovered around eighty-five degrees.

"Why didn't her husband come?" Grief, possibly. But this was a prayer service for his missing daughter and three others. A show of faith and strength to the general public in hopes of garnering information from anyone who might have seen or heard something about one or more of the missing girls. Strange that he would be a no-show.

"One of Patterson's deputies said he overheard the wife say her husband was very ill. This is the second tragedy the family has experienced this year. They lost everything in the April tornadoes."

Jess remembered well that devastating day in April. She'd worried about her sister and her family. And Dan, though she would never admit that out loud. She'd had one of her colleagues check in on him twice that day. Just because she no longer felt the way she used to about him didn't mean she didn't care what happened to him. Those crazy emotions that had been playing havoc with her ability to think the past forty-eight hours tried to resurface.

She mentally hit delete and filled her mind with lines and lines of information from the numerous statements and reports she had reviewed. Wells had pointed out the families of three of the missing girls. Andrea Denton's family hadn't arrived but was, according to Burnett, on the way. Significant friends of all four girls had gathered to hear various clergymen representing the community offer hope and solace. The service took place in the enormous main chapel, the subtle music and expansive stained-glass windows setting a somber tone.

Reanne's father and the delayed Dentons had missed an emotionally wrenching forty-five minutes. Afterward the crowd was herded here, the praise and worship hall, for refreshments. That part, Jess had learned, was Burnett's idea. He hoped the stirred emotions combined with the spiritual setting might prompt someone to come forward with information during this less formal gathering. Sort of like those who often threw themselves before a minister whose thunderous sermon had hit just the right emotional chord.

So far that hadn't happened.

"Let's follow up on the missing father." His absence didn't sit right with Jess. Not that she believed every man, woman, and child who lived in the Bible Belt was of a God-fearing nature. Certainly not, or there would have been no need for this particular prayer service. When a man's daughter was missing, however, and his obviously God-fearing wife showed up at an event held on behalf of the victims and he didn't, something was off. Unless Mr. Parsons was hospitalized or beyond standing up, he should be here.

"I'll get on that ASAP, ma'am."

Jess winced. "Don't call me ma'am. I hate that."

"Sorry." Wells scrunched her face in uncertainty. "Agent Harris?"

"God, that's even worse." Jess winced again. Six hours in the area and she already sounded like she'd never left. The accent she'd buried half a lifetime ago had descended upon her like the second coming.

It wasn't that she hated the South or Birmingham. What she hated was her past here. Throwing off that past, all aspects of it, had served as an emotional launching pad for her future. For the new Jess. It had gained her the respect of those who deemed a Southern drawl and the term *y'all* indications of intellectual deficiency.

The emotional drama of the past few days had done a serious number on her head. She felt out of place, out of sorts...out of options. No matter that this function was about the case, it was the social interaction she didn't have the powers of concentration to cope with at the moment.

Somehow she had to get her head back on straight. Any

mistake she made could prove devastating to the outcome of this case.

"How would you like me to address you?"

Jess shook her head. She'd gotten completely off track and left Wells hanging. "I'm sorry, call me Jess or Harris or whatever."

She puffed out a big breath of self-disgust. She had never exactly been a social butterfly, but current circumstances had rendered null and void what few social skills she generally managed. Wells no doubt thought Jess was a little peculiar.

"The problem is, Detective Wells"—her fingers tightened around the cup of punch, making the Styrofoam squeak—"I'm a little off my game."

Wells slowly nodded her understanding, which meant she didn't understand at all. "The chief can be a little intimidating at times. After I made detective last year, he sat me down in his office and told me that he expected more from me than the other new detectives. I've been terrified of screwing up since."

Oh good Lord. Wells obviously had drawn certain conclusions after finding Burnett in the ladies' room. Since the detective was quite perceptive, the likelihood that she had missed Jess's red, puffy eyes was slim to none.

"Trust me, Detective, my being out of sorts has nothing to do with Daniel Burnett. He's the least of my worries."

As if destiny had determined to make a liar out of her, across the room Dan hugged a tall brunette. The kind of female who made being a woman look easy. The kind all other females disliked on sight.

Apparently noticing her interest or her slack jaw, Wells hastened to explain, "That's Annette, his ex-wife."

"He got married again?" That was one Jess hadn't heard about. She had to hand it to him, he never gave up. Apparently the third time hadn't been the charm.

"Briefly." Wells cleared her throat. "Oh, and that's Annette's ex. I mean the ex she went back to when she and the chief split. They're Andrea's parents."

"She's Andrea's mother?" Jess had picked up on an intimate connection when Dan talked about the missing girls. Andrea was his stepdaughter. "Burnett shouldn't be involved in this case." Her attention rested on the man, his ex-wife, and her former ex who was...wait..."Did Ms. Denton and Andrea's father remarry?"

"Yes. About six months ago."

That still didn't provide the emotional distance needed to be objective in a case like this.

Jess wanted to go right now—or as soon as Burnett finished talking to the Dentons—and rant at him for leaving out that little detail.

But she wouldn't. If she were completely honest with herself, she would probably do the same thing if someone she cared about were missing. But, damn it, this was exactly the kind of seemingly insignificant information she needed from these people.

How could men with the experience under their belts that Patterson, Griggs, and Burnett had not see that omission was precisely the problem with this case? The small-town mentality. No matter that Birmingham had grown to be one of the largest cities in the South; the small-town mind-set that everyone *knows* everyone else lingered. The truth, however, is that no one ever really knows anyone's deepest, darkest secrets. Not even after two or more years of marriage.

This she had experienced firsthand.

"Is there something between you and the chief?"

Jess hauled her attention to the younger woman and lifted an eyebrow as much in a show of skepticism as in surprise at her boldness.

"I shouldn't have asked." Wells held up both hands, palms out, and waved them side to side as if she could erase the question. The telltale display of embarrassment colored her high cheekbones.

Jess could lie but she suspected Wells would see right through her. "Yes, Detective, there is something between us. We've known each other our whole lives, went to school together, and all that. What's your point?"

Chet Harper appeared behind Wells. He flashed Jess a smile. "Excuse me, Agent Harris, but I need a moment of Detective Wells's time."

Harper was the second detective from BPD on the task force. In terms of time on the force and grade he had seniority over Wells. His personnel jacket was loaded with high praise. He was also tall, dark, handsome, and charming. A faint Hispanic accent lent an exotic flair to his voice. Exactly the man one would want questioning college-age girls. Precisely the reasons—beyond his skill as an investigator, she suspected—he had been handpicked for this task force.

"Of course, Sergeant." Jess was ready for a moment alone without distraction and interference now that she had the most relevant faces committed to memory. Plus, Harper's intrusion prevented Wells from pursuing her line of questioning.

"I'll be right back, Agent Har...ris." Wells winced.

Jess waved her off. She'd made a mess of her first time

in the field with the detective. While Wells and Harper huddled by the row of refreshment tables, Jess's attention settled on Dan and the Dentons. The woman certainly didn't mind hugging her ex in front of her other ex-now-husband. But then, the circumstances were incredibly painful. Jess couldn't imagine the agony a parent suffered when a child was lost. There had been a time when she'd considered having a child. She blanked the memory. Not now. Not ever.

Deep breath. She was here for reasons that didn't include Dan Burnett's personal life or her own. Surveying the crowd, she decided the time was right to approach Reanne Parsons's mother. The poor woman lingered near the punch bowl, a cup in her hand. She looked lost, forlorn. Unlike the other parents, she appeared to avoid the friends of her missing daughter who had gathered to show their support.

Jess considered dragging Wells with her, since Parsons might feel more comfortable with a familiar face. But the two detectives had inched closer, the smiles exchanged obviously unrelated to police business.

"I guess I'm not the only one with a secret or two," Jess muttered. She downed the punch in her cup and headed for a refill. There was more than one way to skin a cat. She cringed. Damn it. *There was more than one strategy for any maneuver.*

Lorraine Parsons stared blankly at the mass of people scattered in conversational clusters around the hall and didn't appear to register Jess's approach. Jess poured a little more punch into her cup and turned back to the crowd. She paused for three beats.

"The service was very moving." She had missed the

first fifteen minutes. Dan hadn't been happy, but appearance was an important element in investigative methodology. Jess was glad she'd chosen the conservative white dress. A plain sheath with no embellishments, neckline practically at her throat and the hem all the way to her knees. Not a soul would recognize that she hadn't graced the pew of a church since she was twelve except the time she'd interviewed a priest related to a case.

"It was." The faint sound of the woman's voice was nearly lost in the hum of conversation.

Jess shifted the cup to her left hand and stuck out her right. "I'm Jess Harris."

Lorraine stared at Jess's hand before taking it, her movements stiff. Her hand was like ice, the contact brief. "Lorraine Parsons."

"Oh." Jess put a hand to her chest. "Mrs. Parsons, I'm so sorry that you're going through this awful time. Bless your heart." That phrase she'd thrown in on purpose.

Lorraine wrapped her slight arms around her thin body. "It's a nightmare." She shook her head. "I can't believe Reanne would do something like this."

The revelation sent a little shockwave through Jess. "You believe she ran away from home?"

Reanne was the only one not in college. She worked at a sandwich shop in Tuscaloosa near the University of Alabama. Detectives Wells and Harper had learned the young woman had a few secrets of her own, like the tattoo her parents didn't know about. Friends were always happy to tell those little secrets. The power of knowledge rarely failed to make an appearance in situations like this. Everyone wanted to be the hero or the star if only for a moment by passing along some previously unknown information. The broader the interview list and the more questions asked, the more likely that single piece of relevant information would be discovered.

"Did her boyfriend talk her into running off? I swear." Jess shook her head. "Kids these days."

"No...I meant that she allowed herself to get in this position." Lorraine stared at her, the abrupt retraction of her words telling. "My daughter didn't have a boyfriend."

Didn't? "My goodness," Jess offered, "I'm sorry. I just assumed she did. She's so pretty and all. And Lord knows, young girls these days usually have plenty of boys chasing after them, whether they're looking for a boyfriend or not."

Lorraine looked away. "Not our Reanne. She's too immature for a relationship like that. She's not ready."

Says who? The woman was deep, deep in denial. A denial that had likely started around the same time her little girl blossomed into a young woman. Too bad for both mother and daughter. Mother also thought daughter had run away from home, it seemed, but clearly hadn't meant to say as much.

"More parents should tell their kids how important it is to wait until they're ready for such a commitment," Jess agreed. "Everything happens so fast and with cell phones and such, it's nearly impossible for parents to keep up with what's going on in their kids' lives."

"We don't use cell phones. Or computers. They're the devil's tools."

Jess had decided that herself, at least where cell phones were concerned. She had a feeling Reanne's tattoo was only the tip of the iceberg as far as what Lorraine didn't know. "It sounds like you've set a good example for your daughter. I'm sure she'll come home soon. Her father is probably beside himself with worry. I just can't imagine."

If Jess hadn't been looking directly at Lorraine she would have missed the vague nod.

"He feels guilty. He's sick with it. Between losing the house and now this." She shook her head. "That's why he couldn't be here tonight. He's had all he can take." A big breath crossed her lips. "He's weak."

"That's a shame." Jess put her hand on the other woman's arm. "This must be even more difficult for you to do alone."

Lorraine looked at her, her numb expression suddenly animated with fervor. "I'm not alone. I have my Lord with me. I trust Him completely. Whatever He has in store for my daughter will be."

"Of course." Jess moistened her lips and worked to keep any sign of judgment off her face and out of her voice. "Perhaps He'll help your husband with his guilt as well. The Bible does tell us to put our burdens on Him." The concept had never worked once for Jess. She'd learned the hard way that relying on anyone other than herself was a mistake.

Lorraine shook her head, the gesture adamant this time. "This is his fault," she said in a near whisper. "His faith wasn't strong enough. After we lost our home, he stopped trusting his faith. He let our girl down, but worst of all he let His Heavenly Father down, and now we're all being punished."

For about two seconds Jess was at a loss as to what to say. Did the woman have no compassion for her husband? She went with an old reliable line. "That happens to the best of us sometimes. We just have to get through it."

Lorraine gestured to the crowd. "These people don't understand that they have no control. If this is His will, then all the police in the world won't be able to stop it."

If Reanne had run away, Jess could definitely see why. "Amen."

Wells broke the huddle with Harper and headed down the line of white linen-draped tables that ended with the one crowned with the punch bowl.

Jess patted Lorraine Parsons on the shoulder. She summoned the expected words. "I'll keep y'all in my prayers."

She hurried away to prevent the detective's interception in front of Parsons.

"The York family left immediately after the service," Wells told her. "Mrs. York lost it and her husband felt it best to get her home." She glanced past Jess's shoulder. "You talked to Mrs. Parsons."

Jess wrapped an arm around the detective's and ushered her into the crowd. "I need someone watching the Parsons's home. Right now. Can you get that done without going through Chief Patterson?"

"I can, but"—Wells took a visual of the crowd, no doubt searching for the chief from Tuscaloosa—"there'll be hell to pay when he finds out. He goes to church with the Parsons." Wells turned her oval-shaped green eyes on Jess. "You haven't been gone so long that you've forgotten what we're dealing with here, have you?"

Jess turned her attention to the man in question. Patterson was one of the good old boys. "No need to worry, Detective. I know exactly what you mean." She gave Wells a nod. "I'm giving you a direct order. The fallout will be on me."

Wells didn't question whether Jess had the authority to

give such an order; she pulled out her cell and made the call.

Jess left her to it and drifted into the crowd. Like a sponge, she intended to soak up every conversation within earshot. And to absorb every visual detail in the room—particularly the one playing out near the side exit. Burnett and Mr. Denton looked deep in conversation and, like the one she'd observed between Wells and Harper, Jess doubted it had a hell of a lot to do with official police business.

10:35 p.m.

Burnett parked his SUV in front of the lavish entry of his parents' home and shut off the engine. Jess stared at the dark house and absently wondered if Dan Senior and Katherine, dear, queen Katherine, had any idea that their only son had lent out their home. More important, to whom he had lent their home.

"I should come in with you and check the security system."

Jess snapped to attention and snatched up her bag. "You gave me the code, I can handle it. I have a security system back home."

She did not want him to come inside. The barrage of questions that hovered on the tip of her tongue needed answering but in her present state of mind the asking would be the problem. She needed some distance. And some sleep.

She reached for the door. He placed his hand on her arm. The feel of his palm sent a burst of heat scurrying across her skin. She really was exhausted; otherwise, she would have averted that ridiculous reaction.

"You sure you're okay?" He shrugged. Between the landscape and security lighting she didn't miss the worry in his expression. "You haven't said much since we left the church."

"I'm processing." She moved her arm. "What about you? You haven't said much either." *Stop, Jess.* Taking that path right now was not a good idea.

"I guess I'm processing, too."

"Well, then, I'll see you in the morning." Her fingers made it all the way to the door handle this time.

"Jess."

Why did he have to do that? She closed her eyes for a second to clear her head before meeting his gaze. "Yes?"

"At some point, we need to clear the air. Put the past behind us once and for all." He exhaled a breath that was as burdened with multiple concerns as it was weary from days of intense focus. "I don't want ten years to go by before we speak or see each other again after this case is solved." He squeezed her arm. She flinched, hoped he didn't notice. "I'd like to be friends."

Jess typically turned off her analytical side at times like this. It really wasn't fair for her to be in assessment mode all the time. Especially among friends. But then, she and Dan Burnett weren't friends, not in the true sense of the word. "Fine."

Another big sigh escaped him. "I know what fine means." He waylaid her again, this time curling his long fingers around her forearm.

Tension raced through her body, bumped her pulse rate into a faster rhythm. Was she never going to be able to get out of this damned vehicle?

"What does fine mean to you, *Dan*?" He'd done it first, no reason she couldn't say his name to his face, too.

"It means," he said, unmistakably annoyed now, "that it's not fine at all. You're just going to let this *thing* stand between us like a brick wall forever."

"Forever is a long time, Chief. I dare say that's one timeline we won't have to worry about." Unlike the one she'd drawn on that case board this evening.

"Why do you want to leave it this way?" He threw his hands up, hit the dome light of his fancy SUV.

A Mercedes. The man drove a *Mercedes,* for crying out loud. He certainly hadn't ten years ago. He'd driven a Chevy almost as old then as her Audi was now—which she had purchased pre-owned and only after talking the salesman out of his commission.

When had police chiefs started making that kind of money? He lived in Mountain Brook. She didn't have to know the exact address. The neighborhood said it all. Big house, big money. Or maybe Katherine and Daniel Senior bought the Mercedes for him. After all, who wanted an old worn-out Chevy rolling up in *this* driveway?

"You'll leave," he accused before she could gather her defense, "just like you did last time. And forget everyone back here exists."

The unwarranted exasperation in his tone *almost* deferred the realization that she had nothing to go back to. Her career with the bureau was over for all intents and purposes. The so-called relationship with the man she'd almost trusted was over. Even as the thought breached her already compromised defenses the band around her finger burned her skin.

It was over. All of it.

"Fine," he muttered. "You're right. *Fine.*"

She jumped at the harshly uttered words. She'd gotten lost in her own worries and he'd assumed she had nothing to say to his comment. Truth was, she doubted he would want to hear what she actually had to say.

Breathe, Jess.

"We will talk. I swear. This case has me distracted and that's as it should be." She gambled and reached over to pat his hand. It wasn't her smoothest move on record but it seemed to satisfy him. "First we have to find these girls."

He nodded without meeting her gaze. "You're right. I apologize for dredging up the past. This has been a tough evening."

Because you saw your ex-wife with her new/old husband? Jess held her tongue. That he didn't look at her as he said the words related loads about just how much he was holding back himself.

"It has," she agreed. The conversation with Lorraine Parsons rushed to the front of the long parade of thoughts and theories cluttering her brain. "We have an early day tomorrow." Calm, collected. Good. *Now say good night and get the hell out of this vehicle.*

"Wells and Harper made all the appointments after the service so we're set for the family interviews," he said, shifting the subject back to business.

"Good. We can convene the team at seven and go from there." Her fingers curled around the door handle. "Good night."

"G'night."

She emerged into the humid night air and shut the door before he could toss something else at her. He started the engine as she climbed the steps and relief finally washed over her. Thank God this day was over. Cramming her hand into her bag she tried to remember where she'd put the house key he'd given her.

Her cell phone blasted that *old phone* clang that she disliked immensely but that differentiated her ring tone from all the other chirps and melodies.

"Damn." Where was that stupid phone?

Dress hiked up her thighs and squatting in a manner that would no doubt appall Katherine Burnett, Jess shoved around the stuff at the bottom of her bag. Two more blasts and she still hadn't laid her hand on the damned thing. The Mercedes hadn't moved. Why the hell hadn't he driven away? She'd said good night. What else did he want?

The image of tangled sheets and hot, damp skin flickered in her fatigued brain. "Idiot," she muttered.

"Jess!"

Dan was out of the SUV and yelling at her over the hood. "I'm fine," she assured him without looking. "Just trying to find my phone." *And the key you gave me!*

"Get back in the car, Jess."

Thought, sound, even the ability to breathe faded into the background. Jess couldn't see his eyes from her position near the front door but she didn't need to. She knew every nuance of his voice by heart. *This was bad.*

"Reanne Parsons's father is dead. His wife found him when she got home tonight."

...now we're all being punished.

Tuscaloosa, Thursday, July 15, 2:18 a.m.

Chief Patterson had been trying to interview Lorraine Parsons for the past two hours but she kept grabbing her minister's hands and bursting into fervent prayer with her spiritual leader adding his own brand of passionate harmony. Patterson had finally sequestered her in the kitchen away from the activities in the bedroom and leaving the minister waiting in the living room. Dan had supervised the necessary duties related to the victim.

He'd sat behind a desk for so long he'd almost forgotten what it was like in the field. *Damn.* This was one aspect of police work that never got any easier.

Bob Koerber, the Tuscaloosa County coroner, and his assistant had suited the victim in a body bag and loaded him onto a gurney for removal from the premises.

"We'll get on the autopsy right away." Bob removed his Crimson Tide cap and scratched his forehead. "The wife isn't going to be happy." He made a face that broadcasted his mixed feelings on the subject. "She's one who doesn't believe in going to the doctor much less having some medical examiner slice and dice her kin."

"I'm not certain we have a choice here, Koerber." Dan shook his head. Determining the exact cause of death was essential. No matter what it looked like, they had to be certain. Even if Parsons had committed suicide, if the act had any connection whatsoever to the missing girls, they needed to know ASAP.

Jess had followed the evidence techs around the room, scrutinizing every step taken. No sooner than Bob had turned his back to confer with Dan, she had opened the body bag to have a final look at the victim.

The stool and rope Parsons used to hang himself from the bedroom light fixture, not to mention the note he'd left behind, made the situation relatively clear, if not the motive. Dan doubted the meticulous work by the techs would reveal anything useful.

There was no sign of forced entry. No indication of a struggle. The bedroom, as well as the rest of the house, was pristine. Rigidly so. Perfect order. Not a single item out of place. The furnishings were Spartan, to say the least. Only one small television in the living room. The channel had been set on a local station when the uniformed officers arrived. Still was. Someone had muted the volume.

Other than the numerous crosses and the pictures depicting Christ and angels, there were few interruptions in the flow of white walls throughout the house. He supposed that one explanation was the devastating tornadoes back in the spring. Most personal belongings, including family photos, had been lost according to Patterson.

"Well, we gotta do what we gotta do." Koerber pretended to ignore Jess.

"I appreciate you putting a rush on this." Dan understood that his appreciation wouldn't fully cover the blow back Koerber would have to deal with. The media would have a field day with every angle. A dozen news crews were already camped outside on the street. Patterson had insisted he would make a statement to the press when the time was right. Since this was his jurisdiction, Dan had no problem with staying out of the limelight. He got more than his share back home.

"We'll be on our way then." Koerber hitched his head toward the door and to his assistant tossed, "Let's load up."

His announcement prompted Jess to step back, giving the assistant an opportunity to secure the body once more.

The wheels squeaked as the gurney was guided through the door and out of the room. The sound drove home the point that a man was dead. A man who, apparently, could not bear the burden of having lost his daughter. Jesus Christ, Dan had to find these kids. Parsons's note had been a mere two words. *I'm sorry.* His wife had confirmed his handwriting.

The cop in Dan was stuck on the *sorry* issue. Sorry that he hadn't protected his daughter? Sorry that he was the reason she'd fled—if that turned out to be the case? Or sorry that he was the one responsible for her disappearance? And why now? That his daughter could be found alive was not completely outside the realm of possibility. There was still hope. Maybe waiting to learn her fate had been too much.

Exhaustion clawing at him, Dan rubbed at his raw

eyes. There were questions that needed to be asked and he wasn't sure Patterson was the man to get the job done. He was too close to this family.

Like Dan had any room to talk. Andrea wasn't his daughter but they had grown close during his one-year marriage to her mother. Faulting Patterson would make him a hypocrite. When Jess learned that piece of information, she would accuse him of jeopardizing the case. He'd have to tell her soon or risk her finding out from another source.

He surveyed the room. Speaking of which, where was she? He checked the closet and the small en suite bath. No Jess. He wouldn't put it past her to barge into the kitchen and start asking questions she knew as well as Dan did that Patterson wouldn't straight up ask. Since Dan hadn't heard any bellowing from Patterson, he assumed Jess hadn't made it that far yet. With his luck she would be grilling the minister.

"We're finished here, sir," one of the techs announced.

Dan nodded. "Let me know as soon as you process the prints."

There was little else to process. If they learned anything beyond the likelihood of suicide, it would be gleaned from the body. Even that was doubtful, unless drugs were involved. Since there had been no signs of a struggle or foul play anywhere in the house or on the body and Mrs. Parsons insisted the door was locked, lights out, when she arrived home, this tragedy might very well be nothing more than that. A *tragedy.*

Dan followed the techs into the narrow hall that divided this end of the modest ranch house. The door to Reanne's bedroom stood ajar, and light crept through the narrow crack between the plain flat panel door and the frame. He paused to check it out. The room had been gone over three times since the girl disappeared. Jess may have wanted to see it for herself. Who was he kidding? Of course she would.

He eased the door open and stalled. Jess was stretched out on Reanne's bed. He closed the door to prevent anyone who walked by from seeing her. "What're you doing?"

"Look around." She waved one arm. "This is the most generic room I've ever seen. How could a nineteen-year-old girl live here?"

"As true as that is"—he walked to the bedside and extended his hand to pull her up—"this is where she lives and we've gone over every inch of this room multiple times. There's nothing here except her clothes and a couple of dolls."

The carpet had been removed to make sure there wasn't anything beneath. The ductwork leading from the heating and cooling system to the room had been examined. The bed had been taken apart, as had the dresser and chest of drawers. Even the two dolls her mother stated Reanne had kept since she was a baby had been thoroughly inspected.

There were no secret hiding places in this small bedroom. No nothing. Just plain white walls and pink sheets and bedspread, along with a thrift-store wardrobe. And a single wooden cross hanging over the headboard.

"But there is something not quite as it should be." From her supine position on the twin bed, Jess pointed to the ceiling directly above her. "See. I would have checked it myself but I couldn't reach it."

The ceiling was covered with twelve-inch-by-twelve-inch generic acoustic tiles used in many sixties and seventies houses of this style. The tiles hadn't been painted since installation, allowing the yellowing of age to show. Other than a few dents and dings, he didn't see anything to get excited about. "See what?"

"See the one tile that sticks down just a smidge lower than the others?"

He frowned, glanced at her, mentally jarred all over again at the eyeglasses tucked into place on the bridge of her cute little nose, then back at the ceiling. He didn't see it. These kinds of tiles were installed by hand, one at a time. It wasn't surprising to find one or two not quite level or square with the others.

"Right there." She shook her finger and aimed it straight at whatever the hell she thought she saw.

Maybe he needed glasses, too. Then he saw it. The slightest disruption in the flow of tiles. "Okay. I see what you're talking about." He toed off his loafers. Jess scooted over as he climbed onto the bed. Gripping the tile at the edges was impossible. It didn't protrude enough beyond the level of the others around it to get an adequate hold with the tips of his fingers.

"I'll get a nail file." Jess scrambled off the bed and went to the dresser. "Reanne had to have used something to pry it loose."

The metal nail file and wooden hairbrush were the only grooming tools in the room. No hair dryer, curling iron, no perfumes, and no makeup. Also, as Jess pointed out, strange for a teenager.

She handed him the file and he wiggled it under the edge of the tile. A rip like tearing cloth sounded as he lifted one side far enough to get his fingers beneath it. *Velcro.* The tongue sides of the tile had been cut free of the ones around it; the precise divide would have required a box cutter or X-Acto knife. With this tile cut free from the others, Reanne or someone had used Velcro to reattach it to the narrow wood strips beneath.

The wood strips were secured to the ceiling joists, the spaces between allowed for reaching into the darkness that was attic space. The bat of insulation that should have covered the strips was missing. He could see the insulation all around the area, indicating there had, in fact, been insulation and this particular strip had purposely been moved.

Jess stood beside him now. "Can you reach high enough to see if anything's hidden up there?"

He stretched and felt around on the layer of rough textured insulation on either side of the opening. His fingers encountered a small package or boxlike shape. He snagged the object without any trouble. Cigarettes. Camel Lights. The pack was half empty and a disposable lighter was tucked inside.

"Bet her mother doesn't know about that."

"You'd win that bet." He passed the pack to Jess and reached up again. His fingers curled around another small rectangular object. Metal or plastic. Recognition flared and adrenaline lit inside him. He brought the item down and Jess gasped.

"A cell phone!" She snatched it out of his hand. "Oh… my… God."

She fiddled with the phone while Dan felt around the space for any other surprises.

"The battery's dead."

"She's been missing for eighteen days. I'm not surprised." He carefully replaced the tile, pressing it firmly against the Velcro to ensure it stayed. "Come on."

He stepped off the bed and helped Jess down. They'd searched the house and this room numerous times with the Parsons's permission. With a dead body only recently removed one door down the hall, he didn't feel compelled to request permission now.

While he stepped into his shoes, Jess tucked the Camel Lights and the cell in her bag and tidied the bedspread.

"We need to run those through evidence," he reminded her as she tugged on her high heels. The woman's legs were more shapely now than they'd been at twenty-two and... not for his viewing pleasure.

"Yeah, yeah." She smoothed her hair, slung her enormous bag on her shoulder. "I'm ready to do that right now."

"Don't you want to talk to Mrs. Parsons?"

Jess reached for the door. "Patterson will brief us later. Besides, I spoke to her after the service. Right now I need a Walmart."

"You what?" Why hadn't she told him about that? He started to demand an answer but she was already out the door. He heaved a sigh, turned off the light, and closed the door as he exited. He had an idea what was on her mind. He nodded to the uniform waiting in the living room and hesitated. The minister was no longer seated on the sofa.

"Chief Patterson asked the reverend to join them in the kitchen," the officer explained at Dan's questioning look.

"Have Chief Patterson call me when he's finished here."

"Yes, sir."

Patterson was going to be seriously unhappy about him and Jess leaving without sharing their find. From a legal standpoint it wasn't a problem. The Parsons had authorized a search of their home when Reanne went missing.

None of the parents involved in this case had insisted on a search warrant. Patterson would be pissed but if this discovery got them one step closer to solving this enigma, Dan didn't care if the man made his life miserable for the next month.

Outside, the coroner's wagon was gone. The crowd at the street had tripled in size. Shrewdly, Jess had already climbed into his SUV. The local news hadn't made her yet. Once her identity was uncovered, a whole other facet of this nightmare would begin. Accusations that local law enforcement couldn't get the job done would fly. Something else Dan couldn't care less about.

More uniforms were holding back the news folks and sightseers. Questions were shouted in Dan's direction but he ignored them. This was Patterson's territory. He had no wish to step on the man's toes any further than he already had.

"Dan!"

He stalled. One of the reporters rushed to the secured perimeter. She'd gotten the word fast and hustled on down here. Then, that was her job. Gina Coleman had connections. Connections she had worked hard to cultivate. Her methods often skirted the boundaries of propriety, but he couldn't knock her for that. He'd been known to skate around that precarious perimeter himself.

He motioned for the officer to allow her through. Protests rumbled through the crowd. Reporters hated it when cops played favorites. What could he say? He'd shared a hell of a lot more than a story with this woman. He owed her. He glanced at his SUV, where Jess waited. She would have questions and she wouldn't be happy he'd made her wait.

"Thanks." Gina's gaze swept over him the way it always did, as if they hadn't seen each other in ages and she was prepared to take up where they'd left off. "I realize most of whatever happened in there can't be released yet."

But that wasn't going to stop her from asking. "Chief Patterson is going to make a statement shortly." Dan hoped it would be soon. "That's all I can give you, Gina." He held up his hands. "You know the drill."

She smiled, the smile that had captured his attention the first time they met in a situation not unlike this one. "I appreciate that. But you're Birmingham's chief of police. Your citizens want to hear from *you*."

Oh, she was good. That she had the look and attitude of a runway model had gotten her a long way, but her skill at getting the story had launched her to the top and kept her there. "Ms. Coleman, I can tell you this. If you come by my office around noon I'll give you an exclusive scoop on a possible break in the case. You have my word."

There went that smile again. "I'll be there."

He had about nine hours to figure a way to give her something that would satisfy her insatiable appetite for the breaking story. It never hurt to have an ally in the media, no matter that their personal differences would never permit anything other than a professional relationship. That seemed to be his life story.

Dan walked back to the SUV, surprised that Jess hadn't stuck her head out the window and demanded that he get his ass in gear.

"Take your time. It's not like we're in a hurry or anything," she complained as he settled into the driver's seat.

"Yes, ma'am." Dan started the engine.

"Who was that reporter?" Jess twisted in her seat to get

another look at the woman in question as Dan backed out of the driveway. "I thought Patterson was making a statement. Why were you talking to her?"

Was that mere curiosity or jealousy he heard in her voice? Oh yeah, now there was a thought. He'd definitely gone too long without sleep. "Gina Coleman, Channel Six. She's the hottest television reporter in Birmingham right now. We need her on our side."

Jess made a sound that boasted her low regard for his explanation. "Does she have any other talents besides being hot?"

Now that definitely sounded like jealousy. He stole a peek at his passenger as he guided the SUV between the dozens of vehicles gathered on the street. "She has many talents."

"I'll bet she does," Jess muttered. "I was thinking," she said as if she'd just cast Gina out of her head and was on to more important subject matter. "We should find out what's on this phone and how it impacts the case before we pass along the discovery to Patterson. It may be nothing. No need to get him all worked up for nothing."

"He won't like it."

"He's a big boy, he can take it."

She was right about that. If finding that phone got them a step closer to finding one or more of those girls, Dan would dance on Patterson's toes any day of the week and twice on Sunday.

Birmingham Regional Lab, 3:45 a.m.

"It's one of those pay as you go phones." The young forensics expert, Ricky Vernon, wore a rumpled shirt that wasn't buttoned properly and ragged blue jeans. "You know, *prepaid*. They're all over the place. We probably won't be able to track down who bought and activated it, unless they actually used their real name and address. But we can snatch the call, text, whatever history between this phone and others from the carrier."

Jess heaved a sigh. "But that takes time." And a subpoena, she didn't bother pointing out. All the calls and texts and contacts had been deleted from the cheap phone. Probably in case Reanne's parents found it.

"Definitely," Vernon agreed.

After picking up a car charger at a Tuscaloosa Walmart, Jess had charged the cell phone on the way here. Burnett had called in a favor and gotten Ricky Vernon, an electronics forensic expert, to meet them at the Birmingham Regional Lab. Technically Vernon was a forensic biologist, but he'd taught himself the other. Jess decided he was like her; he needed a real hobby.

"I have a SIM card recovery product, so depending upon the network and how the info was deleted, I might be able to retrieve the last fifteen or twenty calls, text messages, and some of the contacts."

"That would be great." If Jess weren't so utterly drained she would hug the guy and fix his buttons. The need to find a break in this case was all that kept her upright after little or no sleep for way too long. She hadn't slept more than an hour here and there in days. *Don't think about it.* Complete focus on this case was paramount.

"Give me a few minutes and we'll see what we get."

"Thank you so much, Mr. Vernon."

He gifted her with another of those lopsided smiles. For a twentysomething geek who'd been rousted out of bed at three o'clock in the morning he was incredibly amiable.

That word, however, did not describe Chief Patterson. She watched Burnett pace the corridor on the other side of the glass wall that separated them. He'd gotten a call from Patterson about the time they arrived at the lab and the two had been talking since. Judging by the grim face Burnett wore, it was a monumental battle with no peace treaty in sight.

"Here we go."

Jess scooted her chair closer to Vernon's. "Any calls, specifically in the last week of June?"

He shook his head. "Only text messages. Here." He passed her the phone. "You can read them."

ICW

I <3 U

SYS F2F

4ever

She hated text language. What the hell did any of this mean? Frustrated, she handed the phone back to him. "Why don't you read it to me?"

"Yeah, texting is a whole language of its own."

Why couldn't people just communicate in English? Real English.

"The user of this phone sent a text saying *I can't wait*." Vernon flicked a key with his thumb. "Received one, *I love you*. Sent, *see you soon face-to-face*. Received, *forever*." His gaze connected with hers. "That's all there is."

As numb as Jess felt from the sheer mental and physical exhaustion of the past few days, anticipation roared through her. "She intended to meet someone."

Vernon confirmed her statement with a nod.

That changed everything. The possibilities of just how dramatically this changed the investigation spiraled wildly in her brain.

"Can you determine when those messages were sent?" Her heart skipped a beat as he thumbed through the keys.

"June twenty-sixth. That's all we got. Nothing before or since."

A new rush of adrenaline launched her out of the chair. "What about the other number?" She shook herself, reached for calm. Had to think straight. "The number of the person she was communicating with. Can we find and trace that number to its owner?"

"Roger that." He scribbled on a notepad then tore off the page. "Here you go. The number and the contact name as it appears on this phone. I warn you that if it's another prepaid phone, you may discover the owner's info is stolen or made up. When a person doesn't want to be tracked down, that's what they do. It's incredibly easy."

"Yeah," Jess agreed. "Makes life a lot easier for drug dealers and terrorists." She studied the note he'd given her. *Tim.* Her brow furrowed, no doubt making permanent wrinkles. Had she seen that name in the list of associates? She didn't think so.

"I can't thank you enough, Mr. Vernon." She was backing toward the door as she spoke. The list of questions she needed to ask anyone who might have been close to Reanne—discounting her mother—stacked deeper and deeper.

He flaunted another of those cute smiles. "Anytime, Agent Harris."

Burnett was still on his cell. Jess paced the corridor as he had done. She was aware that he and Patterson were still arguing about something but she didn't care about that right now. Reanne Parsons had a boyfriend. Tim. On the day she went missing they discussed meeting face-to-face, which might mean they had not met in person before.

Trepidation mingled with the anticipation twisting in her chest. This discovery set Reanne apart from the others. Patterson wouldn't like where that steered this investigation in terms of her disappearance. It punched a massive hole in what Burnett, Patterson, and Griggs believed had happened in this case.

Jess needed to talk to Reanne's associates at work. She didn't have any real friends, according to her mother. But people talked at work. Jess was banking on human nature. It rarely failed her.

"There won't be an autopsy."

That was the problem with investigators. They sometimes failed to see what their minds wanted to overlook. Patterson knew these people. In his brain, an opinion already existed, which caused him to skip past certain possibilities.

"Jess, did you hear what I said?"

She didn't realize Burnett was talking to her until he said her name. "What?" She shook her head, replayed the words he'd said. "No autopsy? Why not?" Wasn't an autopsy standard operating procedure in an unaccompanied death of possible suspicious origin?

"The coroner's preliminary call is that the death was a suicide and the wife doesn't want an autopsy. Patterson won't push for it and that is his jurisdiction."

Well, hell. "Can we at least get toxicology? Find out if he was on any undisclosed medications?"

"SOP. We'll have that in a couple of days with the rush Koerber is putting on getting this done."

"Good." Jess held up the number Vernon had given her. "Reanne had a boyfriend or boyfriend candidate. The day she went missing she exchanged text messages with a Tim." Jess briefed him on the details.

"Harper can track down the name assigned to the number. See if it leads anywhere." Burnett sent his detective a text that included the number. "Now." He slid his phone into the holster he wore on his belt. "We are going to get some sleep."

Was he out of his mind? "I don't want to sleep! This changes everything. I want to talk to her coworkers. *Now.*"

"Jess, it's four in the morning. People are still in bed. We should be in bed."

The last prompted a shiver. Jess was too tired to deal with her less intellectual side. Or maybe she was hung up on all the beautiful women who appeared to be a part of his life. Wells, his ex, the reporter who was so hot—his word. Maybe she did need sleep. One way or another she had to recoup her perspective.

"We won't be any good to anybody if we don't get some sleep."

She held up her hands in surrender. "Okay, okay. I'll sleep at your office." Surely there was a shower somewhere in the building. There hadn't been time for one before the prayer service. A quick change of clothes had made them late as it was.

"No you will not." He grabbed her by the shoulders and pointed her toward the exit. "You'll sleep at my parents' house and I'll pick you up at eight thirty."

"Eight thirty?" She whirled on him. "Our task force meeting is at seven."

He was ushering her toward the exit again. She was too exhausted to put up a proper fight, verbal or otherwise. "Patterson and I rescheduled to nine considering we've been up all night. Now let's go before I call him back and change it to ten."

"Fine."

"Fine," he echoed.

She loaded into the passenger seat of his shiny Mercedes and buckled her seat belt. There was too much to do to sleep. But she needed the whole team, including herself, sharp and ready if the job was going to get done right. Doing it alone was always a mistake. Something else she'd learned the hard way. Besides, the only thing sharp about her right now was the pain in her feet from these damned shoes.

She almost drifted off as Dan drove across town. The city was asleep as he rolled through the quiet streets. The downtown lights reminded her of all the times they'd ridden through here in the middle of the night as crazy teenagers. He'd had that old convertible Thunderbird. She'd loved the feel of the wind in her hair and his arm around her. She'd been completely stupid. Sitting huddled up next to him, no seat belts. It was a miracle they survived.

She stole a glance at the man behind the wheel, all the way on the other side of the console. He didn't drive that old T-Bird now. He drove a Mercedes. Wore his seat belt and had the most prestigious cop job in the city. And lots of gorgeous lady friends.

What would he think when he learned the truth about her?

Jessie Harris. Almost former FBI. Former wife.

Nobody.

This case was all she had at the moment. She could not fail. Those girls were counting on her.

For the first time in a very long time, Jess was counting on herself, alone, without the shroud of the bureau and the career that had defined her for most of her adult life.

Metal rattled against metal.

Andrea jerked awake.

Opening wide, the door's hinges groaned. A dim light filtered into the room, but not enough to see more than the outline of the dumpy figure that entered. It was the woman. The man was taller and thinner.

Her heart pounding, Andrea drew her knees to her chest and told herself over and over not to cry out... not to move. If the woman realized Andrea had managed to spit out most of the pill she'd forced her to take last night at feeding time she might punish her.

A *click* split the silence and a flashlight's blinding beam swept over the room. Andrea squeezed her eyes shut and tried to stop shaking. The other girls didn't make a sound. Zombies.

The one named Macy couldn't explain what they had done to her when she'd been brought back last night. Tests, she had said. Andrea had shaken her hard and tried to snap her out of the drug haze but it hadn't worked. She was too far gone. Andrea didn't want to turn into a zombie like that. But she had to pretend or *they* would know.

The light landed on her face.

Don't flinch. Relax. Pretend to be asleep.

The smell of hot oatmeal invaded her nose.

Morning. The light moved on to the next bunk. Another day had passed. A sob swelled in her throat. Andrea struggled to hold it back. How long had she been here? Why didn't someone come to rescue them? Where were her parents? The police?

"Which one?" he growled.

The man had come in too but Andrea didn't dare open her eyes to look.

"That one."

The harsh command made Andrea jerk. At first she thought the woman meant her. But the squeak of rusty springs came from beneath her. They were taking the girl named Reanne. Andrea's lips trembled. What would they do to her? Macy seemed okay. She'd come back clean, like they'd given her a bath, but totally zoned out.

Reanne moaned.

"Get up!" the man snapped.

Andrea cracked her eyes open just far enough to get a peek. The back glow from the flashlight allowed her to see the man as he dragged Reanne to her feet. He looked old, like the woman, just taller and skinnier. Older than Andrea's mom and dad. Older than Dan. But not much older. She pressed her lips together to hold back the fear. Her body trembled violently. These crazy people didn't try to hide their faces. Did that mean they intended to keep them forever?

Or...when they were done, would they kill them?

"Time for your next test, Reanne," the woman said. She clutched Reanne's chin and shook her face. Reanne's eyes opened, rolled drunkenly beneath the cruel glare of the light shining in her face. "If you fail, you'll be in trouble. You don't want to be in trouble, do you?"

Reanne whimpered, fell against the tall man.

Part of Andrea wanted to jump out of the bed and fight them. But there were two of them and the other girls were in no shape to fight. Maybe they wouldn't hurt Reanne. Macy came back okay.

"This one was a mistake," the man said. "She's not like the others."

"I like her," the woman argued. She turned off the flashlight. "He'll like her, too. You know he doesn't take after you."

Andrea blinked, tried to adjust her eyes to the sudden darkness. Who were they talking about? Who would like Reanne? The idea that they might have been brought here for sex wailed through Andrea, reverberating in her brain like a shriek. She closed her eyes tight. Tried to stop the thought. No! No! No!

"What about that tattoo?" The man snorted. "I won't stand for that."

The drag of Reanne's feet and the soft clomp of the mean people's footfalls against the dirt floor warned that they were leaving, taking Reanne the same way they had Macy.

As much as Andrea wished they would leave Reanne alone, she was glad they were going.

"I can fix that tattoo," the woman said. "You'll see. She's a good girl."

The door slammed, the key twisted in the lock.

Andrea didn't move until the thump of footsteps on the stairs had faded. She jumped off the top bunk. The plastic bowl of oatmeal tumbled to the dirt floor. She didn't care. They could be putting anything in the food. Since they didn't force a pill into her mouth this morning like usual, she'd bet anything the drug was in the oatmeal. She'd eat more dirt before she'd touch anything else from those creeps.

Water. She needed water. Andrea felt her way to the corner, braced for running into another rat. She'd heard them scurrying around during the night. She shivered, felt for the plastic, and grabbed a bottle of water. She gulped down half of it, fought the urge to puke, then downed some more. She needed a clear head. No matter how hard she'd tried, some of the pill had dissolved in her mouth before she'd had a chance to spit it out last night and bury it.

She moved around the room. Desperation made her want to scream. There had to be a way out of here! Andrea wanted to wake the other girls and make them help her but it wouldn't do any good. They were too doped up.

Think, Andrea! There had to be a way out of this hell-hole. She felt around the walls again, even though she'd done it bunches of times already. Brick and dirt except for the part around the door, as if that section had been added later. The door was cool like steel. She hesitated at the door. The floor was dirt.

The rats . . . they got in and out somehow.

If the floor was dirt in here it probably was on the other side of the wood wall. She hadn't felt any holes in the wall. They had to be digging tunnels in the ground.

Andrea dropped to her knees. The floor was packed

down like it was old. She felt around the door, moving toward the corner. Anticipation burst in her chest. A hole...not very big, but it was a hole. She held her breath and started to dig, using that small hole for leverage. She had to scratch and pull at the dirt to loosen up even a handful of it beyond that little tunnel. But she could do it. If she dug close to the wall next to the door on the side with the hinges, maybe they wouldn't notice. When the door opened it would probably hide the bigger hole she made.

She scratched with all her strength. Had to get out of here. She would not die in this dark, stinking place. Never surrender, that was what Dan told her. She had to be smart and strong.

A scream ripped through the silence.

Andrea's head shot back, her gaze focused on the ceiling. More screaming. Andrea's body shook with terror. They were doing something bad to Reanne.

No. No. No!

Andrea had to hurry. If they didn't get out of here soon, they would all die. No one escaped alive from people like this. Especially after seeing their faces.

She tried to block the awful screaming. Just dig. Dig faster. Harder. If the rats were anywhere around, they stayed out of her way.

The other two girls, Macy and Callie, started crying. They were awake. Maybe they had been all this time but, like Andrea, were afraid to move.

Damn it! She needed something to dig with. The stupid plastic bowls and bottles wouldn't work. The evil people didn't leave spoons or forks. When Andrea ate she had to do it with her hands.

She sat back on her heels. There had to be something she could use. Crawling around the room, she searched the floor with her hands. She slid under the bottom bunks. Nothing.

Desperation and defeat crushed her.

She collapsed, her legs crossed, her head in her hands, and cried. The sobs rocked her body, echoed in the room. The sobs of the other girls multiplied, reaching a terrifying crescendo along with hers.

They were all going to die.

"No." Andrea swiped her eyes and nose, the dirt from her fingers smearing on her face. Anger swelled inside her. She would not die here. They needed help, but help might not find them in time.

The screaming above stopped as suddenly as it had started.

Was Reanne dead?

Had she failed the test?

Andrea wasn't going to fail their damned test. She was getting out of here.

She struggled to her feet and went to where the others still cowered in bed. She grabbed Macy and shook. "Get up," she muttered. "I need your help."

Macy just kept sobbing.

"Get up," Andrea said a little louder. She dragged Macy off the top bunk. She crumpled to the floor. "You have to help me. We gotta get out of here." She helped Macy to her feet, then reached for Callie.

When she tried to stand, Callie's knees gave out. Andrea steadied her. "Come on. I'll show you what to do."

One by one, she led the girls to the spot next to the door. She got down on her knees between them. "We'll dig our way out, but I can't do it alone."

"What if they catch us digging?" Macy cried. "They'll do bad things to us."

Andrea wondered if that awful man and woman had done bad things to Macy during all those hours she was up there. "What did they do to you?"

Macy made a desperate sound. "They made me take a bath. She washed me with a scrub brush."

Andrea felt her tremble.

"It hurt. Then they did . . . like a doctor's exam. They checked me *down there*."

Fury lashed through Andrea. "They didn't . . . ?"

"They just looked."

Callie rocked back and forth. "That's . . . what . . . they . . . did . . . to me," she said between sobs. "They make you do the lessons over and over and over."

What kind of freaks were these people? Andrea licked her lips, wished the anger would keep the fear away. "You've been here longer than me. What else have they done . . . to you?"

"They made me memorize the names of people in pictures," Callie said. She sounded straight for the first time since Andrea's arrival. "You know, like family photo albums."

Macy made a keening sound. "If you make a mistake, they lock you in the box."

The shaking almost got the better of Andrea. She hugged herself. "What's the box?"

"It's like a coffin. There's bugs in the box," Callie said, her voice distant, quiet. "If you can't recite the Bible verses right, they put you in the box, too. Call you a loser."

"Spiders, too," Macy murmured. "There are spiders in the box. I think they put them in there to make you scream."

Andrea shuddered. She hated spiders. "You didn't see anyone else? Just the woman and the man?"

"That's all," Macy said. Callie confirmed, "No one else."

"What does it look like up there?" Andrea should be digging, but she needed to know.

"Rooms." Callie cleared her throat. "Like a house." Her voice still sounded rusty. "There're curtains and shades on the windows. They keep them closed so you can't see out."

"I don't want to talk," Macy murmured. "I want to dig."

"Okay." Andrea grabbed Macy's hands and pressed them to the ground. Then did the same with Callie's. "I think we can dig under this wall."

Their movements were stiffer and slower than Andrea's, but they didn't give up. While they dug, she explained how they could pretend to swallow the pills by holding them under their tongues. Even if they couldn't dig their way out, when they were strong enough they could fight the man and woman. Callie and Macy promised to try.

On their knees side by side, the trench turned out wider than Andrea had envisioned but it was getting deeper by the minute. The door would probably hide it sufficiently when those awful people came back. They never closed the door while they were in here so they weren't likely to notice what was behind it. And they didn't move around the room checking stuff.

Her fingers scraped across something that wasn't dirt. Fear ignited in her heart.

Macy jerked back. "What's that?"

"You feel it, too?" Andrea prayed they hadn't hit something that would prevent digging farther under the wall.

"It's a box," Callie whispered hoarsely.

Macy scrambled away. "I don't want to touch it."

Andrea tried to measure the box or whatever it was. She found two corners. The box or whatever felt hard, like metal. "It's not very big. Like a shoe box only metal and a little bigger."

"A toolbox?" Callie said.

"Yeah." Andrea dug around the sides, tried to find the bottom.

Callie helped. Macy stayed back. Too afraid of what it might contain, Andrea supposed.

Andrea grunted as she tugged. She'd gotten her fingers under the bottom of the box on one end. Callie kept digging on the other end, grunting with the effort of clawing and tugging.

The box came loose from the dirt. Andrea toppled over, bumped Macy. She righted herself.

"I think it is a toolbox," Callie said.

They couldn't see it in the dark, but their hands roved over the metal box with its handle on the top.

"Maybe a tackle box," Macy whispered. "Like my dad uses when he goes fishing." Her voice trembled on the last.

Andrea knew what a tackle box was. She and Dan had gone fishing a couple of times. Her dad was always too busy. But this was bigger than the ones she had seen. She picked it up, shook it, and something inside rattled. She felt around for a latch. Anticipation raced through her as she found two latches, one on each end of what she decided was the front. She fumbled with them until the levers flipped down.

Upstairs, Reanne started screaming again.

Andrea froze.

Macy started to cry. Callie scrambled around Andrea and tried to comfort the other girl.

Andrea struggled to ignore the awful sounds and to focus. They had to get out of here. Maybe there was something in this toolbox that could help them. If nothing else, getting it out of the ground would give them a deeper hole for the effort of removing it.

The lid opened with a squeak of protest. She wished she could see. The thought of sticking her hand in that box without seeing what was there first made her stomach churn.

Okay, get over it, Andrea. The box had been buried for who knew how long. It had been shut tight. Nothing inside it could be alive.

She sucked up her courage, held her breath, and reached inside. Sticks or something like sticks. Different sizes. Andrea frowned. Smooth. Her fingers jammed into a cluster of the sticks. They weren't loose and were lined up together in what felt like two rounded rows. She felt around some more, found something solid and roundish. About the size of baseball. There were holes, like in a bowling ball.

She tried to pick it up, but it was attached to...

Her mind created images to go with what her fingers felt.

She recoiled in horror.

A skull...attached to a tiny body.

A baby.

Andrea screamed.

BPD Main Conference Room, 9:50 a.m.

We can't be sure what this means," Dan reiterated. He'd been attempting to get that point across for nearly half an hour to no avail.

Chief Patterson stood behind his chair, his shoulders reared back, his spine stretched to his full height, refusing to join the others seated around the conference table. "Lorraine told me her husband had been extremely depressed since the tragedy in April. How can anyone in this room be surprised that his daughter going missing would push him over the edge? What's wrong with you people?"

Dan wanted to tell him to sit down and just keep quiet for a minute but the man was upset. His pain was palpable. No one assembled this morning understood that pain better than Dan. This case hit damned close to home.

The rest of the team, Jess, Sheriff Griggs, and Detectives Wells and Harper, kept quiet, waiting for his next move. "Patterson," Dan said with as much composure as he could muster with his patience so close to snapping, "we can't assume anything just yet. We move forward but we must look at all sides of this new development."

"Dan's right, Bruce," Griggs rallied despite having stayed out of the disagreement so far. "We can't pretend this didn't happen. There are steps that need to be taken and the results analyzed."

"The man killed himself," Patterson roared. "His death is not relevant to the abduction of these girls! We can't waste time making his suicide something it's not. We need to move on. If Lorraine had any reason to believe this tragedy impacted our investigation, she would tell me."

Jess turned in her chair and set her full attention on Patterson. Dan braced for the proverbial shit to hit the fan. The two had clashed like oil and water from hello.

"Did she also tell you that her husband blamed himself for Reanne's disappearance?" Jess asked. "That she believes Reanne may have run away from home? Possibly because she wanted to escape her parents' strict rules?"

Patterson shot a loaded look at her. "You questioned her without my knowledge? It's not bad enough you put surveillance on her home without consulting me first? Or that you removed evidence from the scene without informing me? I don't know how they train you people at Quantico but down here we learn to respect the chain of command."

Jess had mentioned something about having talked to Lorraine Parsons at the lab but Dan had been too distracted and too exhausted to follow up. Now he wished he had. Giving himself and her grace, if Jess had learned anything earth-shattering from the woman she would have told him right away. An agent didn't move as high up the ranks as she had without doing her job, even if her methodology was a little off-putting.

"I talked to her in passing after the service, yes." Jess stood and planted her hands on her hips, ready to defend her actions. "And yes, I found a cell phone that Reanne had hidden from her parents. The day she went missing she intended to meet someone named Tim, whose phone we've learned was registered under a nonexistent name and address. By her own mother's account, Reanne wasn't happy at home. Her father felt guilty enough about what happened to her, as well as other events in his life, to hang himself. This is a genuinely dysfunctional family, Chief Patterson. We have to seriously consider that Reanne's disappearance may have nothing to do with the others."

"That said," Dan put in, hoping to defuse another explosion, "we're not making any decisions until we know more. For now, nothing's changed. We have a new avenue to consider. That's what we'll do."

"None of this negates the fact that you withheld information from me. But you're in charge of this task force, Burnett," Patterson said. "You conduct your investigation the way you see fit and I'll do the same with my own."

He walked out.

Visibly stunned, no one said a word.

Disgusted, Dan followed, catching up with his longtime friend in the corridor. "Bruce, I know this is tearing you apart." Patterson paused but didn't give Dan the courtesy of meeting his gaze. "You're too close and that's adversely influencing your objectivity."

Patterson pointed his building anger and frustration at

Dan. "And you're not? Who do you think you're fooling, Dan? Christ's sake, Andrea Denton was your stepdaughter. Don't try to tell me you two weren't close and that this case isn't tearing you apart inside, too."

"I'm not denying that." God Almighty, did either one of them have any business being involved in this case? The answer to that was unacceptable. "But we have to consider every possible lead, otherwise we may overlook the most significant detail."

Patterson shook his head. "You said Harris was the best. That she'd make a difference. You had all of us believing she was some kind of miracle worker. The only thing she has done is rip to shreds what little we had in less than twenty-four hours."

"Maybe that's a sign," Dan reminded him. "We had nothing to speak of and you know it. The truth is we don't even have a case. Technically we're abusing city and county funds devoting this many resources to a nonexistent crime. Jess is forcing us to look beyond our emotions and see what we've missed. She found that cell phone and we missed the whole notion of Reanne's unhappiness at home. Jess is trying to help. Hell, man, she took vacation time to come here and do this."

Patterson laughed, the sound one of defeat and misery. "Is that what she told you? That she took leave from her fancy career to come down here and help us redneck cops?" He shook his head. "Now who's talking out of both sides of his mouth?"

The degree of fury that whipped through Dan was irrational, but there was no beating it back. "What the hell are you implying?"

"I don't know what went down at Quantico, that part's

confidential. But I do have a few sources of my own and the way I hear it, your friend is finished at the bureau. If she's the backup plan you're counting on to find these girls and solve this case, you've failed already."

When he walked away this time, Dan didn't try to stop him. He was too ticked off...too stunned. As much as he wanted to believe Patterson was way out of line, he was no fool.

Why hadn't Jess told him about trouble at the bureau?

Because he hadn't asked. He'd had his own agenda for getting her down here and nothing else had mattered. Desperation had driven him. He needed to find those girls alive and every minute that passed without success narrowed the odds of a single one of them being found alive.

He walked back to the conference room, his steps slowed by uncertainty as to how to proceed. Did he pull Jess aside and demand answers? He had no right to demand anything from her. Had his dissatisfaction with the results he'd gleaned from the local bureau office been nothing more than an opportunity to try to connect with her again?

Jesus Christ. He braced himself against the wall. Four young women were missing and he was questioning his motives in this investigation. He had to pull it together for their sakes if not his own. Andrea and the others needed him to do this right. There was no room for distraction or indecision.

Jess's voice drew his attention back to the conference room. He moved to the open door but didn't go inside. Detectives Wells and Harper, along with Sheriff Griggs, remained in their seats, their collective attention focused forward. At the case board, Jess frantically scribbled notes, then faced her rapt audience. She didn't like wasting time and she felt no qualms about stepping in when the momentum slowed.

"Detective Wells and Sergeant Harper," she announced, "interview everyone you can find who knows Andrea, Macy, and Callie. We need to know if those girls have interacted with a Tim. Go back over every detail with the parents. Those arrangements are already made so work the others in between appointments."

"Ma'am, begging your pardon," Harper spoke up, "none of the girls has a contact named Tim listed in their cells, computers, or social networks. Macy York has a cousin named Timothy but we eliminated him as a person of interest since he lives in LA."

A faint smile cracked Dan's frustration. Harper was a good man. He'd worked in Crimes Against Persons for five years now. He'd tried harder and achieved more than most with twenty years of service on their records. Most of his life had been spent proving he was as good as his Caucasian colleagues. His mother was Hispanic, his stepfather a murder victim in an unsolved case.

Harper's life hadn't been easy. Though he was born right here in Alabama, his mother had been an illegal alien. David Harper, a hardworking blue-collar man, had made the desperate woman and her son his family. Harper's mother had become a proud American citizen shortly thereafter. There was still a stigma and Harper had gone above and beyond the call to prove himself. As unjust as that was, the BPD had benefited tremendously. The man was nearly unstoppable. He'd received a promotion from detective to detective sergeant two years ago. Dan hoped like hell he could afford to keep him on this case for as long as it took. They'd been lucky the past three weeks. Nothing major enough to require all hands on deck in his division.

"But you didn't know to ask before now, did you Sergeant Harper?" Jess pointed to the name *Tim* on the case board. "You'd be surprised how many names folks forget unless you mention a specific one. Ask them again, every one of them. Just because a Tim isn't listed as a friend or contact doesn't mean one or more of the girls doesn't know someone with that name. We have to cover all bases."

"The job will go faster if I conduct some of the follow-up interviews," Griggs offered.

Dan took that as his cue. He entered the room. "Same goes for me. I'll go over this new development with the Dentons."

Jess's attention swung to him. "Actually, I planned for you and me to pay a visit to Reanne Parsons's coworkers."

Something else to fuel Patterson's antagonism. "We may need to coordinate that with Chief Patterson." The rift widening between him and Patterson needed mending, not broadening.

Griggs gathered his notes and stood. "I've known Patterson a long time." He glanced up at Dan. "He'll come around when he cools off. That said, we can't compromise our investigation waiting for him to see what's right in front of his face. You're in charge, Dan. Patterson agreed to that decision days ago. It's your call. I, for one, don't care to waste any more time."

Being reminded of the facts should be unnecessary; Griggs was right. They all had a job to do. Everyone in this room was counting on him to do his. "All right. Let's get it done." He gave his detectives a nod. "You find anything, I want to hear about it ASAP. Coordinate your efforts with Sheriff Griggs."

The buzz of renewed enthusiasm vibrated in the air as those gathered prepared to move out. Dan cleared the static from his head and did the same. At some point he and Jess had to talk about Patterson's accusation. Just not now. The last thing he needed was her bolting. He needed her. Andrea, Macy, Callie, and Reanne needed her.

Griggs hesitated on his way out. "You made the right decision, Dan."

"Thanks, Roy. I appreciate your support."

Griggs patted him on the back. "We'll find these girls and then all this will be behind us."

"Chief." Detective Wells approached him next. "I can speak with Andrea's parents if that's okay with you."

"Make sure Annette understands we've got this covered," Dan said for Wells's ears only. "I don't want her freaking out over this new development."

"Got it," Wells assured him.

When the room had cleared and Jess had gathered her notes and bag, she asked, "Ready?"

"We calling for appointments en route or are we hoping to catch them off guard?" He already knew the answer, but it was the one subject he could broach without having it segue into those other questions he couldn't risk asking just now.

"What do you think?" She headed for the door but stopped short. "I'm wondering." She turned back to him, her notepad clutched to her chest, pencil still in hand. "When did you plan to mention that you were married to Andrea's mother, making you an unreliable resource when it comes to investigating this case?"

He'd waited too long. That she got straight to the heart of the matter was no surprise. "We were divorced more than a year ago. That relationship is irrelevant."

Jess pulled off her glasses with her free hand and turned profiler, assessing his expression, his posture. "Is that so? Then I suppose you're equally concerned for the safety of all four of those girls. Andrea is just another alleged victim? No personal feelings one way or the other?"

He looked away. Suppressed the fire of frustration she so easily kindled in him before facing her once more. "Yes, Agent Harris, part of my agenda here is personal. But only part of it. I can do my job if that's what you're asking."

That assessing gaze didn't let up. "Do you still love her? The mother, I mean?"

That frustration she'd ignited flamed into anger. "Are you asking as a profiler or as my ex-lover?" The words were scarcely out of his mouth before he wanted to beat his head against the wall.

If he struck a nerve she did a hell of a job concealing any reaction. "Our past has nothing to do with how I view this case or the steps I will take in conducting this investigation. Besides, ten years is a long time, Dan. I'm certain your ego understands that I haven't been moping about wondering when I'd see you again."

An annoying tic started in his jaw. He unclenched his teeth and grabbed his self-control with both hands. "In that case, my feelings for Annette are irrelevant, are they not?"

She shrugged. "That's yet to be seen. After the way

you and her husband went at each other last night, I can't say for sure at this time."

The gloves came off. "Brandon Denton is a pompous jerk who didn't have the time for his daughter when she was around and now that she's gone, he wants to play the doting, protective father. I don't need him questioning my ability to get the job done."

Jess gave him one of those looks. The one that said she had just made her point. "I can see how you would consider his opinion as significant even though he's a civilian, is likely operating on pure emotion, and has no clue how the duties of your office are accomplished. Bearing all that in mind, of course his scrutiny would move you to strong emotions of your own."

That she was right rallied not an iota of difference. He lost it. "You mean, the way your emotions related to *your* situation at the bureau cannot possibly be affecting your decisions on this case?"

The slight widening of her eyes warned that Patterson was, at least in part, correct. Oh damn. Dan held up his hands. "Let's just stop. I had no right to go there."

Her face cleared of readable emotion. "But you did, didn't you? You wanted to make your point. You did a bang-up job, Chief."

Hell. "Jess—"

"I screwed up." Her bag slid down to the floor. She bent down, tucked her notepad and pencil inside it, then straightened and looked him dead in the eye. "I thought I was infallible. After all, in twelve years as a profiler I had never been wrong. If I created the unsub's profile in a case, I was spot-on every time. The unsub was always found. The case always closed successfully."

Another of those listless, one-shouldered shrugs spanned the silence. "We had the guy. I knew it was him. But I should have recognized his game."

He wanted to stop her right there. The pain in her eyes, on her face, almost undid him. Yet, selfishly, he wanted to know all of it. Whatever had hurt her like this, he *needed* to know.

"The bureau had been tracking this guy for five years without a break. Until this time. I started receiving anonymous tips from a person I suspected to be his partner." She shook her head, her lips trembling. "The others were skeptical, but not me. I knew this was no nutcase vying for attention. I could feel it."

Her hand went to her hair, tucked a tuft behind her ear. "I saw what they couldn't." For the first time since she started talking, her gaze drifted to his. "I wanted to nail that son of a bitch so badly that I didn't recognize he was hiding from the others what he deliberately showed me. When I interviewed him it was crystal clear. A sense of utter self-confidence radiated in his posture. No fear whatsoever in his voice or his eyes. Instead, there was challenge. He practically dared me to try to prove it was him."

She shook her head. "He tortured, raped, and murdered six women this go around. We suspect there have been dozens of others in the past five years. But like this case, there wasn't a lick of evidence. He was too smart. Too prepared. None of the murders have ever been connected to an unsub."

"*The Player.* Oh my God." She was on that case? Eric Spears, the man suspected in that high-profile case, was one sick SOB. Not only did his torture last for days, near the end he would release his victim, giving her hope of survival, only to track her down and finish her off. "The investigation is all over the news. They may have to release their primary suspect."

She nodded. "Because of me." Jess turned away from him, hugged her arms around herself. "I screwed up and the worst kind of murderer is most likely going to get off scot-free."

"Jess, you should have said something." He moved up behind her, wanted to touch her but he wasn't sure she would appreciate that kind of intrusion just now. "I wouldn't have asked you to do this if I'd known what you were dealing with up there."

"Don't you see?" She turned to him. "If I'm not working I'll spend all my time focused on what I can't change. There's something I can do here. I need to do this, Dan. I need to find these girls."

Not only did he understand, she was right. The last thing she needed was to be sitting around obsessing about a situation over which she had no control.

"Whatever happened up there, I know one thing for certain. Without your help, we were getting nowhere. You've already shown all of us that you can see those little, seemingly insignificant things we miss. We need you."

"I should've been up front with you when you called." She closed her eyes and gave a little shake of her head. "I skirted the law because I was so certain I had him. His psychology screamed at me. He's the one. Somehow he knew that and he had his accomplice set me up."

"That part wasn't on the news." But he wouldn't have expected it to be. The first rule of politics was to cover one's ass. He searched her face, wished he could relieve the worry and frustration he saw there. "You sure you're okay?"

That fragile side she'd allowed to surface vanished. "I'm fit to work this case, if that's what you're looking for."

"Sounds like you got damned close." The idea of how close she may have gotten to that kind of monster scared the hell out of him. Unlike the fictional portrayals, as a profiler her fieldwork shouldn't have been dangerous. "I'm asking if you were touched by this guy." The reports about the Player's work were gruesome, sadistic.

"He didn't touch me," she said as if she regretted that admission. "Not like that." Her lips tightened as if what she intended to say next soured on her tongue. "He hasn't been released yet, but that will change by next week." She drew in a big breath. "My actions sealed that deal." She shook her head. "When those anonymous tips began, I decided to follow up on my own."

Dan had a sickening feeling where this was going.

"The anonymous source led me right to the evidence we needed." That distant look he'd seen more than once since her arrival claimed her weary features. "It was all there. Little treasures he'd taken from each victim. All of it. Only it didn't connect to him. It didn't even connect to the anonymous source who had covered his tracks with so many layers even the F-fucking-BI couldn't trace any of it back to anyone. A ghost." Fury seared across those weary features. "But I knew who he was. Spears reveled in showing me. He wanted me to screw up. Wanted me to feel..." She shook her head, fury tightening her lips. "This guilt and helplessness."

She stared straight into Dan's eyes. "He led me straight to what we needed but it was a setup. I was so caught up in his games that I didn't see where it was going. I couldn't produce the anonymous source. I damned sure couldn't prove the alleged source was connected to Spears. I broke into a storage locker that was traced to a dead man and found the evidence we needed. Only I didn't have a search warrant or reasonable cause, so none of it's admissible in the case against him even if I could connect a single shred of it to him."

"He used you to prove he was untouchable." The revelation shook him. "Damn, Jess. I'm sorry."

Tears she would not shed glittered in her eyes. "They train us not to let that happen. I knew better." She went for a laugh that came out more like a groan. "But I did it anyway because I was absolutely certain it was him. Spears will never be tried and convicted for those six murders, but it was him."

"It's no consolation that you were right."

"None at all when you consider that a sadistic killer is about to walk." She reached down and picked up her bag. "So." She squared her shoulders. "I'm days away from being unemployed along with ten percent of the country and my reputation is in the crapper."

His resistance shattered. His fingers curled around her upper arms. "You listen to me, Jessie Harris. You said yourself the bureau had no evidence against him. What you found couldn't be connected to him, inadmissible or not. The guy was going to walk whatever happened. You made a mistake that set back your career, but it doesn't change who you are and how talented you are at painting a picture of the bad guys. If the bureau doesn't wake up and recognize your value, then they're the ones who are screwing up."

Jess patted him on the arm and presented a smile as counterfeit as any he'd ever seen. "I appreciate the sentiment, but we both know how this will end. Sure, they'll probably offer to ship me off to the middle of nowhere." She shook her head. "But that case will haunt me for the rest of my career. Walking away is by far the best choice." She squared her shoulders. "Now, we have work to do."

She turned for the door; he stopped her. "Is there any chance Spears still wants to play?"

If this bastard had connected with Jess on some sick level, he could make finding her and finishing his game a priority once he was released. Dan had left her alone at his parents' house this morning. The possibilities of what could have happened had fear banding around his chest. Even with Spears still in custody there was the anonymous accomplice.

"Who knows? He's a sociopath. All I can say is if he comes near me the bureau won't have to worry about connecting him to his crimes."

"You need protection, Jess."

She laughed; this time it was real. "I might be just a profiler, but the last time I qualified at the firing range, I was considered an expert there, too. You don't need to worry about me, Chief. I can take care of myself."

"I take it you're armed." If she wasn't, she needed to be.

"And dangerous. Now let's go. Before I go without you." She headed for the door, giving him one last warning over her shoulder. "I have a reputation for failing to acknowledge the chain of command, you know."

Patterson would be livid when he found out they were nosing around in his jurisdiction again. The mayor and numerous council members had confided that one asset that set Dan apart from the competition for appointment to chief of police was his ability to inspire teamwork among his peers and subordinates alike. Somehow that skill had eluded him on this case. He'd infuriated a ranking member of the task force and he had no control whatsoever over Jess.

Worse, she was in trouble, more so than perhaps even she realized, and he had no control over that either.

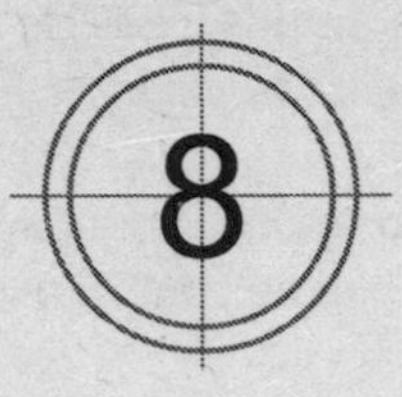

City Parking Garage

What's your take on Harris?"

Ignoring the question, Lori Wells slid into the passenger seat of Harper's sporty black Rogue. Maybe if she ignored him, he would let it go.

The SUV was new, a big change from the minivan he drove just six months ago. The sporty look extended to the interior with front bucket seats and a streamlined dash including lots of sleek gadgetry. Just beyond the console, reality staked a claim in the rest of the vehicle.

The child-safety seat and scattered toys in the backseat reminded her that he was not just her colleague and a man interested in a personal relationship with her, but the father of a young child. Though he was divorced, Lori was well aware how relationships with divorced fathers of young children ended. Badly. His ex-wife would always be his son's mother, consequently deeply entangled in his life. More often than not, one or the other used the kid to make a point or get their way. Maybe it shouldn't, but that major detail prevented Lori from giving in to the feelings he so easily stirred in her.

Her career came first anyway.

She didn't need that kind of messy complication.

Since Harper was assigned to Crimes Against Persons and she served on the Terrorists Task Force, a personal relationship wouldn't be a real issue. But her goal was to eventually move to Crimes Against Persons in order to work cases like this one. Why start something she couldn't finish? She had priorities and as hot as this guy was—she stole a look at his profile from the corner of her eye—she had no intention of getting distracted. Sex was one thing, a relationship entirely another. And Harper wasn't a no-strings sex kind of guy. He'd liked being married and he wanted more children.

At twenty-six, Lori's five-year plan didn't include either.

He started the engine but didn't move from the parking spot, waiting for her to answer his question. She might as well get it over with.

"Her reputation speaks for itself."

Harper backed out of the slot. "Patterson is pissed at her, that's for sure."

Lori stared out her window as he exited the garage, mostly to avoid looking at him. His comment about Patterson confirmed that no matter the date on the calendar, some things hadn't changed. Men still believed they ruled the world and women. Though often respected and admired, women weren't supposed to cross certain boundaries. That Harris had challenged Patterson's conclusions had crossed that testosterone-driven line.

"You disagree with her strategy?" Lori stared at him full-on now. Harper was only four years older than her; his thirtieth birthday was next month. How could he embrace that good old boy mentality?

With the ease and confidence of a lifelong Birminghamian, Harper navigated morning traffic. As she had done, he took his time getting around to an answer. "She's right. Patterson is wrong."

"Is that how you really feel or are you saying that because you think it's what I want to hear?" She narrowed her gaze and watched for an indication that he was patronizing her.

He flashed her a grin. Her pulse sped up. She looked away. That night should never have happened.

"You really think I would compromise my professional principles to make you happy?"

Now she was the one pissed off. "You mean those principles that allowed you to fuck me that night after the shooting?"

He said nothing. Took the fifth, apparently. Lori shook her head and turned her attention back to the passing landscape. She resisted the urge to rotate her shoulder. The ache wasn't real. The injury had been nothing more than a nick. The bullet had grazed her upper arm, a little rip to the deltoid muscle. A few stitches. An ugly bandage. Not a big deal. Except the shot had been meant for Harper. She'd thrown her whole body at him to get him out of the way. It wasn't like she'd had a snowball's chance in hell of moving the guy otherwise.

After the perp was in custody, Harper had insisted on staying with her at the ER and then driving her home. Things had gotten out of control from the moment he walked her to her door.

Lori banished the memories.

He made the turn onto Montclair Road. "I think your memory is a little foggy." His wide, strong hands maneuvered the vehicle with the same ease and precision with which they had guided her that night. "I *fucked* you that night because we both wanted it."

That was such a guy excuse. But he was right. Damn. She closed her eyes and blocked the images. Six months and he still made her throb with need just being this close, listening to his voice, smelling that subtle sexy aroma that was as much him as the Kenneth Cole Reaction he wore. She'd even bought a bottle the last time she was at Saks. She sprayed it on her sheets sometimes. But she would never give him the satisfaction of knowing that every time they were this close she wanted to rip off his clothes.

"I still want you."

Lori ignored his softly murmured confession and checked the calendar on her phone. She would die before she let him pick up on the full extent of the power he wielded over her with nothing more than his presence.

"Annette Denton shouldn't take long." When Lori had made the appointment the chief and Harris were scheduled to conduct the interview. She hoped the chief's ex wouldn't have a problem with the change.

"We can catch the Yorks before lunch and then dig into that long list of extended family and friends," he offered.

She should appreciate that he had moved on from the subject of their one-night stand, but somehow she resented that, too.

"Looks like the husband is home," he announced as he guided the SUV into the Dentons' driveway.

"Awesome." Lori didn't look forward to meeting with

the man. He was arrogant and completely uncooperative. "You can talk to him. I'll take the wife."

"Sounds like a female chauvinist decision to me. Because you're a woman you get to interview the female?"

Lori released her seat belt and reached for the door handle. She flashed Harper a big smile the way he'd done her a few minutes ago. "Don't say you didn't get fucked today."

She got out, shoved the door shut, and strode up the winding walk. Harper didn't hurry to catch up with her. Knowing him, he would say he was enjoying the view from a few paces behind her. He was a good detective but this assignment would have been a lot easier for her if someone else had been picked for the task force.

Maybe this was the universe's payback for allowing that night to happen.

It would not happen again.

The Denton home was large, stately, and probably valued at about two million, even in today's crappy real estate market. Similar homes lined the street. Two matching BMWs sat in the circular drive.

Lori pressed the doorbell and the door opened immediately. Brandon Denton had been waiting for their arrival. He glared first at Lori, then at Harper. "Where's Burnett?"

Harper exchanged a glance with her to confirm she wasn't taking this guy on. "Chief Burnett was called away, sir. Detective Wells and I will be conducting your follow-up interviews."

Without acknowledging the explanation, Denton stepped back for them to enter. Once inside he led the way to the great room. Annette Denton waited there. She sat on one end of the white sofa, a sea of color swirling around her in the form of lush carpets and bold walls. The chairs and sofa were stark white, an almost shocking contrast. Lori suspected that the white seating served as a canvas to display the owners of the home. Both were beautiful, dressed in lavish attire and with egos to match. How had the chief ever fallen for this woman? She could be nice but her entire existence seemed to revolve around money.

"You've found something new?" Annette asked.

"We have a new detail we need to run by you," Lori explained. "I'm sorry to have to intrude on your morning."

Annette managed a small, weary smile. "Don't apologize. I'm thankful there's new information. I want you to find my daughter. Nothing related to the search for her is an inconvenience."

Mr. Denton sat down by his wife and gestured to the two chairs directly adjacent to them.

"Does your daughter have a friend, acquaintance, or relative named Tim?" Harper asked. "It could be as seemingly insignificant as someone to whom she might have run into in the course of picking up dry cleaning, stopping by the store for milk, or at her favorite restaurant."

After due consideration, Annette shook her head. "Not a single person I can think of."

When Mr. Denton said nothing, Harper asked him outright. "No one named Tim that you're aware of, sir?"

Denton shook his head. "We supplied a complete list of her friends and family already. Burnett has this information. Why has he sent the two of you to backtrack?" He glared at his wife. "I knew we couldn't depend on him. We should have hired that private investigator as I suggested."

The agony that pinched his wife's face tugged at Lori. "Sir, I'm confident there's nothing anyone can do that we're not already doing." When Denton aimed a fierce glare at her, she met it with equal intensity in her own. "Chief Burnett was able to obtain the assistance of one of the FBI's top profilers. She has already made great headway in broadening the scope of our investigation." To Mrs. Denton, she added, "We will find your daughter."

The interview lasted a few minutes more, with Lori reviewing the original interview questions. No new answers. She feared that would be the case with most on the list to be reinterviewed. If a single bit of data were gained, the effort would not be for naught.

Harper didn't speak as they drove away from the home. He had something on his mind. Lori could sense the frustration simmering in him. She waited. Still he said nothing.

"What?" she demanded.

"You made that lady a promise." This he said without making eye contact.

"I didn't say we'd find her alive." She winced at the words. God, the idea of finding one or more of those girls dead was unacceptable, but the possibility grew stronger with every passing hour. They had to find them soon. Maybe she shouldn't have given that assurance, but the families needed something to hang on to.

"But we will find them alive." Harper braked for a red light. She met his gaze. "I refuse to believe otherwise."

"Then why are you busting my chops about making that promise?" What did he want from her? And why the hell couldn't she control herself around him?

"Saying it to you is different from saying it to the vic's family."

"Okay, okay. Point taken." She still had a lot to learn. Lori readily admitted that. In truth, this case was the hardest, in terms of emotions, she'd been assigned. She needed it to turn out right. "You really believe we'll find them alive?"

"When you feel strongly enough about something," he went on, his eyes, the sound of his voice, preventing her from looking away, "you make it happen."

Was he answering her question about the case or talking about this personal relationship he was hell bent on initiating? She wanted to warn him that she would not be badgered into a relationship, but she couldn't do it. Whether he was talking about the case or about them, his words weren't prompted by his male ego...he meant what he said and what he said came from his heart.

Lori was in serious trouble.

Tuscaloosa, Noon

Jess surveyed the mobile home court as Dan rapped on the door of the small trailer rented by Kelli Moran. Judging by the shabby landscaping and state of disrepair of the manufactured homes lining the one narrow drive, Shady Court lived up to the boast on its welcome sign proclaiming the date of establishment as 1968. She doubted luxury living was the motive for life at Shady Court. According to Dan, the number of drug busts among the dozen or so rentals was matched only by the domestic dispute calls.

In jarring contrast, many of the vehicles nestled close to the small porches and stoops were undeniably high-end. The mark of dirty money. Kelli Moran, on the other hand, drove a VW Bug. Not the resurrected version of the nineties, but an original from the sixties. A rusty yellow with a license plate registered to her and this address. According to Reanne's supervisor at the sandwich shop, Kelli was her closest friend.

"She's got to be here," Jess argued when Dan sent her a doubtful look. "Her manager said she wasn't scheduled to work today and her car is right there." Jess pulled off her sunglasses and swabbed at the perspiration threatening to drip down her forehead. She had spent far too many years in the Northeast to acclimate to this heat.

Dan knocked again.

A minute passed, every confounded second ticking off in her head. Jess rolled her eyes. Enough waiting. She marched up to the door and banged like she meant it, not the polite knock that Dan had employed.

"Miss Moran, I know you're in there. We need to speak to you."

A door opened across the lane and a head poked out. One look and the guy quickly snatched his head back inside and slammed the door.

Still no answer at the Moran home.

"If she's here," Dan suggested, "she's not inclined to chat."

"That's so strange. Why would anyone not look forward to chatting with the two of us?" Jess shrugged and dropped her arms back to her sides. One hand just happened to land on the doorknob, which she accidentally turned. The door opened, making her step back since it swung outward. She turned to Dan. "Oops."

"Jess," he warned.

Ignoring his caution and since no shots were fired, Jess stuck her head inside. "Miss Moran! I need to speak to you about your friend Reanne. We know about Tim. If you talk to us now we won't have to press charges against you for obstruction of justice."

She surveyed the cluttered living room, listened for any

sound in the rooms beyond. Looking wasn't necessary to know that Dan would be barely containing his frustration at her tactics.

Walking through the door would constitute entering the premises without the proper court order. She had that one down pat.

What had possessed her to tell him the *whole* story . . . that her career was over? He'd caught her at a weak moment. Now she could feel all that sympathy oozing from his every pore. She did not want his sympathy.

Or anything else.

Too bad that assertion fell way short of providing any confidence in her ability to be that strong.

"She's not coming to the door, Jess."

Jess would just see about that. "Okay. I guess we'll have to take the next step and get a warrant. It would be so much better if you spoke to us voluntarily."

One turn and two strides, Jess hadn't even made it to the steps of the rickety old porch when the reaction she'd hoped for materialized.

"I don't know anything. I told that to the cops already."

Jess turned back to the door and produced a smile for the young woman. "Hello, Miss Moran, I'm Agent Harris and this is Chief Burnett." Dan had moved up behind her. "We'd like a few minutes of your time."

The girl shook her dark head. "I don't know what good it'll do."

She walked over and collapsed on one end of the battered sofa. Her clothes were rumpled as if she'd slept in them. The holes in her jeans revealed a knee and a splash of thigh. Her black T-shirt sported the logo of the sandwich shop where she worked. Bare feet sported black toenails, which matched her fingernails as well as her heavy eye makeup. Ears, nose, and eyebrows were pierced. Probably the tongue, too.

"Well," Jess offered, still standing outside the threshold, "Kelli. May I call you Kelli?"

"Whatev."

"Kelli, thankfully we won't need that warrant, but we're sort of like vampires. We need an invitation to come inside." Behind her, Dan cleared his throat. If Patterson complained about their efforts, at least they could say Kelli Moran issued an invitation.

Kelli rolled her eyes. "Come in." She waved her arm. "Have a seat."

"Thank you." Jess took the other end of the sofa. Dan sat on the edge of the armchair. He looked like a high-class lawyer from one of those sexy television series. She'd almost told him this morning how flattering the suit was. Another elegant one, apparently tailored just for him and in a cool gray that made his dark hair and blue eyes even more distinct. Which was an idiotic and senseless observation. Proof positive that she had not regained her professional equilibrium. Or her emotional one.

"Your friend Reanne Parsons...," Jess began, surprised Dan was letting her lead. Maybe that took the heat off him with Patterson. "...is still missing."

"Yeah," she commented, too busy studying the chipped paint on her fingernails to look up. "I saw that on the news."

"We found her cell phone."

Kelli's fingers stalled but she didn't look up.

"The day she disappeared," Jess continued, "she exchanged text messages with her boyfriend, Tim."

Kelli glanced at Dan, then resumed her rudimentary manicure. "Reanne didn't have a boyfriend."

"Maybe she and Tim were just friends."

Kelli shrugged. "No clue."

Jess and Dan exchanged a look that indicated he agreed with her assessment. Kelli Moran was afraid to talk. She had no arrest record. Though she had dropped out of high school, she had a reliable work record and had supported herself since. Which explained her lack of taste in housing. She wasn't afraid of the police; that came across loud and clear in her attitude. But she was afraid of something.

"Kelli, I know Reanne confided in you. And we need your help. She may be in danger."

Another covert peek at Dan. "I'll tell you what I know." She lifted her gaze to Jess. "Just *you*. I'm not talking in front of officer friendly."

Jess looked to Dan. He stood. But before excusing himself, he asked, "Miss Moran, are you here alone?"

She gave him a dramatic eye roll. "Whenever I'm not at work, I'm here alone. Guys don't know how to appreciate a smart, independent chick like me."

"You won't mind if I confirm that before I go outside?"

Jess clamped her jaw shut rather than say the words poised on the tip of her tongue. She could take care of herself. *This* is what happened when a female member of law enforcement showed the slightest hint of weakness. Suddenly she wasn't capable of taking care of herself. She shouldn't have told him. Damn it.

"Have at it," Kelli authorized.

Jess waited, her pulse jumping with anticipation, as Dan did the protector thing.

Finally, he paused at the front door. "I'll be right outside."

"Thank you, Chief." Jess forced a smile even as she threatened his ability to continue breathing with her eyes. When he was out the door, Jess turned her attention back to Reanne's friend.

"You cannot tell her folks," Kelli pleaded, the obnoxious attitude gone. "There's no telling what they would do. She does not want them to find her. She's nineteen, she has that right."

Having that conclusion confirmed set Reanne apart from the others but did nothing to solve this case. Not what Jess had hoped for. "Can you tell me about Tim? How he and Reanne began their relationship?"

"First"—Kelli leaned toward Jess as if she didn't want to talk above a whisper—"you need to know that Reanne was desperate to get away from her folks. Her mom and dad are crazy strict."

Obviously the girl hadn't watched the morning or noon news. "Did she say she wanted to get away from her parents?"

Kelli nodded. "She loves them but they go too far with the religious stuff. She'd had enough. Reanne wants her own life. After she started talking to Tim, she was happy for like the first time in her life."

"How did she and Tim meet?" Jess wanted her to believe they knew Tim's identity, in an effort to hopefully get as much of the truth as possible. What they learned from this young woman could make the difference in how this case moved forward.

"It was wild." She smiled, looking away as if to hide the expression.

When she smiled, the dark, brooding girl was very pretty. Jess wondered if she realized how attractive she was. "How do you mean?"

"She got notes at work for weeks. From a secret admirer. The envelopes would be on a table or on the counter. *Reanne* would be written across the front. It was super exciting for her. Finally, he gave her his number. Reanne bought one of those prepaid phones so they could text. His parents are weird, too, so they couldn't *talk* talk. They had to text. His folks hovered over him worse than Reanne's."

"Really?"

"Yeah, he warned her to never call. His parents wouldn't understand the texts but a call would be different."

Jess could appreciate that. She couldn't decipher text language either. "How long have they been communicating?" Apparently she had been right to assume the two hadn't met in person . . . at least not until the day Reanne disappeared.

"Nearly two months."

"But she never shared his last name or address with you?"

Kelli shook her head. "I'm pretty sure she didn't know anything but his first name. Putting that kind of info in a note or text was too risky. Their plan depended on careful preparation."

"Their escape plan?" Jess suggested.

Kelli nodded. "They planned it down to the minute."

"Where did she pick him up?"

A frown furrowed the girl's brow, accentuating the row of small hoops in her left eyebrow. "Reanne doesn't have a car. One of her parents took her everywhere."

"Of course, you're right. He picked her up."

Suspicion crept into her dramatically embellished eyes. "I guess."

"You haven't heard from her?"

"No."

There came the fear. Jess felt another surge of anticipation. Kelli was either lying or she was concerned about some aspect of Reanne's disappearance. "I appreciate your cooperation, Kelli." Jess stood. "I guess we can take Reanne off our list. You've confirmed for us that she left of her own free will. No need for the police to get into her business."

Jess was halfway to the door when the girl spoke again, "You said she might be in danger."

Jess turned back to her. "Looks like we were wrong." She shrugged. "You said she and Tim had made their plan. Very carefully. They appear to have accomplished their goal. You're her best friend." That was a guess. "And you said she doesn't want to be found. That hardly leaves us anything to investigate."

Kelli stood and hooked her thumbs in her back pockets. "I don't exactly know for sure. That was the plan... but..."

Jess closed the distance between them. "This is your chance, Kelli. If you know any reason we should continue to look for Reanne or should suspect foul play, you need to tell me right now."

The fear escalated. Her pupils flared with the blast. "I...don't know for sure." She shook her head, tears brimming on lashes caked with black mascara. "I mean, it's not really a big deal."

"Three other girls around Reanne's age are missing. She could be a victim of whoever took them. Every minute we waste could mean the difference between life and death for those girls. For your friend."

Two seconds, three, then five. "I'll show you."

Kelli grabbed her hand and led Jess back to the bedroom. There was only one in the small trailer and like the living room a whirlwind appeared to have gone through it. Kelli reached into the disorganized closet and pulled out a suitcase. She placed it on the unmade bed and opened it.

Jess moved to the bed and stared at the contents.

"She bought all this stuff at the thrift store." Kelli picked through the items. Two pairs of jeans. Five cute little feminine blouses. Sexy bras and panties. And a slinky nightie. "For when they took off." From the zipper compartment inside the suitcase, Kelli pulled out a few folded bills. "She had been saving part of her tips." She tucked the cash back into its place. "After he picked her up they were gonna come by here and get this."

"Maybe you weren't home when they came by."

A single tear streaked down her cheek. "She knew where the key was hidden."

Jess played devil's advocate. "It's only clothes and a few dollars."

Kelli reached into the suitcase again, this time withdrawing a cross on a silver chain. "Her daddy gave this to her when she was twelve." Kelli fingered the small cross. "She said it was the last time she remembered being happy." Her gaze locked with Jess's. "Her period started the next month and everything changed. It was like they expected her to turn into a whore or something."

"If," Jess ventured carefully, "you're that convinced that Reanne wouldn't leave without picking up her stuff, why didn't you call the police?"

More tears followed that dark trail down her cheeks. "I was scared to say anything. I didn't want to get her in trouble. Her parents are insane. I didn't want to be the reason they found her if she and Tim got away."

"What are your instincts telling you, Kelli?" Jess searched her eyes for any flicker of emotion other than fear. "Do you think she would leave without this stuff?"

"She might." Kelli held out her hand, the cross and chain in her palm. "But she wouldn't leave without this. As crazy as her folks made her, she loved them. She never took this off, not until the day before she and Tim were hitting the road. She told me to put it in her suitcase so she wouldn't get excited and forget to come by and get her stuff. It was her reminder." Kelli touched her throat. "She was always messing with it, straightening it. There is no way she forgot about it or left without it. Even if she hadn't been able to come get it for some reason, she would have found a way to call me and let me know how to get it to her."

Jess lifted the delicate chain from her palm. Her heart pounded. "Kelli"—she met the girl's terrified gaze—"did she keep any of the notes from Tim?"

"She always got rid of them at work."

Jess flinched. She'd hoped that wouldn't be the case.

"But..." Kelli hurried to the scarred dresser at the foot of her bed and rummaged in the bottom drawer. She removed a white, folded piece of paper and brought it to Jess. "I got this one out of the trash." She shrugged. "I figured I'd keep it for her. She might wish later on that she'd kept at least one."

Smart girl. Jess's fingers trembled a little as she accepted the note that had obviously been crumpled and then smoothed out and folded. She opened it and studied the bold, sprawled words.

Tomorrow it's our turn.

Jess lifted her gaze to Kelli's. "You didn't get the envelope?"

She shook her head.

Jess should have known she wouldn't be so lucky. "Just a couple more questions, Kelli."

The girl waited, terror making her eyes huge.

"Has anyone contacted you? Been following or watching you since Reanne disappeared?"

Kelli shook her head.

"No strange vehicles in and out of here? No one who behaved oddly came into the shop?"

She shook her head again.

"Okay." Jess nodded, searching for a way to ask the final question that wouldn't scare the girl worse than she already was. "Is there any place else you can stay for a while? With a friend or family member?"

After more than two weeks there was really no reason to believe Kelli was in any danger, but Jess wasn't prepared to take that risk.

"I could go to my brother's in Moundville," she offered, her voice trembling. "As long as my boss'll let me off work and my Beetle holds out."

"Trust me. Your boss won't give you any trouble."

Dan waited on the porch right outside the door. The somber face, despite the designer sunglasses shielding his eyes, warned that he was either annoyed that she hadn't gotten him a pass inside or something else had happened.

"Kelli," Jess said to the wary girl hovering in the doorway, "you get whatever you need for a few days."

When the girl had gone to get her things, Jess gave

him the condensed version of what she'd learned before he could ask. He inspected the note, which had probably been too contaminated to hope for any prints or trace evidence left behind by this Tim person. They hadn't gotten any evidence at all from anyplace else. She doubted they would suddenly get lucky.

"We're about to have company." He slid his sunglasses back into place. "Patterson is on his way here and he's mad as hell."

"Good." Jess tucked the note and the cross necklace into her bag. "He can make sure Kelli gets to her brother's house in Moundville. I don't want her staying here alone."

As promised, Patterson arrived posthaste. Kelli waited in Dan's Mercedes. At Jess's prompting Dan had shown her how to operate the music system. Jess hoped she wouldn't overhear whatever Patterson said when he exploded.

Dan pulled the Tuscaloosa chief of police to the side and brought him up to speed. Jess tried to focus on anything else but she kept drifting back to the way Dan handled the situation. He was very good at negotiating problems. Both Patterson and Griggs appeared to respect him, even though they had a decade or more on him in police work. Try as she might, she had to, yet again, admire the cut of his suit and the strong, confident bearing that was so much more mature than even ten years ago. Fortysomething looked damned good on him.

She, unfortunately, had not held up so well. The glasses had become a requirement last year. Surrendering to the use of moisturizers and fastidious use of sunblock was now the bane of her existence for fear more lines would appear around her eyes. She'd tried joining a gym to stay in shape but with her work schedule that had been impossible.

Her work schedule was no longer a problem.

And *he* knew.

Her stomach roiled with a big dash of humiliation and a faint signal of hunger. She hadn't bothered with breakfast this morning. She'd even done without coffee until she arrived at Dan's office. Knowing Katherine Burnett, she would recognize if her high-tech coffeemaker had been touched. Jess wouldn't put it past her to count the coffee beans in that fancy crystal container gracing the marble countertop in the *butler's* pantry.

Jess snapped to attention as Dan and Patterson headed for the small porch where she waited. She braced to have her head bitten off. It wouldn't be the first time and as long as she kept breathing it wouldn't be the last.

"You think Reanne ran off with this Tim."

Jess couldn't ascertain whether he was asking or accusing. "No. Absolutely not."

Something like relief lit in the man's eyes. "Why is that?"

"That girl is Reanne's friend." Jess nodded to the Mercedes where Kelli waited. "She doesn't believe Reanne ran anywhere. She believes she was taken. That's the only proof I need."

Patterson nodded, whether in acknowledgement or approval, she hadn't a clue.

"She needs a ride to her brother's house," Jess told him. "Can you see that she gets there safely?"

Patterson nodded again.

What was wrong with him? Where was all that piss and vinegar he usually sloshed around?

"I owe you an apology, Agent Harris."

It took a second or two for his words to penetrate the denial that was her brain's first response.

"Lorraine admitted that she thought Reanne had run away. She didn't tell me because she was afraid we'd stop looking for her since she's old enough to leave if she wants. She's so convinced her daughter ran away that she's already decided she's dead to her." He shook his head. "It's the shock. First Reanne, then her husband." He heaved a big breath. "Anyway, there is no excuse for my behavior."

"You're a friend of the family," Jess offered. "You wanted to believe your friends. As for Mrs. Parsons, I imagine any mother would have done the same in a desperate situation like this."

Dan stepped away to take a call.

Patterson glanced at the girl waiting in the SUV. "I have a bad feeling about this. Reanne may not be connected to the other girls." He shook his head. "God only knows if she's still alive."

Dan ended the call and tucked his cell away. The look on his face had the bottom dropping out of Jess's stomach. He climbed the steps to rejoin them on the porch. One look at his eyes confirmed her assessment. Bad news.

"That was Wells. We have another girl missing."

That sinking sensation went through her again. "Where?"

"Warrior. Wells and Harper are headed there now."

"Just like the others?"

Jess held her breath as she waited for Dan to answer Patterson's question.

"Pretty much. No history of trouble of any kind. College student. Left for a friend's house last night and never made it. When she wasn't home by noon today, her mother called the friend, who said she hadn't shown. They found her car parked in front of a flower shop."

Damn. If a fifth girl disappearing didn't draw out the bureau's resources, then something was wrong with the law.

"We may have gotten a break this time," Dan went on. "A witness saw the girl get into a vehicle. We don't have a license plate but we've got color and make and the exact time of the abduction."

That was a start.

10

Andrea leaned forward and tried to snag the tape covering her mouth with her thumb. She grunted. Frustrated. She'd been trying to get loose all day and nothing worked.

If she hadn't screamed she might be out of here now. For two girls half out of their heads on drugs, Callie and Macy had saved her ass. They'd quickly reburied the toolbox and dragged Andrea back to the bunk beds. When that crazy bitch and her husband had stormed into the room, flashlight blinding them all, they'd found Andrea on the floor with her scattered oatmeal. The other two pretended to be asleep.

Grabbing her by the hair, the bitch had stuck her face in Andrea's and warned that she would not tolerate disobedience. She then stood over Andrea until she scraped up every drop of the oatmeal she'd spilled and ate it. What she didn't know was that Andrea had been eating dirt for days. What was a little more? After that the man had duct taped her hands, securing her to the metal leg of the bunk bed. For added punishment he plastered tape over her mouth so she couldn't scream anymore.

Andrea was glad it hadn't been worse. She squirmed around to get in a better position. If she could just get the tape off her mouth, she could chew her hands loose. Callie and Macy were out. They'd had their pills and apparently both had forgotten what Andrea told them about spitting the pills out. She hadn't been given one. That was probably part of her punishment. Those creeps wanted her wide-awake while she was bound to the bed like this.

A-holes.

She closed her eyes and braced her forehead against the cold metal. Since it was dark, she couldn't say for sure that those were bones in the toolbox, but she had a bad feeling. She just didn't want to believe it. She shuddered. No use pretending. Definitely bones. Little ones. Like a baby.

Bile surged in her throat and she struggled to swallow it back or risk choking. Why would anyone kill a baby? Maybe it had been born dead. But why bury it in the basement like this? In a damned toolbox or whatever?

Okay. No giving up. Andrea refocused her efforts on getting her thumb under the tape over her mouth. Her fingers and wrists were mostly covered, but her right thumb stuck out. She dug at her face some more; her skin around the tape was raw from her thumbnail raking over it again and again. If one of the others would wake up they could help her. She couldn't call out to them, and all the grunting and groaning she'd done at first hadn't gotten through their drug-induced sleep.

Thank God the rats hadn't come back. Maybe since she'd excavated their tunnel they had decided to stay clear for a while.

One corner of the tape lifted. Hope thrilled through her. She caught that corner between her thumb and her bound hand and pulled her head back slowly. The burn had her holding her breath as she slowly dragged the tape away from her mouth. She gasped for air and then coughed.

Thank God.

A minute to recover from the burn and to relax her muscles, then she'd tear loose the rest of the stupid tape. She moistened her raw lips and started chewing at the sticky band around her wrists. It would take a while but she was determined. If she got lose she could start digging again. Her fingertips were sore from clawing at the dirt but she wasn't going to let a little pain slow her down.

She hadn't heard any more screaming from overhead. Was Reanne okay? They hadn't killed Macy or Callie. Maybe they wouldn't kill Reanne either. Maybe they weren't going to kill any of them.

Maybe…Andrea slowed in her efforts to get free. In the movies the hostages were kept alive until the bad guys were finished with them. She figured they wanted money. If they got what they wanted, would they let them go home? If she and the other girls didn't give the crazy man and woman any trouble, why would they hurt them?

Because they had seen their faces.

Andrea chewed harder at the nasty-tasting tape. She wanted out of here. Dan and the cops might not find them in time. Waiting to be rescued would be stupid. A big strip of tape pulled free of her wrists, giving her hope. Tugging harder with her teeth, another loosened. Psyched now, she kept at it. Another and another tore loose. Yes! A little more and she would be able to twist her hands free.

Last one! She did it. Her hands fell to her lap. She squeezed her fists, released, and squeezed again. She shook her arms and hands to get the feeling back; both had gone numb hanging like that.

She scrambled back to the door and listened for a few seconds before moving to the hole and digging. Thank God those awful people hadn't noticed the loose dirt. This time she carefully piled the loosened dirt to one side so she could shove it back in if necessary.

A shudder rocked her when she grabbed hold of the handle on the metal box. She lifted it out of the hole and set it aside and started digging under the wall. The hole seemed wide enough on this side of the obstacle that stood between her and freedom. Now she needed to get underneath and out the other side.

It took a while—her fingers were sore—to clear a tunnel wide and deep enough under the wall. As she had hoped, the wood wall just sat on the dirt floor. Had to be attached overhead because it didn't feel as if it was attached to the ground with cement or anything. Her fingers scratched a rocky chunk.

Damn. Maybe it was cemented in the ground. She felt around the hole, dug a little more. Now she understood. There was concrete on either end of the hole she'd started. Chunks maybe two feet apart. Andrea had watched the guys build the big arbor in the backyard for her mother's climbing roses. They had concreted posts into holes in the ground before attaching all the other wood to those posts.

She sat back on her heels. This wall must have been built like that. Lucky for her it felt as if there was space enough between the cement chunks holding the posts to continue digging toward the other side. Anticipation allowing her to ignore the pain in her fingers, she kept going.

The space behind the wood on this side of the wall was hollow. She reached deeper. There was more wood on the other side. She needed to dig maybe six more inches to get beyond the wall and then hope she could reach far enough and dig fast enough to get out the other side before those awful people came down here for some reason. Lunch had passed. They had brought the other girls sandwiches instead of oatmeal. Andrea's stomach rumbled. Not for her. She was being punished. Maybe the menu change was to drive that point home.

Bastards. She focused her anger on the hole.

She didn't know how long she'd been scratching at the dirt, but Andrea sat back to evaluate the situation. Could she squeeze through that space? It felt wide and deep enough, but she had to bend her body far enough to wiggle under the wall.

Only one way to find out. She tried to stick her upper body down and under the wall. She jerked back. Wouldn't work.

Wait. She needed to go under with her back to the ground.

She lay on her back and started to scoot her head and shoulders into the hole.

"What're you doing?"

Andrea jumped. Hit her head on the wall. She lay still long enough for her heart to stop jumping. "Callie, you scared the hell out of me."

"They'll hurt you if you go out there."

"I don't care. I have to try."

"But...what will you do? Do you think you can get out?"

"I don't know." Andrea pushed, wiggled, turned her head to one side, and dug her heels into the dirt to push harder. She'd dug all the way through to the other side. Now all she had to do was fit her body through the space.

Her head and shoulders squeezed through, but her boobs were stuck. She tried to arch, pressing her back harder into the ground. Another inch or so. *Keep pushing!* The wall burrowed into her boobs. She bit her lips together to prevent crying. She pushed hard with her legs.

She scraped through to her waist. Hope blasted through her. Andrea relaxed. Took a breath and listened for trouble.

All quiet.

Okay. She got one arm and then the other out. Using the heels of her hands she braced against the dirt floor and wiggled and tugged until her hips were free. Giddiness made her lightheaded.

She was out!

"What's out there?"

Andrea blinked, ordered her eyes to adjust to the eerie glow of dim light.

"Are you okay?"

"Yeah. I'm gonna look around."

She got up, staggered a little. Beyond the stretch of wood wall, brick steps led upward. Andrea shivered. That was where the bad people were. Maybe they were gone somewhere. Her body shaking, she eased toward the steps. Up one step, then another. She stalled.

Pull it together, Andrea.

One step at a time, she kept going until she reached a small landing. The stairs resumed in the opposite direction. A door waited at the top.

"Don't be afraid," she whispered as she climbed to the top.

If she turned the knob and they heard her...if she opened the door and they were waiting on the other side...

Andrea grasped the worn brass knob and twisted.

It was locked. She held her breath and released. The knob whined. Fear punched her in the chest. She froze.

She didn't know how much time passed before she could move. No one came busting through the door or screamed or anything.

Going back down the stairs, she stumbled but caught herself. At the bottom the basement stretched out in front of her. The prison with its wall of wood was on her left. The brick wall to her right. The far end lay in near total darkness. Probably wasn't a way out down there. But maybe she could find a weapon. Her lips tightened. Something she could use to beat the hell out of those crazy people.

She moved cautiously in that direction. It was hard to see; the farther from the stairs she got the darker it was. Glass jars lined rows of rustic shelves. She got close enough to make out the contents of the jars. Beans. Peaches. Canning jars. Her grandmother on her mom's side canned fruits and vegetables.

These looked old. She touched one. A thick layer of dust coated the jar. Really old. She searched the dark, squinting in an effort to see. No tools or pieces of loose wood that could be used for a weapon.

Andrea moved to the far end of the basement. Definitely a basement. She could see the wood joists that supported the floor above. The basement walls were all brick except the part that divided their prison from the rest of the space.

At the farthest end from the steps there were more shelves and a big wooden box. Something dragged across the top of her head. She ducked. A string hung from a small round light fixture that held a bare bulb. Andrea reached up and pulled the string. The light came on and she blinked to adjust her eyes before starting forward again.

She stalled a few feet away from the box. Not a box. *A coffin.* Andrea stumbled back. Hit the ground on her bottom. Her lungs seized, refused to allow air inside.

Was this the box the others talked about?

"What's out there?" Callie whispered from the hole.

Andrea found her voice. "Junk." She swallowed back the fear. "Just junk." Andrea didn't want Callie screaming like she had that morning.

She got back to her feet and made her way to the box... the coffin. The wood looked rough and old. Maybe it was just a coffin-shaped handmade box for storage. On the wall above it there were pictures of angels and crosses and pages from the Bible. Parts of one of the verses were highlighted in yellow. Andrea squinted to read the highlighted words: *fallen... one is... not yet come.*

Andrea drew back. Shook herself. *Freaks.* She stared at the coffinlike box. Something was written on the top. Hand shaking, she reached out and cleared away the dust.

Loser.

Andrea snatched her hand back.

Run. Just run.

Her feet felt mired in the hard-packed dirt.

No. She needed to know what was in the box. So far

these nutcases hadn't hurt them. Not bad enough that anyone was dead. What about Reanne? a tiny voice argued. And the baby? Andrea squeezed her eyes shut.

She had to do this. She needed to know as much as she could to make an intelligent guess about what these freaks might possibly have planned.

Finding her courage, she reached out again and lifted the lid.

Clothes. Girl clothes. Pinkish or purple flowers. At first nothing besides the faded dress registered, then the rest trickled through the denial in her brain. *A skeleton.*

Andrea slapped her hands over her mouth to hold back the scream that surged in her throat.

Noooo!

She collapsed into a squat, afraid to move her hands for fear of the sound of horror escaping.

Her heart hurt from the pounding. Her stomach felt as if it had risen into her throat and clumped there.

A creak overhead jerked her gaze upward.

Oh God.

Andrea closed the lid, her entire body shaking so hard she could hardly stay upright. She rushed back to the hole.

Above her footsteps echoed.

They were coming!

She got down on her hands and knees at the hole. "Shove some of that dirt into the hole," she whispered to Callie.

"What's happening?"

"Hurry, Callie, they're coming!" she urged as quietly as the fear would allow.

Dirt poured into the hole. Andrea leaned closer to the wall. "Put the toolbox back in and cover it up. Okay?"

"What're you going to do?" Callie's voice trembled.

Andrea listened. Didn't hear the footsteps now. "I don't know."

As Callie pushed more dirt into the hole, Andrea smoothed the pile on her side of the wall. She rushed back to the light and tugged the string. With that light out it was really dark. She prayed they wouldn't notice the loosened dirt.

"It's done," Callie whispered.

What now? What now?

More footsteps. Stumbling or dragging.

Andrea had to do something. "Get back in your bed," she whispered. "I'm going to hide."

But where? There was no place to hide.

The sound of steps overhead progressed toward the other end of the house...to that locked door that led down here.

Shit!

Andrea moved to the steel door that separated her from Callie and Macy. It was locked, she knew. She damned sure couldn't crawl under or over it.

There was no place to hide!

She was fucked.

She smoothed her hands over the cold steel, searching for a hidden latch. Anything! Her fingers bumped something above the top of the door. Wait. A big key hung on a nail. She grabbed it, shoved it into the lock, and twisted. The door opened.

Her heart pounding, Andrea hung the key back on the nail, eased into their prison, and closed the door. She checked the hole Callie had filled. Raked her foot over the dirt to smooth it.

"What're you doing?" Callie cried softly.

Clomping on the steps warned that the bad people were close.

"Lie down and close your eyes." Andrea sat down at the end of the bunk bed and grabbed a piece of tape. She pressed it against her mouth. It fell off. Hands shaking, she grabbed another piece and pressed it hard across her mouth. This time it stayed. She flattened pieces around her wrists as best she could, then felt around for any strips she had missed.

The key rattled in the lock.

Andrea hung her arms around the bedpost as they had been before and rested her forehead against the cold metal. She prayed they wouldn't notice the tape wasn't as tight and thick as before. She prayed they wouldn't notice the loose dirt. Or the unlocked—

"Did you leave the door unlocked?" the woman demanded.

"I'm not stupid," the man groused. "I locked it."

The door creaked open.

Andrea squeezed her eyes shut, pretended to be asleep. She prayed the others would, too.

The light swept over her as they checked their prisoners.

"You didn't lock it," the woman accused.

"Next time lock it yourself. What do you want me to do with Dana?"

"I don't care what you do with her." The woman was mad. "I told you she's not fit for him. She's like the other one, a loser."

"He likes her and that's what matters. Besides, you started this with her."

"I had my reasons," the woman said with a funny kind of ugliness in her voice.

"You always have your reasons."

The man was close, almost on top of Andrea. She shook so hard inside she was terrified they would see her vibrating. The man grunted and the bed frame shook with the weight of a body being hefted onto it.

"Maybe she'll fall off that top bunk and break her neck and save me the trouble of fooling with her. Little whore," the woman sneered.

The man stepped away from the bed. Andrea found the courage to breathe.

"You hurt her and I'll tell him what you did before. You hear me?"

"You don't control me."

"No," the man agreed smugly, "but *he* does."

"You're just jealous," the woman taunted.

The man didn't say anything else. The door slammed shut.

"I'll lock it this time," the woman smarted off, her words muffled by the closed door.

"It's time for his walk," the man said. "You want me to bring the other one back down here first?"

"I'm not done with her yet. She has more tests."

Still grumbling at each other, they stamped up the steps.

Andrea threw off the tape and shot to her feet. She braced her foot on the bottom bunk and hoisted herself high enough to check on the girl they'd put on the top bunk. This one smelled fresh, like flowery perfume.

Reanne was upstairs, the woman had said. Testing. At least she was still alive.

They called this one Dana.

She was unconscious. Andrea couldn't see what she looked like but she could hear and feel her steady breathing.

Andrea hopped down to the floor.

"They brought another one." Callie's voice sounded small and tired.

That Macy was still sleeping worried Andrea. She checked her breathing. Slow and steady.

"Reanne was here when I got here," Callie said. "Macy came next and then you. What're they going to do with us?"

Andrea thought about the skeleton in the coffin outside that door. *Loser.* But she wasn't saying anything about that. Callie and Macy would be hysterical. Andrea turned and peered through the darkness at the new girl. The woman had called her a loser, too.

Would the new girl be the first to die? Were the tests some kind of competition that would determine who lived and who died? Had the girl in the handmade coffin failed her tests? What about the baby?

Andrea put her arms around Callie and hugged her. "None of us are going to die," she promised.

She closed her eyes against the images of the evidence that at least one girl and a baby had died here already.

Please, God, she prayed, *help Dan find us.*

Warrior, 5:50 p.m.

Dan watched as Jess worked her magic with Steve and Elaine Sawyer. Her ability to put people at ease under the worst of circumstances was uncanny. Not even the family's concerns and questions about the department's failure to find the other missing girls had prevented Jess from drawing the interview into focus. She was a master at getting what she wanted from the families and friends of victims.

Yet, put her in a room full of cops and the foreplay was over.

Dana, the Sawyer's daughter, had gotten into an older model blue Ford truck at approximately eight forty-five last night. A witness, Jeremy Thompson, had been fueling up his Dodge truck next door at the mini-market convenience store. He might not have noticed her except that the girl was really hot, he'd stated. He'd said the same thing to his buddy, who worked at the convenience store, when he paid for his gas—which was the only reason they now had a witness.

The windows of the Ford were darkly tinted, so he couldn't have seen the driver even if he'd looked. Unfortunately, the convenience store's security cameras' range didn't reach beyond the first parking spot of the floral shop.

Sergeant Harper was running down the trucks registered in Jefferson County, as well as the surrounding counties, for a list of ones matching the witness's description. When pushed and shown photos, Thompson had narrowed the age of the truck down to something between '69 and '74, which was a damned wide gap to try to fill.

Detective Wells was in the missing girl's bedroom exploring her laptop with the help of Ricky Vernon from the lab.

Dan eased into the conversation with the parents by taking the chair next to Jess. Steve and Elaine were huddled together on the sofa. Their minister and family attorney had been called, but the couple insisted that the latter's presence was for peace of mind, while the former's was for peace of spirit.

It worried Dan when folks felt compelled to call their attorney at a time like this. Crime shows had damaged law enforcement's relationship with the public to some degree. Everyone thought they needed to invoke their rights and lawyer up to even sit in the same room with a cop.

"She's in the top of her class at Birmingham-Southern College." Mr. Sawyer managed a vague smile. "Full scholarship."

"I know you're proud," Jess said with a smile of her own.

Dan hadn't seen her smile like that once since she'd arrived. That it disappeared so quickly suggested the expression had been for show.

"Your list of her friends is quite extensive. Dana is a popular girl."

Elaine swiped at her tears with a wadded tissue. "She has always been very popular. Everyone loves her. She's a good Christian girl. She teaches the preschool Sunday school class."

Jess studied the list. "Are any of the boys listed here former boyfriends or maybe present romantic interests?"

Elaine shook her head adamantly. "No. Dana prefers to focus on her studies. She had a long, painful relationship in high school, and she decided that college was going to be different."

"She's a really smart girl," Jess agreed. That she shot a look at Dan from the corner of her eye telegraphed loudly and clearly that she was recalling their tumultuous high school years.

"Is there any contact with the boy from high school?" Dan asked.

Steve shook his head. "He died in a car accident right before graduation. The whole community was devastated."

"No contact with his family? Siblings, perhaps?" Jess asked, pursuing that angle with obvious interest.

"He was an only child," Elaine answered. "Like our Dana." She looked at Steve. "I haven't seen the Murrays in ages."

"Chief?"

Dan turned to his detective. Wells waited at the doorway that divided the living room from the foyer. She gave a succinct nod toward Jess. Dan lifted his chin in approval.

"Agent Harris," Wells said, "I hate to interrupt, but I need a moment of your time."

"Excuse me, Mr. and Mrs. Sawyer." Jess skirted Dan's chair and joined Wells in the foyer.

While the two conferred, Dan distracted the worried parents, whose attention had followed Jess from the room. "I saw the trophies in your daughter's room. Is she still involved with dance competition?"

Andrea had stopped only recently. Her mother said she'd danced before she walked. But after her father dropped back into the picture she'd lost her enthusiasm. The idea that she was still missing after five days twisted inside Dan like razor-sharp barbed wire.

"That changed with college, too," Elaine said, her voice trembling. "She is a very focused student."

Other than Reanne, all the girls appeared to be intently focused on their educations.

"How long has your family lived in Warrior?" Dan already had the answer to that question and numerous others, but he, too, needed to keep his attention in the room when he wanted to look into the foyer just as much as they did. And the more specific questioning was Jess's. The quickest way to put off a pair of terrified parents was to start hammering them with pointed questions from two different sources.

"I apologize for the interruption," Jess said as she returned to her seat. She readied her notepad and pencil. She apparently didn't care for technology beyond the cell phone she appeared to use for nothing but calls.

"We...ah...we've been here all our lives," Steve said

in answer to Dan's question. "Both our families." He patted his wife on the hand. "Dana is the sixth generation of Warriors."

"Mr. and Mrs. Sawyer, you know what Facebook is, I'm sure." Jess gave them a second to think about that. "It's a popular social network for teenagers and, really, people of all ages."

Elaine nodded first. Steve seemed to do so just because his wife did.

"Dana has a Facebook page," Jess explained, "and there was a private message to her from a female friend who calls herself Beautiful Mind. She seemed worried that Dana hadn't called her since yesterday."

The Sawyers shared a questioning look, then shook their heads. "I have always respected my daughter's privacy," Elaine responded. "I have no idea who her Facebook friends are."

Dan wondered if Annette knew Andrea's friends.

"Detective Wells discovered that Beautiful Mind is actually Dr. Maureen Sullivan. She's a psychologist in Birmingham who specializes—"

"We know who she is," Steve said. He looked confused for a moment, then visibly shook it off. "She was Dana's therapist for the first year after the accident. The Murray boy had been a part of her life all through high school. His sudden death was difficult for her even though they had ended their relationship several months prior."

Elaine seemed to have a more difficult time absorbing the implications of Jess's announcement. "Why would Dr. Sullivan be talking to Dana now? Their last session was more than two years ago."

"We'll find the answer to that question for you, Mrs.

Sawyer," Jess promised. "It may very well be as simple as bumping into each other on Facebook. It happens all the time."

The worried parents nodded in unison. Dan hated to see another family going through this nightmare. It was bad enough that four families had been devastated. Fury burned in his gut. Who the hell was doing this?

"I believe I have all I need for now," Jess said. "If you think of anything at all that might help our investigation, please call the chief's office."

It was Dan's turn. "We've had Dana's car moved to the lab to check for anything the evidence techs may have missed. With your permission, we'll take her laptop for additional analysis. Our hope is that we will find any communications with anyone who may know something about who she intended to meet at the flower shop."

According to the witness, Dana had gotten into the truck of her own free will.

"You're aware, I'm sure," he explained, "that considering your daughter's age, technically we have no jurisdiction over her decision to leave, alone or with anyone else, when no coercion is suspected. But we have four other girls who have gone missing in the past three weeks. All around the same age as Dana and under similar circumstances in terms of the abruptness of their departures and the lack of advance warning to even their closest friends."

"Generally," Jess added, "a girl of Dana's age will tell someone when planning a decision of that magnitude. The cooperation of all her friends is essential, as is yours."

"Whatever we can do," Steve guaranteed. "Anything. We have friends all over town looking for her."

Numerous search parties had been organized for each

of the disappearances, to no avail. If Dana was number five in this unnamed case, search parties in the woods and throughout nearby neighborhoods might prove pointless. But Dan appreciated the need to go through the motions. He'd beat his share of bushes for the first forty-eight hours after Andrea went missing.

As if fate had decided he needed a break, he, Jess, Wells, and Vernon were on their way out as the attorney arrived. The minister pulled up behind him.

"I'm going to the lab with Vernon," Wells said. "Unless there's some place else I need to be."

"Keep doing just what you're doing, Wells," Dan agreed. They had to catch a break soon. "Let me know when you've got something." Assuming there was anything to get.

Gina was going to be royally ticked off that he'd had to postpone the scoop he'd promised. She would use that for future leverage, he felt sure.

While he deliberated the way to make Gina happy and keep Jess out of trouble, Jess climbed into the driver's seat of his SUV. He went to the passenger side and opened the door. "Is there a reason you want to drive?"

On the way here he had broken every speed limit encountered. He'd never known her to be afraid of pushing the limits, but then that had been a long time ago.

"Maybe I just want to see how one of these extravagant SUVs handles." She smoothed her hands over the leather steering wheel.

Dan resisted the urge to loosen his tie at the idea of how many times she had run her hands exactly that way over his naked skin. He banished the memories.

"Why not?" He passed the keys to her and climbed in.

As soon as he closed his door, she eased away from the curb.

Jess passed him a note. "Enter this address into your GPS. That's our destination."

He should have anticipated a hidden agenda. Dan looked at the Mountain Brook address. "Who we going to see?"

"Dr. Maureen Sullivan."

No surprise there. Jess had been in a hurry to go from the moment Wells gave her the news. "She won't talk to us, Jess. You know that. Doctor-patient privilege. There are steps we need to take first. And she might not talk then."

"She doesn't have to tell us anything." Jess headed for the interstate. "We tell her and then we watch what happens."

Dan shook his head. She was grasping at straws. "You feel this compelled from a simple *call me* message?"

"No." She flipped open her notepad with one hand while she drove with the other. "I feel this compelled by the one that came after the *call me* message." She passed the notepad to him.

Dan stared at her neatly written notes. Underlined twice was: *Don't do it.*

Mountain Brook, 7:00 p.m.

Jess parked the Mercedes at the curb in front of Dr. Sullivan's home. "Looks like she has company." The doctor was unmarried and lived alone, according to what Wells had passed along while they were en route. She drove an

Infinity sedan. The Volvo parked behind her sedan was the unknown variable.

"What do you want to bet it's her attorney?"

Jess wasn't in a betting mood. "I guess we'll just have to see." No need to run the plate. They would soon know.

With scarcely more than an hour before dark, Jess wanted this woman under surveillance 24/7, but that required additional manpower on a case that wasn't even really a case. Five girls were missing and they didn't have a speck of evidence indicating foul play.

Even if Dan went for it, he had a hierarchy to whom he had to answer. As much as the mayor and every other powerful politician and influential citizen in the Birmingham area wanted these girls found, there was a limit to how far they could bend the law and extend resources. And the Bureau was waiting for BPD to prove there was a connection before doing any more than the cursory efforts already in place. Not even another missing girl had swayed their position.

Jess could kick herself for leaving her car at Dan's parents' house. If she were in her own car, she could do the surveillance. She wasn't on the city or the county's payroll. In a few weeks, she wouldn't be on any payroll.

Dan rapped on the ornate door of the Sullivan home. The door opened immediately. The man who towered in the doorway was forty or better, had an enviable tan, and wore wire-rimmed eyeglasses. But it was the haute couture suit that gave him away. The lawyer.

"May I help you?"

The lavish foyer behind him was empty but Jess, now in the betting mood, would wager that the good doctor was close by listening.

"Yes, you may." Jess smiled and flashed her soon-to-be-useless creds. "I'm Special Agent Harris and this is Chief of Police Burnett. We'd like to speak to Dr. Sullivan."

The lawyer thrust a card at Jess. "I'm Edward Williams, her attorney. You and the chief may speak to me." He acknowledged Dan with a nod.

"In that case," Jess suggested, "may we come in out of the heat?"

"I'm comfortable right here."

Jess supposed he was. He had all that climate-controlled air circling around him. "Since you're here, Mr. Williams, I assume you know a former patient of Dr. Sullivan's has gone missing."

News in small towns traveled at the speed of light, straight to the local news networks, all of which were poised and salivating for actual news. When would people realize that no news was generally good news?

"We have heard, yes. It's tragic."

Jess adjusted the strap of her bag on her tired shoulder. "Your client left a couple of messages for Dana Sawyer on her Facebook page. I'd like to know what those messages mean."

"I'm afraid my client is constrained by doctor-patient privilege. There are steps you will need to take if you intend to pursue questioning." He puffed out his chest and smiled smartly. "Good day, Agent Harris, Chief Burnett."

"Your client is also aware," Jess said before he could close the door, "that Dana Sawyer is one of five girls who have gone missing under similar circumstances."

"As I said, Agent Harris," Mr. Williams returned, "we saw the news and we sympathize with your position. You must, in turn, understand ours."

"Any information your client has," Jess pushed when he attempted to shut her out a second time, "could make the difference between whether those girls live or die."

Movement beyond the fancy attorney drew Jess's attention.

Williams turned to his client. "Maureen, do not allow this agent's dramatics to influence your emotions. We have already discussed these possibilities. Our position on the matter cannot change."

"You can make up your own mind, Doctor," Jess said, ignoring the attorney's glare.

"And lose your license," Williams warned.

Sullivan had been crying. Her eyes were swollen and red. She wrung her hands as if she couldn't decide what to do with them. She wanted to talk but she was afraid of the consequences; that was obvious. Ultimately, she looked away, mouth shut tight.

Jess acquiesced. For now. "All right, Mr. Williams. I'll be sure to notify you and your client first when we find the bodies."

She turned her back and descended the steps. Sullivan launched an argument with Williams but he closed the door before Jess could hear what she had to say.

Fury scaled her rigid backbone as Jess strode to the SUV. She would never understand how a doctor could hold back information when a life or lives were at stake. Wherever Dana Sawyer had been going, her therapist knew something about it. That information could lead them to all the girls.

If they were together.

Reanne Parsons may have gone off with a boy named Tim. Dana obviously had someone she intended to meet.

There was not a single shred of evidence that connected these five disappearances. Only that hard, cold instinct of Jess's that warned this was all tied together.

Jess climbed into the passenger seat and slammed the vehicle door. She didn't want to drive anymore. She wanted her Audi so she could sit out here all night and watch this woman. If nothing else maybe the effort would save Dana Sawyer.

When Dan was behind the wheel, Jess turned to him. He wasn't going to like her request but that would be nothing new. "If Detective Wells or Harper could bring my car, I'd like to keep an eye on Sullivan tonight. If she has any idea—"

"Out of the question." Dan started the engine. "First—"

Her cell rang. She grabbed for her bag. Damn. Damn. Damn. "Why won't you listen to reason, Burnett?" Jess fished for her phone. "Sullivan may very well try to track down Dana herself. If she does something stupid like that she'll need backup—protection, I mean."

Burnett stared at her, his expression somewhere south of furious, but not more than a hop, skip, and a jump.

Her cell blasted another ring. She hit the screen and shoved it to her ear. "Harris."

If she were lucky it was Wells. Jess could persuade the ambitious detective into pulling an all-nighter with her.

"Harris, we have a problem."

The rush of cold and then hot that dashed over Jess's skin soaked all the way to her bones and left her speechless for a moment.

She summoned her voice. "And what would that be?" She refused to bother with the formalities of addressing her superior by the book at this point. Why cater to

Supervisory Special Agent Gant's rank? He had probably already submitted the paperwork for her dismissal. In reality, they had several problems, starting with him. Besides, Burnett was listening. He already knew too much.

"*He* walked two hours ago."

Jess went completely still deep inside where her thoughts usually raced like the Gumball Rally when on a case. She couldn't breathe much less speak.

"You need to watch yourself, Harris. We're doing everything we can to put this case back together but God only knows where he'll be by then. We've got surveillance on him but based on the resources at his disposal, if it lasts the night, it'll be a miracle."

Reality nudged her. Jess blinked. "Thank you. I appreciate the update." She didn't bother with a good-bye. She shoved the phone back into her bag, deep in the bottom, as if that would somehow conceal what she did not want to acknowledge.

"Did Harper find something?"

"No." She shook her head for emphasis and maybe to clear it.

He shifted into drive but his attention failed to shift from her.

Why didn't he just let it go? "It was . . . *personal*." Undeniably, regrettably very personal.

Burnett drove. She sat in a kind of coma. *Eric Spears was free.* At least six women were dead. All brutally raped and murdered with slow, methodical torture techniques. And no one had been able to stop him. The six bodies they had found were probably only the first peek at a much larger, much uglier history of depravity. Spears was forty years old. He'd likely been doing this far longer than anyone other than Jess suspected. Definitely longer than the five years the bureau had tagged.

He was out.

And it was her fault. She had made a terrible mistake. The chances that he would have walked anyway had been stacked deep in his favor. But her role had ensured that, barring a miracle, none of the evidence he'd stockpiled could ever be used against him. The only way he would be stopped now was if some of his old work, assuming she was right about that, was uncovered or if he killed again and got caught.

Otherwise he would just keep killing and his victims, all women, would keep dying horrific deaths.

Because of her.

How could she possibly believe for one second that anything she was capable of doing would save these girls?

Jess stared out her window, focused on the blur of trees and houses. *Don't think about it.* There was nothing she could do. The damage was done. She couldn't go back and make it right.

When Burnett dropped her off, she would drive back and watch Sullivan's house. Jess doubted the woman would risk leaving until her attorney had taken his leave and she had the cover of darkness. Then again, she might not take the risk at all. Not every woman was as rash as Jess.

"Burnett."

She started at the sound of his voice. If she hadn't been so distracted she would have noticed he'd gotten a call. Could be Harper or Wells with an update. Or Patterson. Griggs, possibly. Maybe there would be a real break and they could find these girls and wrap up this case. Then Jess could disappear into nowhere. Someplace where *he* wouldn't find her.

There were many times in a woman's life when she wanted to be the object of a man's desire. His total obsession. But this was not one of those times.

Would Spears really take that kind of risk? His intelligence level would indicate otherwise...but the part of him that could not control the impulses driving his obsession with achieving pleasure in the only way he could ruled him to a large degree.

Burnett's cell phone slid back into its leather holster, the sound not unlike that of a weapon easing back into its keeping place. She shivered. If Spears came after her, no one close to her would be safe. Not her family...not Dan.

Focus, Jess! She kicked Spears and Gant out of her head and reached for some semblance of composure. No need to borrow trouble; she had two handfuls already.

"Did you really think you could keep this news from me?"

So the call hadn't been an update. Perfect. One of his people had obviously seen the news. The question was, how would Wells or Harper or any of the others under his command know about her connection to Spears?

"Thanks for blabbing my secrets to the world." You couldn't trust anybody anymore.

"Wells," he clarified. "I told her to keep an eye on any press releases related to the guy. I didn't tell her why."

"That's something, I suppose." Jess hated, hated, *hated* anyone knowing her secrets. Wells was no dummy. She would figure it out.

"You'll stay at my house tonight."

"No." She glared at him. "I will not! I am a trained agent. I can take care of myself." Not to mention she wasn't going to be caught in his house alone with him under any circumstances. Life or death included.

"Jess, you have two choices."

That was a tone she hadn't heard in half a lifetime. Before she could set him straight, he laid down the law according to Dan Burnett. "You will either stay with me or I will assign a uniform to you. One who won't take any of your crap."

"Fine."

"Here we go with the fine again."

"You can stay with me but we will not stay at your house. We'll stay at your parents'." As much as she dreaded the idea of spending 24/7 with him, she preferred that to another stranger knowing her business. Better the devil she knew.

"Fine," he conceded.

Her car was at the senior Burnett's house. Chances of persuading him to change his mind about the surveillance were greater in an environment that was not his usual habitat.

"We'll stop by my house so I can get a change of clothes."

That she could do. "Fine."

"God, I hate that word."

He made the next right and Jess's interest level in the area rose despite telling herself over and over that she did not care where he lived.

The house wasn't as massive as his parents' home. It was one of those English Tudor styles that reeked of grandeur no matter that the house on either side of it was much larger. A cobblestone drive stretched beneath a portico that offered entrance to the side door without tackling the elements, then flowed back to a two-car garage. The landscaping alone had likely taken the same size dent from his bank account as the Mercedes had.

He parked beneath the portico and hopped out as if he couldn't wait to show the place off. There really was no need for her to go in. He could grab his change of clothes and come right back.

He opened her door. "Come on. I'll show you around."

She opened her mouth and he interrupted, "Don't say fine."

She exhaled a big, disinterested sigh. "Okay. But, for the record, we're wasting time."

He shook his head and headed for the side entrance. Jess shoved the car door shut and followed. By the time she reached him he had the door unlocked and the security system disarmed. "Would you like something to drink? A glass of wine? Coke?"

"No, thank you." Wine and Burnett did not go together at any time, under any circumstances.

The side door led through a mudroom–laundry room. She shadowed him into the kitchen.

Her breath hitched before she could stop it. She'd expected nice but this was incredible. If he had picked out the surfaces, colors, and textures—not to mention the amazing cabinetry—she was impressed.

"I see you have a decorator." Maybe his ex-wife had done his decorating. Not that Jess cared. Annette could be beautiful and have an eye for decorating. As long as she wasn't smart and nice. Jess gave herself a mental kick and retracted the cat claws.

"My mother." He grabbed a soft drink from the enormous side-by-side fridge with its glass doors. Top of the line. More big bucks.

That the mastermind behind the gorgeous decorating was his mother was almost worse. "She did a beautiful job." Of course she did. Spending money was a fine art to her.

"Make yourself at home." He downed another swallow before setting the can down. "I'll be right back."

He removed his sport coat as he walked away, the imagery reminding her of that time ten years ago. Only his place had been a stylish apartment downtown then. And there had been no slipping out of anything. They had practically torn each other's clothes off.

Jess chased the memories away and wandered through the rest of the downstairs. The great room was just that. Big, comfortable furniture was artfully arranged. A massive fireplace and flat-panel TV. Homey but elegant. The dining room was extremely well done. Not too formal, more an eclectic blend of lavish and simple.

The hall powder room was iron and marble and glass. Very masculine. Sexy almost.

But the coup de grace was the staircase leading to the second floor. Grand, yet the inviting textiles climbing the steps gave it a soft, welcoming appeal.

Her phone made that funny little sound that signaled she had a text. She hated texts. Only Gant sent her text messages. Most of the time to relay an order without suffering any lip from her.

Jess sat down on the second step from the bottom and dug around in her bag. She needed to organize this monstrosity that housed her life. She needed to do a lot of things.

She swiped the screen, allowing the message to open fully. Private number. She frowned and reached for her glasses. With the frustrating eyewear in place she visually scrolled down the screen.

I'm celebrating. Wish you were here.

The phone slipped from her hand and bounced on the thick Persian rug gracing the sleek marble floor.

Reaching deep inside and hauling her courage back from the pit of her stomach, she considered the situation with as much objectivity as she could amass. She shouldn't be surprised. Spears had a hard-on for her. She'd wanted so badly to get to him that she'd allowed herself to be vulnerable. She'd opened too far to entice his curiosity if not his trust.

Now he had turned his powerful obsession on her.

Wish you were here. But he was there and she was not. She refused to let him get to her with his head games.

"How about we grab some dinner before—"

She snatched up her phone and shoved it into her bag. "Fi—sounds good." She stood, hoisted a reasonable smile into place. "Then can we drive back to the doctor's house and just admire her neighborhood while we eat?" Her voice cracked only once. She was tired. Who wouldn't crack a little after a day like today?

He nodded slowly. "Why not? What kind of host would I be if I didn't show you a little of the city's nightlife." Suspicion hovered in his eyes. "Chinese or Mexican?"

"Chinese." She did an about-face and strolled through the house, using the same path she'd taken on her tour. If she worked hard enough and kept her cool, the whole Spears situation would fade into the background of their investigation. She did not want Burnett hovering over her.

"Harper called."

"How many blue Ford trucks from that era are registered in the area?" That was the ticket. Play it cool. Nonchalant.

"One hundred and three."

Jess laughed, the sound groused out of her. "Harper should have fun with that."

"And that's only the active ones. If he has no luck on those, he'll have to go digging in the archives for those not currently registered."

"I don't even want to think how long that will take." Jesus, couldn't anything about this investigation be simple?

At the door Burnett stopped her, stepped outside, and surveyed the area, before allowing her to cross the short distance beneath the portico to the car.

This was exactly what she did not want.

When he'd armed the security system and secured his home, he slid behind the wheel. As he backed out onto the street he braked, set those blue eyes directly on hers. "There's nothing wrong with being afraid, Jess."

Dear God. "I am not afraid, Daniel Burnett." Where the hell had he gotten that idea?

"You should be."

She laughed. He didn't even know the half of it. "Well, Dr. Phil," she leaned back into the lush leather seat and turned to study him, "if you give me a chance, I'll explain why I'm not afraid."

"By all means. I would love to hear how you came to that conclusion, considering what that evil son of a bitch has done." The fury simmering in him spilled over in his words. He really was worried.

"I built the man's profile. I'm not his type. All his victims were brunette, tall, young." Jess was none of the above. She was barely five four, weighed all of a hundred pounds, and she hadn't run or really worked out in ages.

"The scumbag is just curious about me because I see him for who he is when no one else seems to. He likes to play with those he perceives as interesting. But I'm not the type who gets his motor running. I don't evoke that level of desperation and desire in him. When he grows bored of analyzing me he'll move on."

Burnett didn't need to know this but that was the part Jess actually was afraid of.

As long as the Player was entertained by her, maybe no one else would have to die.

10:40 p.m.

Dan stuck his half-empty cup of dark roast in the holder on the console. With no restroom handy, any more coffee would be a bad idea. He hadn't pulled this kind of surveillance in years. He could easily have assigned someone else, but he wanted to do this. First, if Dr. Sullivan did have some idea where Dana Sawyer was and decided to attempt an intervention, he wanted to know immediately. Second, Jess had made a deal with him and he wanted to keep her cooperative.

He wanted to keep her close. The Player was one messed-up bastard. Whether Jess took the threat seriously or not, Dan wasn't taking any chances.

"Did Harper say he would have that list of Ford trucks worked by tomorrow afternoon?" Jess scooted around in her seat, trying to find a more comfortable spot.

Dan imagined that her butt was numb, just like his. The thought went off on a trek of its own with him dwelling on the idea of just what a cute butt hers happened to be. *Dumb, Dan.* "He'll do his best. Older models like that sometimes fall off the radar when they end up in junkyards or in some collector's garage."

"I can't believe Wells and Vernon didn't find anything else on that computer. I was hoping for more exchanges between Dana and the therapist. Or some interaction with a friend that alluded to something we could use."

"Speaking of the therapist," he ventured, "I don't think she's going anywhere tonight." They had been parked across the street from her place for two hours.

And though Dan couldn't say he hadn't enjoyed becoming familiar with Jess's unique scent and soft sighs again, it was different now. She was a married woman. Somehow that intrigued him all the more. Twenty years ago her fragrance had been wild and ferociously ambitious. Her sounds mostly of impatience. She'd tasted wild and sweet, too. Untamed and unstoppable. In the early days she'd made him feel as if anything were possible.

But reality had shattered the dream she'd inspired in him a long, long time ago. That she somehow resurrected those feelings of anticipation made him wonder if his most recent failed marriage had precipitated a midlife crisis. There was no other reasonable explanation for how she seemed able to stir those less rational sensations. He'd denied the responses for better than twenty-four hours now.

During the last two he'd run out of excuses.

Case in point, the interior of his SUV felt considerably smaller now than it had two hours ago. The space was filled with her. The sound of her voice... the smell of her skin. All those little sighs and soft sounds she made while considering some aspect of the case.

History and experience should serve as better defenses. He and Jess were far too different, each too focused on their own goals and definitions of who they were to compromise. How had twenty years of experience and understanding of the way life works evaporated in hardly more than that same number of hours?

"I'm surprised," Jess complained, intruding into his self-deprecation. "I'm sure Williams probably told her to stay put before he left." She stuffed her Pepsi can in the cup holder next to his coffee. "But I had her pegged for having more moxie than that."

Dan heaved the last of his thoughts from the forbidden to the reality of what was and shot her an *are you serious* look. Didn't matter that she couldn't see his skepticism had she bothered to look at him—which she did not—it made him feel better to do it.

"You haven't even met her. How did you peg her as having moxie or not?" He wasn't actually trying to be a smart-ass. He was curious. About her...the Jess of the present.

Just another item to add to the growing number on the bulleted list of examples proving his inability to control his baser instincts where she was concerned. The same thing had happened in about five minutes ten years ago. There was a pattern here and he hadn't figured out a way to change course before repeating it.

"I did so meet her." Jess twisted in the seat to face him, kicked off her racy high heels, and curled her legs under her. "She was in the entry behind that bull-headed attorney. I saw the look on her face."

Her tone had taken on that pouty quality that said she was tired but right, whether he believed her or not. Just listening to her evoked images of the way she used to scowl at him when he annoyed her, lips puckered in frustration. She glowered at him that way right now. The faint light from the streetlamps and the moon prevented the full impact, but his imagination filled in the missing details. The fitted suit she wore was an earthy brown. Elegant, conservative. But whatever she wore under that jacket was lacy and sexy. The lace adorned her cleavage, allowing the tiniest peek at her lush breasts.

And she belonged to someone else.

Okay, time for a walk. "I'll be right back." Clearly, one date in six months was not sufficient bonding time with the opposite sex.

"You're not going anywhere," she argued. "You ask me a question, the least you can do is listen to my answer."

Don't look at her. "Fine. I'm all ears."

"I thought you hated that word."

"Jess, you had a point to make."

She released a big, frustrated exhale that filled his senses with the smell of mints and chocolate M&M'S. She carried both in that huge bag of hers. "I read her professional bio. Scanned a few of her contributions to psychology journals. She's very type A. She's not married, which tells me that a traditional relationship is too confining. Her house is ostentatious, indicating she needs to display her success for the world to see. And she doesn't like to be wrong. Otherwise she wouldn't have crossed the line with a patient by sending a personal plea through a social network. Moxie should be her middle name."

If Jess had concluded all that from a little reading and a fleeting look, what did she deduce about him? "When did you have time to do all that research?"

"I didn't." She leaned her seat back a little farther and snuggled into the leather. "Detective Wells sent the info to my e-mail."

"Do you walk around profiling everyone you meet or just the persons of interest in a case?" He hadn't exactly meant to ask that. Now that he had, he wanted to hear the answer. For his own peace of mind.

"Depends." She drained her Pepsi can.

"On what?" Tension tightened the few muscles in his body that weren't already wound to the max.

"Whether the person is relevant to me or not."

He shifted his attention back to the street. Oh yeah. She had analyzed him all right.

"Are you asking me if I've created a profile on you, just for my own amusement?"

Now she was a mind reader. "I imagine it would make for fairly dull reading."

"To the contrary, Chief. It's rather intriguing."

Now she was teasing him. He kept watch on the house and the street, didn't spare her a glance.

"Based on what I know about you from your childhood and what I've read and learned since coming here—"

"You've been reading up on me, too?" He laughed. "I should've known."

"Like you didn't check up on me before calling me down here," she challenged.

"That was different. I needed your help on a case." Not exactly accurate, but she couldn't prove it. He'd wanted to know all he could for purely personal reasons as well. As crazy kids they had both been very competitive, even with each other.

"What did you find?" Her seat powered up to a more erect position.

"We were talking about what you found," he reminded her.

"All right then. You're driven, like always. You know what you want and you go after it. Those in your world believe you're a nice guy but in reality you're a hard-ass. You like things done. And you like them done your way. Your organization skills are top notch."

"I'll take that as a compliment." Not too bad.

Silence thickened in the air like the humidity after a rain when the sun roared its victory, scorching everything in its path. Seconds turned to a minute and she said nothing else.

"That's it?" He was a glutton for punishment.

"You mean besides your commitment issues?"

She hit a nerve with that one. "That was a long time ago, Jess."

How could she still hold that against him? They were kids. Another extremely vivid memory zinged him. Nope. She was referring to ten years ago. He hadn't called. He hadn't had the guts. She hadn't called either. They were even, in his opinion anyway.

With nothing more than the moonlight, he could see her face pinch into a frown. "I'm not talking about us, Burnett. I'm referring to three ex-wives. No children. Twelve-hour workdays. And though your home is lovely, you've lived there for what? Three years?"

"Five," he groused.

"And it looks like you moved in last week. I didn't see

a thing connected to you personally besides the framed five-by-seven your mother probably stuck on the mantel when she did the decorating."

Damn. She was good. "I'm impressed." Uncomfortable as hell, but impressed.

"Why did you and Annette split?"

His gaze lingered on hers in the faint light, trying to glean some motive. It wasn't a smart move but he couldn't resist. "I enjoyed her company. She enjoyed mine. At least for a while. Her top priority is her daughter, as it should be. Annette felt the family unit was best served intact." The last came out chock-full of resentment. His ego had been damaged, and it still stung.

"You and Andrea were close."

"Still are." As hard as he worked to keep that aspect of his life out of this part, it didn't always work. He adored Andrea and the idea that she was out there somewhere hurting, maybe worse, ripped him apart inside. But he couldn't do the job if he let that eat at him. Maybe the need for distraction was what made him so susceptible to Jess and their history.

"How would she handle this?"

"She would be strong. Careful. Smart."

"Smart enough to properly assess her situation and make a move to escape?"

"Yes." His voice sounded hollow. He missed that kid. A week didn't go by without her calling, or dropping by the office if she was home from school.

"Careful enough not to take too big a risk?"

"I think so."

"That's good." Jess nodded. "The others will need her."

"The others are hardworking, high achievers, too.

Reanne might not have made it through school but her employer praised her reliability and work ethic."

"True, but the others aren't like Andrea. There's still a lot of little girl in the others. Their rooms. The statements made by friends and family. The way they live reveals a great deal. They haven't made that last little emotional leap into adulthood. Andrea is far more mature. She's a leader."

"I can see that." He'd read the same reports Jess had. Hell, he'd been there. Listened to the family and friends firsthand. Saw the girls' rooms. And he hadn't been able to put his finger on an analysis so exact. Her precise isolation of points lifted those traits from the deluge of information right to the surface.

The last of the lights went out in Sullivan's house. Eventually Jess would have to admit defeat on this surveillance gig.

"My turn." There he went again, treading into personal territory.

"For what?" She leaned forward, close enough for him to smell the jasmine scent of her shampoo. "Seems the doc's going to bed."

"We'll give her a little more time," he offered, "just to be certain." Now why the hell had he done that? Maybe because his brain had stopped functioning properly with her so close.

And he wanted to know . . . a whole lot more.

She resettled in her seat. "Maybe she has a reason for waiting." She grabbed her Pepsi can again, shook it, then stuffed it back into the cup holder.

To avoid the silence and because the suspense of all he didn't know was killing him, he resumed his turn at the business of profiling. "I kept up with you for a long time."

Maybe it was that damned moonlight, the proximity, or a combination of both. The confession wasn't planned but it needed to be said. Too many things hadn't been said for too long. If this case wasn't enough to make a man realize that life was entirely too short and fragile, that man was an idiot. Dan had made his share of dumb moves in his life, but he wasn't stupid.

Gave credibility to his unprofessional curiosity.

"My career, you mean," she countered.

He shook his head, kept his gaze on the house. "All of you."

The little catch in her breath disrupted the rhythm of his.

"From the time you graduated from the academy, all the way through your last promotion. My liaison at the local bureau office kept tabs on you for me."

"You kept tabs on me until two years ago?"

"That's right."

She faced forward. "Two years ago, I got married."

"Yeah, I know." That was when he'd stopped asking and started moving on. He resisted the impulse to shake his head. *Stellar job, Burnett.*

"Things didn't work out with that."

There was a distinct sadness in her words. Not that tortured, rip-your-heart-out sort, but the regrettable acceptance-of-fact kind.

"You still wear the band?" He glanced at her, kept it brief. Was she saying that the marriage was over? Why the hell did he feel relieved?

"Habit."

He laughed. "Now that's a good one, Agent Harris."

"At first I assumed we would work things out."

She didn't say anything for a bit.

"Eventually I realized it wasn't going to happen. Funny thing is, I could never figure out why. He asked me to marry him and two months later he started accepting assignments that would take him the farthest away for the longest periods. It was only a matter of time before he accepted a permanent assignment on the West Coast. One day I got home and the divorce papers were waiting in my mailbox. I guess it just wasn't meant to be."

"Ouch." What a heartless bastard. She made the statements with little or no emotion. Did that mean she was over the guy? Not in Dan's estimation. She still wore the ring he'd given her.

"There's a shop downtown that'll pay you top dollar for gold." He tapped his left ring finger. "I've used it more than once."

"The ring comes in handy." She held up her hand and considered the plain gold band. "No one asks what went wrong until the band disappears. No unwanted advances. Makes life simple."

Sounded like BS to Dan. But that was as far into personal territory as he intended to go. That she was no longer in a relationship changed the mental boundaries he had unconsciously set. Which meant he really had to get a grip on this need-to-know compulsion before he made a mistake.

"She's not coming out, Jess."

"Let's give it another hour just to be sure."

He'd made it this long. Surely another hour cramped up in here with her like this wouldn't kill him.

Friday, July 16, 1:48 a.m.

The girls in the five photos spread across the sleek surface of the coffee table stared back at Jess.

"What're you trying to tell me?" she muttered.

She had gone over the statements, the photos. Every detail. If these young women had been abducted by the same unsub there had to be a connection that linked their lives. A common thread existed. No link through the schools they had attended or the neighborhoods where they grew up. No church associations or clubs or sororities in common. No related work history or volunteer involvements.

Since they were in the same age group, it was likely that they shopped in some of the same stores. Music, movies, books... leisure activities... all those near-impossible-to-trace categories. Jess made a note to look into shopping habits and leisure time hangouts. That aspect had been looked at already but a second, closer look couldn't hurt.

Dan had gone to bed, finally, half an hour ago. She had no desire to venture into that wing of the house until she was certain he was asleep. Those three hours in the Mercedes with him had drained her emotionally.

She threw down her pencil and rubbed at her blurry eyes. Exhaustion pulled at her. Sleep was what she needed. She shuffled the photos back into a stack and stuffed them into the file. Her attention stumbled on the band encircling her left ring finger. She hadn't intended to be so honest with him about that. There was no reason to be. But once she got started talking she hadn't been able to shut up. Never a good thing.

He'd kept up with her all that time. That part startled her. Didn't make sense. He was the one who had made the decision not to follow her to Quantico, maintaining that he had commitments at home. Lies.

They had planned their futures for years. The plan always included the bureau. But Dan had gotten passed over for an internship that first summer after college. He could have worked anywhere in DC or the surrounding area and tried again, but he'd turned his back on their plans and walked away with his ego dragging behind him.

The ache was still raw. It shouldn't be. All these years she had scarcely noticed it, buried it deep in rarely visited regions of gray matter, until that encounter ten years ago. Apparently, she hadn't been as successful at burying it after that. Not even taking a husband had gotten the job done completely.

What was she doing?

Jess braced her elbows on the table and propped her chin in her hands. She'd been sitting cross-legged for so long, her legs had gone to sleep. But that didn't explain the sudden numbness in her brain.

She had a degree in psychology. The answer to her self-analyzing question was easy. She'd suffered a tremendous blow to her career. Her career defined her, since she didn't have a husband or kids or a life, frankly. The decision had been made her senior year of high school that career would come first. But she'd had Dan then. He'd more than made her career-oriented plan enough.

Twenty years. Two decades. She had pretended her career was enough. An internship each summer for two years before becoming an agent with the Federal Bureau of Investigation. She had worked any available temporary jobs with local law enforcement while getting her graduate degree and waiting to reach the bureau's age requirement.

Was the reason she'd gotten too close on that last case because her life was unbalanced? Her sister swore she was proud of Jess. And if their parents were still alive, they would be, too. No matter what she did. Even when Jess had married a man her sister had never met until the evening before the wedding, her sister had been okay with it. Even when she confessed her decision not to permit children to interfere with her career. Her sister, her only family, loved her anyway.

Why was it no one else had loved her enough? Not Dan and not Wesley Duvall, the ex-husband who'd scarcely been around long enough to meet the definition of the term.

Now here she was. Forty-two and alone.

Jess rolled her eyes and pushed up from the floor. She winced as she walked around the room until the feeling returned to her legs. Any time she started self-analyzing this deep, it was time to go to bed.

The facts were simple. She was alone because no man wanted to take second billing to her career. She had no kids because her career came first and she'd spent more than half that career studying the faces of evil. Eventually her motive for remaining childless had become more about her experience than climbing the career ladder. How could anyone bring a child into this world knowing all that she knew? How could she put a child at risk because of her work? She could not.

She would not.

It was bad enough that with Spears a free man she had to worry about her sister and her family.

And Dan.

Jess gathered her notes and the file, stuffed them all into her bag, and slung it over her shoulder. Maybe she would take one of those posh bottles of water from the fridge to her room again.

Padding quietly through the massive house, she decided this wasn't a home. It was a museum.

The Katherine Burnett museum.

She snagged a bottle of water from the fridge, which looked exactly like Dan's, only larger. The kitchen was a monstrosity, with acres of cabinetry and granite. No one needed a kitchen this huge.

She wandered through the keeping room, a fancy name for a den off the kitchen. She hesitated at the fireplace, adorned with its marble and granite embellishments. Rows of photographs lined the mantel. Dan. His parents. Grandparents. Aunts and uncles. Oh, and one with Annette and Andrea. My. My. Jess switched the framed photos around like pieces on a chess board. She tucked some of the shorter ones in the back.

Feeling wicked, she moved around the room, displacing and repositioning small items. She stood back and surveyed her handiwork. "Better."

Katherine would blow a gasket when she came home.

Jess practically tiptoed down the big main hall. The house was only one floor but it sprawled over the massive treed lot. The bedrooms were in the east wing. The entertaining rooms in the west. With a cavernous foyer and parlor in the middle at the front of the house. The kitchen, keeping room, and dining room held center stage at the rear, opening onto grand gardens and patio venues. Katherine had designed the layout herself.

The Burnetts had built this mansion Dan's high school graduation year. It dwarfed their previous home. Funny how a lucky streak in the stock market could change one's status in life. And how swift maneuvering into more stable options could keep it that way. The Burnetts had always been comfortably wealthy, but that year had changed everything...except Katherine's low opinion of Jess.

Jess took no offense. The feeling was mutual.

Dan had taken his old room to get some sleep. She had used the guest room across the hall the night before. Now, however, she stood outside the door for a long minute, contemplating the proximity. The idea of being this close disturbed her. Had her feeling restless and too warm. She refused to allow a repeat of ten years ago.

The tension had been thick in the car tonight. Didn't help that she'd allowed herself a stroll down memory lane just now.

Decision made, Jess retrieved her wheeled bag and headed for the master suite. There were three other bedrooms. But she figured the last place he would consider crawling into bed with her was in his parents' room.

She opened the towering French doors and stepped inside. The room even smelled like Katherine. Rose. That was her signature scent.

Jess dug out her pajamas and headed for the bathroom. She'd take a shower in the morning. No way was she drying her hair tonight. She brushed her teeth, washed her face, and changed into her pajamas. She'd stopped wearing skimpy nighties months ago. What was the point?

There was no one to impress. Besides, with pj's, if an emergency came up in the middle of the night all she needed was her shoes and a coat.

Had she known all the work she would have to do to unmake the big four-poster bed, she might have picked another room. Mountains of pillows now sat on the richly carpeted floor. She peeled back the comforter and slid beneath it. Her body sighed with relief. It felt amazing to lie down.

She switched off the bedside lamp and tried to turn off her brain.

Her cell chirped.

For a long time she lay there, warring with herself about checking it. She reached over and touched the screen. She ruthlessly squashed the niggling idea that it could be *him* again. She absolutely would not waste her energy worrying about that twisted chain of useless DNA. This case had to be her top priority. Spears was the bureau's problem now.

Another persistent chirp.

Damn it. She rolled over and snatched up her phone, yanking it loose from the charger.

New text message.

She put on her glasses, slid her fingertip across the screen, and the text message appeared: Private number.

It was him.

Good night, Agent Harris.

Jess bolted to a sitting position. How could he know to send that message at this exact moment?

The drapes were pulled. Her car was in the garage.

Another chirp. Then another.

Five pretty girls.

I hope you'll be able to help those girls better than you did the last ones.

Jess scrambled out of bed, grabbed her weapon from her bag, and rushed to the window overlooking the front of the property. She edged the drapes aside and scanned the yard. The landscape lighting provided ample illumination to get a good visual.

Unless someone hovered in the bushes, there was nothing out there. No vehicles on the street.

Taking a couple of slow, deep breaths to lower her heart rate, she moved to the window facing the back of the property. Nothing. She started to draw away, then stalled.

The wind chime hanging from a decorative iron post swayed. With the windows shut tight she couldn't hear the sound it made, but she watched the rods and tubes swirl in the dead air. She surveyed the trees and shrubs. Nothing else moved. There was no breeze. Her heart rate picked up with equal measures fear and fury.

The security system was set. The doors were locked.

Still, she made her way through the house, checking each room and window.

When she reached Dan's room, she hesitated. If she walked in he might wake up. She didn't want to have to explain this to him. Spears was most likely playing a game with her. He'd made a good guess, that's all. He'd have to be an idiot to show up down here. Birmingham, Alabama, would be unknown territory to him, putting him at a disadvantage.

After a moment to steady herself, she padded silently into Dan's room. She'd checked all the others; if she skipped this one she'd only lie in bed wondering if she'd missed anything.

The curtains were open, allowing the moon and the landscape lighting to filter through the gauzy sheers. His clothes were draped over a chair. He lay on his back, one arm resting on the pillow above his head, the other at his side. The comforter partially covered his long legs and little else. He slept in his boxers, like before... when they had been a couple.

The urge to cover him almost had her reaching for the comforter. But the need to take in every detail prevented her from following through. He'd kept in good shape. Nicely rounded biceps, well defined pecs and abdominals. His hair was sleep rumpled and instead of looking unkempt, it looked sexy. His face was relaxed. She knew every angle and plane of that face, each chiseled detail. The square jaw...the classic Greek nose...the dimples when he smiled.

No wonder all these gorgeous women around here flocked to him like he was the last loaf of bread on the shelf before an unexpected winter snow.

Would she be lying beside him, wrapped in those strong arms, if she hadn't been so stubborn twenty years ago and had come back here with him? Would they have children?

An uncharacteristic wave of regret washed over her.

She would never know the answer to that question.

That bridge had been burned a long time ago.

Deep breath.

She had made the right choice.

She turned away, slipped quietly to the door.

"Jess."

Shit. Careful to keep her weapon behind her, she turned to face him. Spears and his stupid messages along with her even stupider response suddenly made her feel like a complete fool.

He was up and walking toward her.

Whatever gasp of air was in her lungs promptly evacuated.

"Are you all right?"

He stood over her, strong and beautiful, with the concern in his voice cloaking her in a warmth that felt familiar and safe. It was the middle of the night and she was weak.

Deep down she was terrified.

Her life was upside down...everything was wrong.

"I'm fine." She backed up a step. "I...was about to go to bed and I thought I'd check on you."

He must have heard the sham in her voice because suddenly his arms went around her and one hand smoothly slipped the weapon from her grasp.

"Is that why you're wandering around the house with this?" He held the weapon up as if it confirmed his suspicions that she was lying.

Problem was, it did.

"I left it in the living room. I went back to get it," she improvised.

"Liar."

That his face was suddenly nearer...that he held her tucked against him as if she were the missing piece of the puzzle that made him whole and he wasn't about to let go confused her. She couldn't think straight with his warm, hard body sending all kinds of wild signals to hers.

"I don't want you making a move without my knowledge," he said fiercely, his lips way, way too close. "I don't want you"—he seemed abruptly preoccupied with her mouth—"out of my sight."

Before she could answer, his lips brushed across hers and a fire ignited so deep inside her that it felt too far away. The yearning to be consumed by those flames made her ache. She leaned into the invitation of his mouth... dared to touch his naked skin with trembling fingers... smoothed her palms upward until her arms entwined around his neck.

The need to lose herself to the wondrous sensations... to reacquaint herself with him in the most intimate ways almost swept her away, but then the memories from ten years ago gathered like storm clouds...showering the chill of reality over her...extinguishing the flames.

This was a mistake.

She flattened her hands against his shoulders and pushed away from him.

"We have a long day ahead of us." She managed a deep breath, grabbed her resolve with both hands. "I should turn in."

He released her, held up his hands, her weapon still clutched in one, in surrender. "You're right." He passed her weapon to her. "Good night."

Jess couldn't tell if he was angry or disappointed or both. He gave her his back and stalked to his bed.

Her movements slower, she pointed herself in the other direction and returned to the master suite.

She placed her weapon on the bedside table and scrubbed at her eyes. How the hell had she let that happen?

Spears. Her lips tightened in fury. The bastard. He'd gotten the exact reaction he'd wanted.

He'd scared the hell out of her.

She would not be afraid.

Damn it. She would not.

Crawling into the bed and dragging the covers over her, she repeated the mantra until sleep lulled her into unconsciousness.

Hoover, 11:00 a.m.

Amy," Jess urged gently, "I want you to think really hard. Did Dana ever mention the young man's name or how she met him?"

Amy, Dana's closest friend and also a student at Birmingham-Southern, shook her head. More tears spilled down her pale cheeks. Her hands twisted together in her lap. "She wouldn't talk about it. But I could tell she felt really bad. It was like she thought there was something she had to do to fix something. She just wouldn't say what that something was."

Amy's parents, Carla and Tim Porter, sat on either side of their daughter on the sofa.

"Amy and Dana have been friends for only two years," Carla reminded Jess. "They met their freshmen year at Birmingham-Southern. Dana is a sweet, sweet girl." Carla shook her head as if still overwhelmed by disbelief. "I can't believe she would just up and run away like this."

"She didn't," Amy snapped, her nerves obviously frayed. "She wouldn't do this."

Tim Porter put his arm around his daughter. "It's going to be all right," he murmured.

As soon as Jess had learned Amy had a father named Tim, she put Wells on ferreting out all she could about the man. It was a long shot but Jess wasn't skipping any steps. The Porters had asked the usual questions. Were there any leads on the other missing girls? Was there a connection between Dana and the other girls?

"We've reviewed all the calls and texts on Dana's phone," Jess went on. "We didn't find any contact with persons not listed as close friends by her parents or you. How do you think she would have interacted with this unknown young man?" They were assuming the unsub in Dana's case was male.

That was the kicker. How was the unsub, or unsubs, in this case reaching the girls? They had the answer in Reanne's instance, but not with the other four. Nothing on cell phones or computers. The possibility that none of these disappearances were connected gnawed at Jess, but she refused to ignore her instincts. Somehow, there was a thread that wove through all five of these young lives.

Amy moved her head side to side. "She never told me." The worry for her friend clouded her eyes with genuine misery. "She always had her cell with her. Always. Checked her e-mail and Facebook that way. If they didn't talk on her cell, it had to be in person."

"And you're certain Dana doesn't have a boyfriend?"

"She doesn't." Amy shrugged. "Guys try but she ignores them."

"Do you believe this other boy is the reason? Or is it

her work at school?" It wasn't that Jess couldn't accept that a girl that age didn't have a love interest, it certainly seemed to be the one glaring theme beyond age, but what did Dana and the others do with their summers when they weren't in school? These were nineteen- and twenty-year-old women, for goodness sakes; biologically their hormones were ripe and raging.

"Until the last couple of weeks I thought it was school. But now I don't know."

Jess put her pencil and pad away. "Thank you, Amy, for talking to me. I realize you gave your statement to the police already but I wanted to speak personally to Dana's closest friends." And she wanted to get some face time with the father, Tim. "If you remember anything at all that you believe might be helpful please let me know."

Amy nodded, the tears starting anew. Her mother pulled her close and hugged her tight.

Jess stood, lugged her bag onto her shoulder. "Thank you, Mr. and Mrs. Porter. I appreciate your time."

The father followed Jess to the door. Burnett and Wells were outside having some kind of conference that Jess felt reasonably sure had been timed to ensure she wasn't a part of the huddle. If he had Wells checking into the Spears situation, Jess was going to pitch a fit. They needed all hands on deck on this case. There was no time for distraction.

Last night's creepy text messages meant nothing except that Spears wasn't finished playing games with her.

Or maybe Burnett had found out Jess had talked Wells into getting a beat cop friend of hers to watch Dr. Sullivan's house today. The man was off duty, it wasn't any of Burnett's business what he did with his free time. The cop wanted to make detective. He'd been eager to do a favor for Wells.

Outside the front door, good-byes exchanged, Jess hesitated. "Mr. Porter, you work in Tuscaloosa, is that correct?" She studied his face, watched for the slightest twitch.

"I do, yes." Suspicion as to her motive for asking immediately made an appearance on his face.

"Have you ever had lunch at the Roll Tide Sandwich Shop near the UA campus? It's a very popular place." It was also the place where Reanne Parsons worked six days per week most weeks, until she disappeared.

"I know the one you mean," he said carefully. "I've never eaten there, no."

"The reason I asked," Jess explained, "is that another of the girls who vanished worked there. I'm looking for any connection between these girls and their families. If you remember a time when perhaps your office had food delivered from that particular sandwich shop and maybe Reanne was the delivery person, please contact the chief's office or me directly." She withdrew Reanne's photo from her bag. "I'm sure you've seen her photo on the news, but just in case you haven't." She showed him the face of the missing girl.

He studied the photo at length without a visible reaction. "I'm sorry. I'm certain I've never seen her, but I'll ask around the office."

"Thank you, *Tim*." She started down the steps but hesitated again when she reached the walk. "It's just a coincidence, I'm certain." She shook her head and breathed a dog-tired sound that wasn't exactly a laugh.

"What's that, Agent Harris?"

Tim Porter stood still as stone, his face paler than before. He might not have any connection to Reanne, but there was something in his life that he was afraid of. His distress at whatever she intended to say next flashed like a caution light.

"The last person to see Reanne is named Tim." She shrugged. "It's a common name. Just a little unsettling." She gave him a big smile. "Thank you again."

Jess left him at the door staring after her. She wanted him to fret over whether he had anything to worry about. Mostly she just wanted him to think. Somewhere, somehow, there had to be a common element of which someone out there was aware. Until she found that link or those girls, she would happily take potshots at every available target.

"What's going on?" she asked when Burnett and Wells looked up.

If the uh-oh expressions captured on their faces weren't enough to tell the tale, the awkward tension vibrating the air as Jess approached warned that whatever was up, she wasn't going to like it.

It wasn't enough that she'd been avoiding eye contact with Dan all day after the incident last night. She'd acted like a total fool. A weak, helpless one at that.

"We need to get you back to the office. There's a storm coming and I don't think we're going to be able to stop it."

What was he talking about? Jess glanced at the sky. The sun was shining and the temperature was way too close to the triple digits for her liking. Of course, his statement had nothing to do with the climate. "What storm?"

"A media storm, Jess."

She shrugged. "So. They've been on top of this case for

weeks. The only reason they're not here now is because we're backtracking over territory already covered."

"It's not exactly about this case."

With him wearing those blasted sunglasses, she couldn't see his eyes. While she was on the subject, where the heck were hers? In the SUV. She shielded her eyes with her hand. "If it's not—"

She stopped short when it hit her. It was about *her*. And the Player.

"We have a short lead time," Wells explained. "The chief has a contact at Channel Six. She heard about the rumor blowing through the networks. Channel Ten is already camped out at the courthouse."

Jess swore under her breath. "I can't go to the office," she argued. "I'm not getting stuck downtown." When the big networks and cable news heard she was here, this case would become a national fiasco. A brief mention was one thing, but hour-by-hour coverage was another. More often than not, that kind of nuisance impeded an investigation. Particularly if the blitz was focused on a different case. "This is a disaster."

"We'll make a decision en route." Burnett touched Jess's elbow in silent direction for her to come along.

Jess read between those lines without a blink. He had already made up his mind. "I'll be right there. I have a couple of things I need to go over with Detective Wells." Maybe he could read between those lines. *Give her some space.*

"One minute," he warned.

A big, fake smile was her answer. When he'd loaded into the Mercedes she turned her attention to Wells.

"Sullivan didn't go to work today," Wells reported.

"She left her residence one hour ago and drove to the Walmart on Lakeshore Parkway in Homewood."

Jess braced. "And?"

"Officer Cook followed her inside. She wandered the book aisle for a few minutes before going to the restroom. So Cook followed her to the back of the store but not into the corridor where the bathrooms are located."

"Oh damn. She's gone, isn't she?"

Wells nodded. "He went back outside and her car is still in the lot. He's waiting there for further instructions."

"She knows someone who works there." Jess bit back a slew of curses. "I'll head over there now. Anything on this Tim?" She jerked her head toward the Porter home.

"Other than the affair he's having with a coworker that his wife doesn't know about? No. Nothing."

That certainly explained Porter's edginess when she asked him about work. "All right. Thank you, Detective." Jess hesitated before joining Burnett, who had powered down his window and was staring in her direction. "I hate to keep asking you for these little favors."

"No problem," Wells assured her. "What can I do?"

"I've gotten a couple of texts on my cell from a private number. See if Vernon can find out where they're coming from."

"That won't be so easy."

Jess understood. The chances of keeping that from Burnett were not good. "Try your best."

"Will do."

Burnett was annoyed when she joined him in his SUV. She ignored him, buckled up, and focused on her notes while he drove.

She waited until he was on Highway 31. "I need a

Walmart. If I remember correctly there's one on Lakeshore Parkway."

"Walmart?" He shot her a look through those dark shades.

"I have a need, Burnett." She flipped to the next page of her notes.

"Jess, we *are* going back to the office." Another shielded look arrowed in her direction.

"Do you have feminine products available at your office?"

"Enough said." He focused on driving.

That did it every time.

Walmart, 1:29 p.m.

Dan was going to have a serious talk with Wells. Not that he could really blame the detective. Jess had worked some major cases; her reputation was nothing short of awe-inspiring. That alone was enough to get any young detective's attention. And, as he well knew, Jess could be damned persuasive. Otherwise he wouldn't have allowed her to completely take over this investigation.

But he couldn't claim to have any better ideas than the ones she suggested.

The store manager wasn't thrilled about marching Jess around to each of his employees on duty in the store, but one flash of her official ID and he caved. They started with the stock employees in the back. No one admitted to knowing Dr. Sullivan or having seen her. From there, they covered one department after another.

Dan hadn't complained about her tactics. After the

temporary insanity that had seized him last night, he'd just as soon stay clear of pissing her off. She'd rushed around all morning, avoiding engaging him in any way.

He deserved that, he supposed.

He'd crossed the line.

They'd both spent the entire day pretending it hadn't happened. No point in changing course now.

"Mary, this is Agent Harris and Chief Burnett. They have some questions for you."

Fear widened the eyes of the fifty-year-old head of the Garden Department. "Sure," she said to her boss.

This was the one. Dan didn't need Jess's powerful discernment skills to see that. The woman was shaking in her blue vest.

"Good afternoon, Mary," Jess said. "We're looking for Dr. Maureen Sullivan. We believe she may have visited you here today. Maybe she borrowed your personal vehicle."

"She's my cousin." Mary dropped the hand-held scanner she was holding onto a stack of bagged grass seed and heaved a sigh. "I don't know what she was thinking." She shook her head. "She wouldn't even tell me what happened." Her watery gaze met Dan's, then settled on Jess. "She just kept saying there was a problem with a patient and she was in danger. She needed to get out of town for a while but she was afraid she was being followed."

"Did you get the impression she meant that she was in danger," Jess asked, "or the patient?"

Mary bowed her head in shame and wagged it side to side before answering the question. "I think she was talking about herself, but I don't know for sure. She seemed scared to death."

"Mary," Dan said, "we'll need the color, make, and model of your car. The license plate number, too, if you can give us that information."

Ten minutes later, Dan had an APB out on Mary Benson's 2008 white Ford Taurus.

Sheila, his personal secretary, sent him a text confirming that the circus had already set up camp in front of the BPD offices. Gina had warned him that they didn't have a lot of time. As usual, she was right.

After waiting for Jess to settle into the passenger seat of his SUV, he fastened his seat belt and started the engine. "I guess you'll get your wish."

"Which one?" Jess buckled her own safety belt. "That the girls are found alive and well? That Spears died of a sudden heart attack?" Her eyes rounded in feigned surprise. "Wait no, that my SAIC got transferred to North Dakota?"

"We can't go back to the office."

"Oh"—she pouted—"that's too bad."

"This thing with Spears is going to become a major issue." Dan sure as hell didn't want the guy watching Jess's every move on the news.

"Maureen Sullivan knows what Dana had planned. That's the only major issue on my mind."

"That, too." Dan wasn't surprised that Jess had been right about the doctor's having moxie.

"Sullivan knows enough," Jess pressed, "to believe she can find her or somehow intervene."

"Maybe." Dan wasn't going that far, but it was clear the doctor felt she could accomplish more on her own than by cooperating with the police. The other side of that was maybe she felt guilty to some degree for not having sounded a warning before Dana disappeared.

"Since we can't go back to the office right now," Jess said with enough offhandedness to almost sound credible, "let's drive past the Sawyer home and see if that white Taurus is there." She twisted the ring on her finger.

Last night's conversation and then that kiss filtered through his thoughts, resurrecting the tension even a cold shower and a decent night's sleep hadn't fully worn off. Her excuses for still wearing that band were bullshit. She had the lowdown on his personal life while she continued to hold back key aspects of hers.

"We could swing by Mr. Gold's first and you could take care of that extra baggage you're carrying around."

"We could," she offered. "But then you'd have to tell me about that pretty reporter you allowed to cross the yellow line the other night down in Tuscaloosa. The one you promised a scoop and who keeps you posted about what her colleagues are up to. Sound fair?"

"I guess we're headed to Warrior." Dan had given Jess all she was going to get. He needed to get a handle on this tension building between them. The stress of recent events in both their personal lives combined with the frustrating and colliding cases was a surefire trigger for crossing another line that had nothing to do with yellow crime-scene tape and a mere kiss.

"I see."

Dan sent her a look. He refused to take the bait. She hoped to goad him into telling her what she wanted to know. Not happening. He also wouldn't ask her why she'd slept in his parents' room last night. Not that he cared, but did that move suggest she didn't trust herself to sleep across the hall from him after the way he'd attacked her in his room?

Frustration twisted a little tighter. What the hell had he

been thinking? Waking from a dead sleep, already semi-aroused by dreams he refused to analyze, to find her in his room had obviously robbed him of any good sense.

Jess settled her eyeglasses into place and focused on her phone, tapping and sliding her fingers over the screen.

Back to business. "What's your assessment of the Porters?"

"They don't know anything, but I want Tim followed up on just in case I'm missing something besides his workplace affair."

"I'm beginning to wonder, Jess"—it pained him to say the words out loud—"whether we might be wrong. There may not be a connection between these girls."

She lifted her attention from her phone's screen. "That is a possibility."

He braked for a light, turned to her. "There's a lot we may be wrong about."

"That's always the case. What we have to bear in mind is whether or not the steps we take are hindering any aspect of the investigation in the event these are five separate abductions by five different unsubs. If the answer is no, and it is, then we're only guilty of wasting resources."

Dan hoped that was the only part of this strategy they would have reason to regret.

"You said Andrea is strong, Dan."

She hadn't called him by his first name but once or twice since her arrival. It shouldn't have made him want to reach across the console and touch her, but it did. "She is."

"Then her chances of survival are better than average. We have to hang on to that."

"With both hands, Jess." He took a deep breath and gained speed on the interstate. "With both hands."

"I think I'll call Mr. Williams."

"For all the good it'll do." Attorneys just loved yanking cops around.

Jess left Williams a voice mail informing him that his client had fled in a borrowed car and that she was now an official person of interest in this case.

As exhausted as he was, Dan smiled. He was lucky to have her on his team for this one. Finding a way to repay her would be difficult. She had dived right in and focused fully on the case.

He wondered if beneath all that determination she worried just a little about Spears. Her explanation that she had no need to fear him since she wasn't his type was more BS. Jess was far too smart not to be at least a little afraid. All the more reason not to let her out of his sight.

And to be a lot smarter than he'd been last night.

Dan slowed for the turn into the subdivision where the Sawyers lived. He rolled down the street, slowing as they passed the Sawyer home. No white Taurus. Disappointment pricked him.

Jess muttered, "Shoot."

"Warrior's not that big. We could drive around just to kill some time," he offered. "Give the news hounds a chance to get restless and go sniffing around elsewhere."

Jess was busy entering information into her phone.

Dan turned around and headed in the other direction. He slowed as he passed the Sawyer home again. If the Sawyers knew anything...if Sullivan knew something that would help find those girls, he wanted to know, too, because damn it, they had nothing. Nothing!

Frustration and fury collided in his gut. He banged his

palm against the steering wheel. How the hell were they supposed to find those kids with nothing?

"Dan?"

"I'm all right." The hell he was. He wanted to find whoever had done this and...

"I'm entering an address on Jasper Lane into your GPS." Jess awakened the screen and started entering information.

"Jasper Lane?"

"The Murray farm." She stabbed a few more times at the screen. "Dr. Sullivan treated Dana for emotional problems related to their son's death. That's the connection between those two as far as we know." She sat back in her seat. "Since that's all we've got, that's where we'll go."

Dan inhaled a deep breath, worked at calming himself. God Almighty, he wasn't sure how he would have gotten through this without her. He blinked. It was true. Maybe it was his personal connection to one of the victims, he couldn't be sure. But he needed Jess to keep him level.

"Thanks, Jess."

"Don't thank me yet. We have to find them first."

Less than fifteen minutes were required to reach the address. The farm was one of only two on this three-mile lane. The two-story Victorian-style house stood several hundred yards from the road, surrounded by mature trees. Between the house and the road was a pond. An old rowboat was tied to a short pier. The dirt driveway ran alongside the pond and disappeared somewhere behind the house. Quiet. Peaceful.

"Keep going so I can get a look at what's behind the house."

"Yes, ma'am."

The road came to a dead end at the second farm. Dan turned around and rolled back in the direction they'd come. He slowed to a crawl so he could get a look as well. There was a barn, probably as old or older than the house.

"I see a tan or light brown minivan. A black truck, newer than the van."

"No white Taurus?"

"Stop!"

Dan hit the brake hard.

"There's a man coming out of the barn. Pull in the driveway. I want to talk to him."

"Jess—"

"We don't need a warrant to ask a small-town neighbor about a missing girl."

Maybe he'd been in administration too long. When had he become more concerned with appearances and following the letter of the law than following leads?

Dan turned onto the long drive and drove all the way to the house. A man, Mr. Murray presumably, rounded the corner of the house.

"Let me do the talking." Jess opened her door and bailed out.

"Don't I always?" Dan muttered.

By the time he caught up to Jess she had already introduced herself and him to the man who identified himself as Raymond Murray.

"Mr. Murray, we're sorry to bother you, sir, but we'd like to ask you a few questions."

"'Course." He looked from Jess to Dan and back. "How can I help you?"

Jess shifted her bag so she could poke around in it. She

withdrew a photo. "Mr. Murray, do you know this young woman?"

He took the picture from her and studied it. "Sure do. That's Dana Sawyer." A frown furrowed his weathered face. "I saw the news. I sure was sorry to hear about that. She's a good girl. My Tate was wild in love with her back in high school. She was always over here."

While Jess continued to question him, Dan absorbed as many of the details about the property as possible. The house had been painted recently. A bright white. Checkered curtains hung in the windows, flanking either side of white shades that could be lowered for privacy but were not. The minivan was a Chrysler. The truck a Chevy. The place was tranquil, a world away from downtown Birmingham.

"All I can tell you," Murray said, "is the same thing I told the other lady who came by right after lunch asking about Dana."

"What lady, Mr. Murray?"

Dan listened up.

"Maureen somebody. Said she was looking for Dana, too." He shook his head. "I think she might have been a little crazy though."

"Why is that?" Jess asked.

"She said she was worried that Dana might try to commit suicide." He shook his head. "Now, I haven't seen that little girl in a good long while, but I don't believe for a minute she would do anything like that. She's a good girl. My Tate couldn't have loved her if she wasn't."

Jess dragged out her cell phone, fingered the screen. "Is this the woman who visited you this afternoon?"

Murray studied the image. "Sure is. She was driving a white car. I felt bad about the dusty driveway."

Jess reclaimed her phone and tucked it into her bag. "Sir, would you call me if you hear from her again?" She passed him a card.

"I will." He shook his head. "I respect the work y'all do. It's the Lord's work."

Jess thanked him; Dan did the same. She made no comments as they loaded up and prepared to go. While Dan executed a three-point turn, she stared at the house, twisting around in her seat as he drove away.

When she remained fixated on the house as he rolled out onto Jasper Lane, he asked the burning question. "You think he wasn't being completely honest?"

Jess finally settled in her seat. "I think he was very neighborly, cooperative, and stated exactly what was in his heart. He believes Dana is a good girl. That his son loved her. And that Dr. Sullivan came by this afternoon in a white car." Jess took one last long look before the farm was out of sight. "Even so, there's one thing he didn't do."

Dan knew her pause wasn't to build the drama; she was deep in analysis mode.

"He didn't ask if we were getting closer to finding the girls."

Dan smiled. She was right. Most folks they questioned asked a few of their own, that question being at the top of the list. He made the next turn. "I guess we face the music now."

"Actually." She reached back into her bag. "We need to talk to the Sawyers. Afterward we need to talk to Amy Porter. If Dr. Sullivan thinks Dana is suicidal, then her parents or her best friend should have at least noticed something was off."

Dan's cell vibrated. He slid it from the holster and

checked the screen. Text. From the mayor himself. That was a bad sign.

My office. Now.

"Looks like we have a reprieve from battling the press." He passed the phone to Jess so she could read the screen. "Unfortunately, we have a bigger problem than reporters."

The political shit was about to hit the fan.

14

They gone yet?"

"They're gone."

"You think they believed you?"

"Think so."

Andrea could hear the man and woman talking. Had someone come? *Oh, please, please let them come back.*

The man had shoved Andrea into the pantry. Her back was to the closed door, so she couldn't even attempt to see anything, but she could hear. What were they going to do to her now? They'd dragged her out of the basement what must have been an hour or more ago.

She fought the urge to struggle against her bindings. She tried not to scream behind the tape. Her body trembled with the effort.

"They'll be looking for that woman now," the man said. "You should've been patient. I told her I hadn't seen Dana. She was gonna leave."

The woman laughed that nasty, condescending sound. "Yeah, right. She didn't believe you and even if she had, all we needed was her going to the police with what she knew. That stupid little bitch shouldn't've told her nothing."

"There wouldn't have been anything to tell if you hadn't been messing with her head about his birthday."

"If you hadn't brought Dana here we wouldn't've had to worry about her. She hurt him too bad. She's nothing but a loser. A bitch loser."

"I got just as much say in this as you," the man growled.

"Just shut up and get Andrea out of there."

The door opened. Andrea's heart swelled with renewed fear. The man grabbed the back of her chair, his fingers snagging strands of her hair. She winced as he dragged the chair, to which she was bound like a rag doll, out of the pantry. Her gaze clung to the normalcy of the rows of canned and dried goods lining the shelves. Probably bought with all those damned coupons. How could people who looked so ordinary be so crazy?

Her chair was dragged back to the table, with her facing forward as if she were about to have dinner.

"Pull down those shades, get Reanne, and we'll move on to the next test." The woman leaned over Andrea as the man left the room. "As much trouble as you've been I think I like you best." She leaned closer. "Don't mess up 'cause he likes Dana better. I don't want her to win."

Andrea shuddered, couldn't help herself.

The man brought Reanne into the room. Her hands were tied behind her back, like Andrea's, and a wide strip of silver tape covered her mouth. He forced Reanne into the chair directly across from Andrea.

What were they going to do now? Andrea had already been tested. They had showered and scrubbed and then examined her. She closed her eyes and tried to block the memories. The woman had announced she wasn't a virgin but still suitable. Her body started shaking again. Andrea forced herself to stop thinking about it. She had to pay attention. She was out of the basement. There were windows and doors. She needed to stay aware in case she got an opportunity to run.

"Okay, girls," the woman announced. "We start the elimination rounds today."

Don't stare at her! Andrea blinked. Tried not to look at her face. The woman wasn't ugly. She was kind of pretty. Short and chubby but pretty. The man wasn't awful looking either. Broad and kind looking. Why was this happening? Why were they doing this?

Reanne sat with her head down as if she'd had another of those pills. There was a big white bandage on her chest, just above her right boob. What had they done to her?

"Reanne," the woman shouted, "hold your head up!"

Reanne didn't react. The man grabbed her by the hair and pulled her head up. "Pay attention, Reanne."

Reanne opened her eyes. She stared at Andrea. Andrea wanted to cry. Her eyes looked blank, as if she no longer cared what happened.

"If you don't try, Reanne," the woman yelled at her, "you forfeit."

Reanne turned to her. She stared at the woman for a second, then she tried to say something. The woman removed the tape so she could talk. Reanne spit in her face.

The woman slapped her hard, then swiped the spit from her face. "I'm done with this one." She turned to the man. "You were right. That tattoo was a sign. She's not fit."

He grabbed her by the shoulders. Reanne went crazy.

She started screaming and biting and kicking her legs. The man slung her over his shoulder and stalked out the back door with her still thrashing.

"Stupid little bitch." The woman walked to where Andrea sat and started to finger comb her hair. "You're so pretty. I want you to work really hard. Don't fail me, Andrea. I'm counting on you." She patted Andrea's shoulder. "I've waited a long time for a daughter."

Andrea couldn't keep the tears from sliding down her cheeks. She tried. She really tried. But she couldn't. She closed her eyes and searched for a way to leave this place . . . she remembered the trip to the beach she and her mother had taken at the end of May. A getaway for girls only. Andrea's lips trembled into a small smile beneath the tape.

Where are you, Mommy?

"Pay attention, Andrea! How do you make those perfect grades dozing off like that?"

The woman slapped her on the back of the head. Andrea jerked her head up. Blinked to focus her eyes. Kitchen. She was still in the kitchen.

Reanne was gone.

A scream rushed into her throat. *Don't scream!*

Someone made a sound. Andrea looked around. Macy was at one end of the long rectangular table. Callie sat at the other. The man pulled out the chair where Reanne had been sitting. He ushered the new girl, Dana, into it. Tape had been plastered over all their mouths and their hands appeared to be bound behind their backs.

The woman ripped the tape off Macy's mouth. Macy cried out but quickly snapped her mouth shut.

"Of all these girls, you've been in training the longest, Macy, so you go first." The woman moved around to the other side of her. "Recite your purpose and your Psalms. Be very careful. You don't want to be eliminated like Reanne."

Macy licked her lips as if she were thirsty. She sucked in a ragged breath. "My purpose is to be a loving wife. To bear children and raise them in the way of the Lord." She cleared her throat, licked her lips again. "The Lord is my shepherd; I shall not want. He makes me lie down—"

"Weaaahhh! Wrong! Strike one!"

Macy blinked back the tears. "He maketh me to lie down in green pastures." Her voice shook hard. "He leadeth me by the still waters."

"Weaaahhh!" The crazy bitch was thrilled. "Strike two." She stuck her face in Macy's. "I think you're going to be eliminated with this round, Macy."

Macy started to cry.

"What comes next?" the woman shouted. "Can't you remember anything? I taught you well!"

Macy sobbed harder.

"You have five seconds, Macy!"

The room spinning, Andrea closed her eyes, tried to block the sounds. This was crazy. It couldn't be real.

That screeching noise that signaled a wrong answer pierced the air again.

"Take her away, Daddy. She failed. Macy's a loser!" The woman danced around the table, shouting *loser* over and over.

Macy screamed. The sound was twisted with the sobs rocking her thin body. Andrea wished she could reach out to her. She watched, in horror, as the man took Macy away.

"Woo-hoo! We're narrowing down the results. Kicking the idiots off the island! Let's see if you can do better, Callie."

Callie began reciting her lessons.

Andrea stared across the table at the new girl, Dana. She stared back at Andrea, resignation in her eyes.

That was the moment Andrea understood the reality of the situation. No one was going to make it in time to help them.

They were totally fucked.

Whatever the goal of these stupid tests, it was a competition. Between the tattoo and her refusal to be submissive, Reanne had been eliminated. Macy hadn't been able to hold it together under pressure. Callie wouldn't either. She was worn down from days and days in that damned hole of a prison.

These people weren't just mean or stupid or crazy nuts, they were twisted, evil. The skeletons in the basement proved that.

Andrea understood perfectly now. The reason the woman liked her was because she was strong. As scared as she was, Andrea paid attention and followed instructions. The woman wanted a winner for a daughter.

When this was over, there would be only one winner and the rest . . . would be losers.

If Andrea tried her best and won, what happened to the others would be her fault.

If she failed, *she* would be eliminated. A *loser.*

In this house, losers ended up dead.

Mayor's Office, 5:30 p.m.

Joseph Pratt had served in Birmingham politics for the last half of his esteemed career. A graduate of Birmingham's prestigious Samford University, he came from old money, had made lots of new money in the business world, and now he preferred power to more money. He was a good man, but one of his top priorities was public perception. Particularly the public's perception of him.

"Dan, this is unacceptable."

He clicked the remote, shutting off the flat screen on the credenza behind his desk. It seemed that every news organization in the country had just aired a clip of Jess, surrounded by Detectives Wells and Harper, along with two uniformed officers entering the BPD building. Jess had insisted she and the detectives had work to do. She had no interest in warming a chair in the mayor's anteroom.

Innuendoes about her part in the failure to build a proper case against the notorious suspected serial killer

Eric Spears had come off as less than flattering. The insinuation that her reckless behavior might somehow damage the investigation into the disappearance of five young Birmingham women had the mayor and anyone else who watched up in arms. Half a dozen staffers were fielding calls. Worse, the local bureau office had given a statement to the press basically throwing Jess under the bus. Agent Harris was on administrative leave. Her affiliation with the BPD was in no way connected to the FBI.

Bastards.

Mayor Pratt sat the remote on his desk, then braced his elbows on the arms of his leather chair. He steepled his fingers. "How do you plan to handle this?"

After twenty minutes of watching various clips and quiet but forceful rhetoric in regards to the media circus performing around the courthouse, this was the mayor's bottom line. How would Dan make it go away?

"We have no control over what the media chooses to broadcast any more than we have over how the bureau conducts its ongoing investigation into Spears and the Player case. That Jess is here brings that scrutiny to us. There's no way around it."

Pratt waited for more, the *right* answer to his question. Dan's explanation of the reality of the situation clearly was not the answer he was looking for.

"Our focus will remain on the five missing young women," Dan added as a reminder of his position and for the emotional impact. "Every hour they remain missing lessens the likelihood of finding a single one alive."

"You still have no evidence that the disappearances are connected."

Not a question. Dan refused to be intimidated by the

man simply because he held the power to remove him from the office of police chief. This was not a theoretical situation. Not a textbook example for future training reference and definitely not a game of political achievement. This was life and death. And it was Dan's fucking case.

"Not yet," he admitted with absolutely no regret that he couldn't set this man's concerns for his reputation to rest. "We are following several leads, two of which are promising. The good news is"—he looked the mayor straight in the eyes—"we have no bodies either."

"This Harris woman...," Pratt began, his hands now resting on the arms of his chair as he casually reclined. "Have her services risen to your inordinately high expectations?"

He had to throw that in, didn't he? "She is the only reason we have any leads at all."

Fury had a muscle flexing in his jaw. This meeting wasn't about the case, not really. It was about whether or not they could dump Jess, thereby shifting the media's scrutiny elsewhere.

Pratt leaned forward, picked up a handful of notes from his desk, and shuffled through them. "Here's what I'm dealing with, Dan. I have two complaints from the families of those missing girls." He glanced over the notes. "And those are just the two that my assistant wasn't able to handle without my intervention. Five complaints from families who have been questioned in connection with the disappearances, the most recent a Tim Porter."

"Did Mr. Porter also tell you that he was having an affair with a coworker?" Dan tried to keep his temper from flaring but he failed.

"Does this affair have anything at all to do with the case?"

"That's yet to be seen." In all likelihood not, but there was no reason to speculate.

"I don't have to remind you that with five lives at stake, we cannot be too careful with the conduction of this investigation. The eyes of the people are on our every move."

Dan's temper got the best of him. "If that's a warning of some sort, you need to be a little more specific."

"Our friends at the bureau tell me that Harris is a bit of a maverick. She doesn't conform well to the rules and her impulsive actions resulted in a heinous killer going free."

"Spears was going to walk anyway. They had no evidence. Jess jumped the gun, that's true, but the evidence she discovered was previously unknown to the investigation and impossible to connect to Spears anyway. Her actions did not damage the case they *didn't* have."

"As far as the media is concerned," Pratt countered, "that's irrelevant. It's the perception of error that matters. Spears walked and an explanation is required."

"A scapegoat is required," Dan corrected. "And Jess is it." Nearly two decades of dedication to the job and she took the fall. Respect and loyalty couldn't compete with public perception.

"Another parent came to me personally with concerns about Harris."

"Jess," Dan challenged. "Her name is Jess. Special Agent Jess Harris."

Pratt said nothing to Dan's pointed amendment.

"Though Andrea isn't my legal or biological daughter," Dan argued in regard to the complaints Pratt listed, "I'm thankful for any help we can get in finding her. What kind of parent would question the tactics of one of the best profilers the bureau has had the opportunity of employing?"

"It was Annette, Dan. She is immensely concerned that your prior relationship with this Agent Harris prevents you from being completely objective in the matter."

The outrage he'd been holding back ignited, whooshing through his veins. "Annette came to you and said this." Dan didn't believe it.

"She and her husband, yes."

"Did she make that claim or did he?" Dan gripped the arms of his chair in an attempt to ground himself. He wasn't surprised at Denton's audacity. He would go to any lengths to make Dan look bad, even if his own daughter proved to be the price. But Annette? Why would she do something so thoughtless and utterly reckless where her daughter's life was concerned?

"They were both here," Pratt argued, "sitting right where you are. Who said what is irrelevant. The consensus is that Jess Harris is an element this case does not need." Before Dan could argue that point, Pratt added, "This is the highest-profile case your department has faced since you accepted the position of chief. What do I have to say to make you understand the ramifications we're both facing? The citizens of Birmingham are watching you. You cannot make a mistake, Dan. That your former stepdaughter is one of the missing is dicey business as it is. Dragging in a former lover whose professional reputation is questionable at this time is simply bad judgment."

Dan wasn't sure he'd absorbed all that Pratt said after "former lover." He was very close to walking out. *After* telling the mayor where he could shove his consensus. But Andrea was counting on him. They were all counting on him. Including Jess.

"Andrea," Dan reminded the mayor, "that's my former

stepdaughter's name. Macy, Callie, Reanne, and Dana are the names of the other missing girls. They need all the help we can summon on this case. I don't care about public perception. I care about finding those girls. I care about doing my job to the best of my ability, not the public opinion."

"Unfortunately, public opinion determines whether or not you are rising to the occasion." He studied Dan for a moment. "Can you, without reservation, say that you're performing at the peak of your ability?" Pratt asked. "That you're making decisions without bias?"

"If you feel I'm failing in either area—if any of my deputy chiefs or captains or detectives feel I am failing in any way—I suggest you take the appropriate steps." Dan stood. "Meanwhile, I have a job to do."

Before Dan reached the door, Pratt asked one last question. "What about Agent Harris?"

Dan turned back to ensure there was no misunderstanding. "If she goes, I go."

"And if the attention the media deluges on her puts her in danger, now that Spears is free, it is of no consequence to you?"

Fear trickled past the anger. Dan refused to validate that ridiculous question with a response. He would protect Jess.

He walked out the door.

The mayor could play his power games with someone else.

BPD Conference Room, 6:17 p.m.

"Tate Murray was killed in a car crash three years ago this past May," Wells read from the notes she had collected.

"He was on his way to school for a seniors' meeting the day before graduation."

Jess studied the notes and photos posted along the timeline on the case board. "Was a cause listed for the accident?"

She couldn't get the connection between him and the latest disappearance out of her head. But the poor boy was dead. His parents could be seeking some sort of belated revenge. But why now? And why these five girls? Then again, their only connection seemed to be to the latest victim. The boy's name was Tate, not Tim, which would seem to eliminate any link to the texts Reanne had received.

Neither Amy Porter nor Dana's parents believed for one second that Dana was or ever had been suicidal. A text from Jess as she and Burnett had left Warrior had gotten Griggs in touch with both parties. Though Jess would have preferred to do the follow-up interview herself, Burnett's command performance at the mayor's office had precluded the possibility.

Since her arrival back here, Detectives Wells and Harper had been bringing her up to speed on the leads she had asked them to follow up on. Now, with Harper settled at the conference table finalizing calls, Wells hovered at the case board with Jess. She felt confident she looked as tired as the two of them. No one was getting any sleep to speak of. The faces of these girls haunted Jess's dreams. That last text she'd gotten from Spears added another layer of apprehension. Not to mention the incident with Burnett and then Sullivan disappearing.

Jesus Christ, she needed a break.

"He was the passenger in a Honda Civic with a friend,

fellow basketball teammate Josh Sever," Wells recounted. "Sever attempted to pass a farm tractor and hit an SUV head-on. Sever survived for a few hours, but he died as well."

Jess elbowed aside all the other troubling thoughts and focused on this long shot of a lead. "Did the Murrays sue?"

"There's no record of a lawsuit. Sever's insurance company may have paid the family a settlement to preclude that kind of action."

Jess tapped her pencil against her chin. If the parents had held a grudge about their son's death, it would surely have been against the driver of the car. And the driver was dead. There was just no logical reason to add the Murrays to the scattered pieces of this puzzle that refused to click together. Except for the therapist and Dana.

And the idea that there was nothing logical about any of the disappearances.

"Still no word from Sullivan's attorney? No sign of her or the white Taurus?"

"Nothing on Sullivan. Williams's secretary insists he's out of the office and unreachable."

"I don't know why I'm surprised." Jess turned away from the frustrating board. "He's probably out looking for her." Hoping that whatever happens doesn't come back to bite his reputation in the ass.

That Sullivan was still unaccounted for was not a good sign. Damn it. What had the woman been thinking? Where the hell was she?

"Ma'am"—Sergeant Harper placed his cell phone on the table—"that was the last name on the list of blue Ford trucks, 1969 to 1974."

"All one hundred three?" She was impressed. Harper

had set out to contact every owner to determine the driver of the vehicle as well as its whereabouts.

"Yes, ma'am."

She winced, then tried to cover it with a smile. "Let me guess, not a single one ties to any of our missing girls or their families, friends, or whatever."

"That would be an affirmative."

Damn it! Was one little break too much to ask for?

"Jess."

She turned to Wells. Finally, the younger woman had broken through the formality barrier. Now if Jess could just convince Harper to stop calling her ma'am.

"You have something else?" They'd gone over new input from family and friends—which was nothing. They'd reviewed call logs from all relevant phones, cell and landlines, yet again. No usable evidence had been found in the Parsons's home, on the note to Reanne her friend had kept, or in Dana's car. They had nothing.

"Here's the information on that *other* phone contact."

Wells was referring to the text messages Jess had received. The air stalled in her lungs. She pushed her glasses up the bridge of her nose and stepped closer. "Let's see what you have."

Wells opened a manila file folder that was empty. Jess smiled. She was learning fast. "What does that mean?" Jess pointed to a nonexistent note.

"It's a prepaid phone," Wells said. "It was registered under a stolen ID." She covertly pointed to Jess.

The bastard had gotten a prepaid phone in her name!

"No harm done," Wells hastened to assure her. "Just the made-up name and a nonexistent address."

"Thank you, Detective." Jess added the number to her

contact list and labeled it *Tormenter.* There were numerous other labels she could use—scumbag, snake, bastard, et cetera—but there really was no one moniker that defined the kind of evil Spears represented.

"Lori."

Jess snapped back to attention. "I'm sorry . . . what?" She shook off the fog of distraction. "Of course, Lori."

"Chet," Harper piped up from his seat at the conference table.

Jess nodded. "Chet, why don't you call me Jess?" Every time he called her ma'am she felt twenty years older.

Harper shook his head. "I can't do that, ma'am, my grandmother would roll over in her grave."

A smile tugged at the corners of Jess's mouth. "We can't have that."

"Wells."

Jess glanced at Lori, who stepped to the far side of the room to take a call. While they were on the whole let's-get-personal kick, why not go all the way? She strolled over to the conference table.

"Chet, are you married? Children?" There hadn't been an opportunity to get to know each other beyond name and rank. Besides, she was curious after the interaction she'd seen between these two at the prayer service.

The look he cut in Lori's direction before he answered spoke volumes. "I've been divorced for two years and I have a three-year-old son." A smile touched his lips. "His name is David Chester, after both me and my father."

Chet was short for Chester. "Marriage seems to be a casualty of this profession." She could vouch for that. As could Burnett.

"Yes, ma'am." Another of those covert glances at Lori.

This time, Jess openly followed his gaze. "Lori has never been married, has she?"

"No, ma'am. She says her career is her top priority right now."

Do tell. "Speaking from the voice of experience," Jess said, "time has a way of slipping through your fingers." She leaned down and said for his ears only, "Don't give up. She won't hold out much longer."

Jess had noticed how Lori looked at him. These two were in deeper than one or both comprehended.

Chet adopted a confused expression.

Jess lifted a skeptical eyebrow.

He cleared this throat, admitting defeat. "Yes, ma'am."

The door opened and Burnett walked in. He looked no worse for wear after his meeting with the mayor. Maybe it had gone more smoothly than he'd anticipated. Either way, wasting time in the waiting room had been out of the question. She and the detectives had accomplished a lot in the last hour or so.

Since he stood there not giving her jack, she demanded, "Well?"

He slid his hands into his trouser pockets and shrugged. "I still have a job. And we still have our task force."

Which meant the mayor hadn't mandated that he send Jess packing. Not that she had been all that worried. It was a free country. He couldn't make her leave town. She felt confident that Harper and Wells—Chet and Lori—would have continued to work with her either way.

"Great." Jess gathered her notes and stuffed them into her bag. "I guess that's all we can get done today."

"Would you like me to continue attempting to get in touch with Williams?" Lori asked.

Jess thought about that a moment. "If Chet"—she turned to him—"wouldn't mind following up on Williams, I have another task for you, Lori."

"Works for me," Chet confirmed.

"Great. Lori, I'd really like you to see what else you can dig up on the Murray family. Particularly the son. Did he have any friends other than Sever who might have decided to avenge his death at this late date?"

The idea didn't even fit into the category of longshot, but the Murray scenario just wouldn't stay out of Jess's head. "I just want to be sure we aren't missing anything on these folks." Good God. She'd given up completely on slowing her digression into her old speech patterns.

"Patterson called me on the way over here," Burnett said. "One of Reanne's coworkers remembers seeing a blue truck, older looking, driving past the sandwich shop several times during those last few days before Reanne went missing." He checked his cell. "The guy's name is Jarod Rimes. He takes his smoke breaks in the parking lot."

"I'll cover that one," Chet offered.

Confirming that piece of information could make a difference. Too bad the sandwich shop didn't have video surveillance. Someone had hand-delivered those notes to Reanne. "You still have those truck photos so you can see if what he means by older and what we mean are one in the same?"

"Yes, ma'am."

"Good deal." Jess loaded her bag onto her shoulder. "Let me know if anything pans out or comes up."

She was ready for a long, hot soak in Katherine's glamorous bubble tub. Maybe she'd pilfer through the wine selection and do a little more reorganizing. Jess really shouldn't get so much glee from the idea.

"Good night, Lori. Chet."

Jess exited the conference room. She didn't slow to wait for Burnett. The sooner she got through the horde outside the happier she would be. She stopped at the elevator and pressed the down button.

Burnett came up beside her. "Chet and Lori? Really?"

Jess laughed. "Really." The doors opened and she stepped inside.

Burnett tapped the button for the lobby and waited for the doors to close.

"They're still out there in full force," he warned.

Jess leaned against the wall at the back of the elevator car. "My mother had a saying, *When they're talking about me, they're letting someone else rest.*"

The car bumped to a stop on the second floor. An alarm sounded.

Jess straightened as she realized that the stop had been triggered by her companion. "Why'd you do that?"

He closed in on her. The intensity on his face made her breath catch. Before she could repeat her question, he moved even nearer and braced his hands against the wall on either side of her.

"Listen to me, Jess."

She flattened her back into the wall but the move didn't help. He was still way too close. The same heat that had ignited between them in the wee hours of the morning blazed.

"I don't care what those reporters out there say or do. I don't care what the mayor says or does."

"Did he say something I should know?"

It was difficult to concentrate on the mayor or anything else with Burnett practically on top of her. That subtle aftershave he'd worn since he used his first razor made her unsteady on her feet. The fervency in his eyes scared her almost as much as it drove her body temperature higher and higher.

"He made one point that I should have considered with far more gravity."

"Whatever it was"—her voice quivered just a little, damn it—"I'm certain it wasn't as important as all that. Relax, Burnett. We're doing all we can and—"

"With Spears out, your safety is compromised. I haven't taken the proper steps to ensure he can't get to you."

"You hardly let me out of your sight. You slept right down the hall from me last night." She shook her head as if the idea were ridiculous. "Like I told you, I can protect myself."

"That isn't enough."

Instead of calming down, his tension visibly mounted.

The text messages. Fury belted Jess. And she had thought she could trust Wells. See if she called her Lori anymore. "Detective Wells had no business telling you—"

His expression changed to one of suspicion. "What about Wells?"

Crap. "She wasn't supposed to tell you that I asked her to do a little digging around in Andrea's father's background." She hadn't but it wasn't a bad idea. Then again, she imagined he'd already done that.

The elevator alarm sounded again.

"Security is going to be calling Fire and Rescue if we keep this elevator stopped any longer," Jess warned.

His suspicion turned to something along the lines of cockiness. "That's funny. Wells had already taken care of looking into Denton's background since I felt I couldn't be objective."

"That is funny." The problem was, he wasn't laughing. "What are you hiding from me, Jess?"

"Is there a problem, Chief?" A deep male voice rattled over the elevator speaker.

"No problem," Burnett answered without moving. "We need a few more minutes."

"Yes, sir."

He leveled the full brunt of his impatience on her. "Tell me now or I will get the answer from Wells."

"I received two texts." She heaved a frustrated breath. "The first one was just what you'd expect from Spears or one of his puppets. *I'm celebrating. Wish you were here*," she mocked.

"What about the other one?"

He was overreacting. "It was stupid."

"Tell me now."

Jess jumped at his growled words. "Fine. He said, *Good night, Agent Harris*." That was all she intended to tell him. For now, anyway.

"When was this?"

She let go a defeated sigh. "When I went to bed last night."

Fury tightened the features of his handsome face. "So that's why you were wandering around the house in the middle of the night with your weapon."

If he hadn't said the words so quietly she might have denied the charge, but there was a lethal kind of fury in his eyes. This was not the time to dismiss his concerns.

"Yes," she admitted.

He pushed away from the wall, turned his back, and stabbed the necessary button to prompt the elevator back into motion.

Damn. Now she wouldn't even be able to go pee without him.

16

10:15 p.m.

Lori hesitated at her door. She told herself again to just pretend she was in bed already.

Chet waited on the other side. He had called and asked to come over. She had said no, but he'd insisted that he had an update they needed to discuss and it couldn't wait until morning.

Deep breath. She opened the door and stepped back. "Come in."

He walked in, his presence immediately diminishing the usually comfortable size of her Five Points loft. He still wore the brown trousers and cream-colored shirt he'd been wearing when they parted ways almost four hours ago. The jacket and tie were gone. That he'd unbuttoned the top two buttons of his shirt shouldn't have drawn her attention, but it did.

She closed the door, wrapped her arms around herself, and faced him. If she'd been smart she would have changed before he arrived. The lounge pants and cami made her feel naked in his presence, particularly since she'd shucked her bra and panties in anticipation of going straight to bed when she'd exhausted herself researching the Murrays.

"You said you had news."

"I interviewed Rimes." He surveyed her one-room space, his attention lingering on the bed. "He confirmed the truck he saw cruising the sandwich shop repeatedly was the same one Thompson stated picked up Dana Sawyer."

Anticipation raced through Lori's body. "Did you let Jess and the chief know?" This was their first real break. They finally had a connection between two of the victims.

He nodded as he looked from the half-empty glass of wine near her laptop to her.

Gesturing to her laptop on the old steamer trunk she used as a coffee table, she hoped to shift his attention. "I'm still working on what the Murrays have been up to."

She hadn't discovered anything relevant yet, but she wasn't giving up. She had all night. The team wasn't scheduled to meet until nine tomorrow morning.

The weight of his stare came to rest on her once more. She suddenly wished she had lit some incense or a candle. Anything that might have overpowered his scent. The clean, citrusy fragrance made her think of that *night.* Which was a really bad idea.

"I'm glad you shared this with me." How did she ask him to leave without being outright rude? "It's good news."

All he had to do was stand there, looking at her as if he wanted to taste her, and her heart rate sped up. This was a really precarious situation, one that needed to be cut as short as possible.

"Yeah." He shrugged. "I figured you'd want to know."

She wanted to look away, but it was difficult. He had beautiful eyes. Deep, rich brown. When they were alone like this he made her doubt her decisions about the future. She didn't want that.

Jess was proof that waiting for kids and other complications could work. Lori wanted that kind of stellar career. Not with the bureau, but with the BPD. And what was wrong with that? She was the first in her family to graduate from college. Her family looked up to her, depended on her. Making detective last year allowed her to qualify for the necessary loans to help her baby sister with college.

There was no room in her life at this time, financially or otherwise, for marriage and children.

"I should go." He gestured to her, then seemed at a loss as to what to do with his hands. "You're ready to call it a night and I'm holding you up."

She nodded, moistened her hungry lips. "Another hour or so on the net and I'll be beyond ready to crash."

He nodded. "Well. Good night then."

She followed him to the door, part of her thankful that he was going, the other screaming for him to stay. How crazy was that?

Her fingers closed around the doorknob and opened the door; she was almost home free.

"I'll see you in the morning."

If she hadn't looked at his mouth...

"Be sure to lock up."

If she hadn't watched his lips move as he spoke...

She might have had a chance.

He took the decision from her. Closed the door and flipped the dead bolt.

Before she could catch her breath, he swept her into his arms and carried her to the bed.

He kissed her until she gasped. His scent, his touch, saturated her senses. Her fingers fought frantically with his buttons... with the fly to his trousers. He peeled her lounge pants down her legs and off, and then settled between her thighs. Her arms and legs wrapped around him; she couldn't resist. She didn't care that he was still dressed with only his trousers open... she needed him inside her.

Without preamble, he thrust fully, deeply.

Her breath caught, her body arched with pleasure, and nothing else mattered. Not her career... nothing. All she wanted just then was for him to kiss her the way only he could... to make her body scream with ecstasy as no one else ever had.

He nuzzled her ear and whispered, "This"—he ground his pelvis into hers, and she cried out with the exhilaration the move aroused—"is not *fucking.* This"—he executed the exquisite move again—"is making love."

Lori took his face in her hands and searched his eyes until he trembled from holding so very still. "Show me more."

She brought his lips to hers and lost herself to this man who was so incredibly dangerous to her independence.

17

Saturday, July 17, 11:00 a.m.

Jess parted the blinds and peeked out the conference room window. "Damned reporters."

After the brouhaha on the ten o'clock news last night, the mayor had insisted on a press conference this morning. Burnett, Griggs, and Patterson had command performances. Chet was there for a show of strength.

Jess wasn't allowed to show her face. Not that she wanted to. Definitely not. The reports made her look inept, pathetic, and evidently they had searched for the absolute worst candid shots of her to use as visuals. Lori had babysitting duty. Burnett's order had been something like: *Do not let her out of your sight.*

Fine. Jess turned away from the window. She had work to do anyway.

On her way to the other side of the room to join Lori at the conference table, her cell vibrated. She'd silenced it at seven this morning after five calls from former colleagues concerned about her. Right. They all wanted to gloat. She was out and they were still in.

Jess groaned when she checked the screen. Lily. Her sister had called twice last night and once already this morning. She was horrified by the news reports. She was incensed that Jess had been in town for more than forty-eight hours without calling. Jess let the call go to voice mail. If she heard one more *I'm so sorry* she might just puke.

Her suggestion that Lily and her family take a vacation out of town had gone unheeded. Jess didn't really believe she had to worry about Spears...but she didn't want to take chances with her family. Lily had insisted that her son had a summer job and her daughter had a thousand things to do in preparation for going off to college this fall. There was no time for a vacation...why did Jess ask?

Explaining that one, without suggesting her own vulnerability, had backfired big-time.

The only good thing about the past dozen or so hours was that no one else had gone missing and they finally had a connection between two of the girls with the blue truck. Sullivan was still unaccounted for. Her attorney had finally called in and said he had heard nothing from his client. So far the press hadn't connected the MIA doctor with the missing girls.

And, incredibly, Jess had managed to steer clear of Burnett last night. The house was huge; it hadn't been so difficult.

Jess sat down across the table from Lori. "Find anything new?" Jess was restless. Sitting here doing nothing was driving her out of her mind.

Lori was completely absorbed in her search. Feeling Jess's gaze on her, she finally looked up from the laptop. "Sorry. Did you say something?"

Jess liked Lori Wells better every day. The woman was driven. Reminded Jess of herself a couple of decades ago. Harper might just have to keep waiting to catch this one. The distraction in her expression went deep but there was a distinct air of excitement simmering in her eyes.

"Did you find something?" Adrenaline lit. Jess felt herself leaning forward in anticipation.

Lori leaned her head toward one shoulder and made an I-dunno face. "May…be. It's a cold case."

Jess was up and around the table before the detective finished her uncertain statement. "Show me."

"Christina Debarros, age thirteen, went missing almost six years ago."

The young Hispanic American girl was listed as still missing. Jess read through the info listed on the database with her photo. "No indication of foul play." Jess grunted. "That sounds familiar."

"You haven't gotten to the best part yet."

Jess leaned closer to the screen. Janie Debarros, the mother, stated that she suspected her daughter was pregnant. Sudden bouts of nausea and the lack of a menstrual cycle for three months were listed as her reasons. Christina had been a student at Warrior Middle School.

Jess's breath hitched.

"Keep reading," Lori urged, the excitement now a full-blown rush in her voice.

Jess's jaw dropped. At the very top of the list of persons of interest in the case was *Tate Murray.* "How the hell did we miss that when we ran the Murrays' names through the databases?"

"He was a minor. And he was cleared of suspicion.

His name wouldn't be in any of the databases. I got this straight from records."

Reeling with the possibilities, Jess took a second to calm herself. "Can you send the photo of the girl to my cell phone?"

"Sure thing." Her fingers flew over the keys. She'd scarcely stopped typing when Jess's cell vibrated.

"While you're at it, send me the file, or at least what you can of it." Jess studied the young girl's face. "Do the Debarros still live in Warrior?"

Lori pecked a few more keys. "Affirmative."

They looked at each other, the unspoken shattering the air between them.

"The chief will have my head."

"Not if what we find puts us on the trail of those girls."

"Could be a coincidence."

Jess smiled, anticipation charging relentlessly through her veins. "You don't believe that any more than I do."

"Tate Murray is dead."

Jess nodded. "Yes, he is. But his parents aren't."

Tate's father had made an impression on Jess. His every word and action had come off as kind and caring. But there had been one element missing, besides the fact that he didn't ask the usual questions. The one concept that had niggled at her all night.

Mr. Murray hadn't shown the slightest inkling of sadness when he spoke of his son. Not a glimmer. Three years wasn't nearly long enough to have arrested that kind of pain. Which suggested one of two things. He was either still in denial or he hadn't cared about his son.

Jess was going with denial—that initial, universal reaction to the sudden, agonizing loss of a loved one.

And denial could be a dangerous defense mechanism

when allowed to linger for weeks or months...or years. In extreme cases one might not feel the emotional impact of events or see the logical consequences of their actions. The conscience would go by the wayside.

"We have to wait until after the press conference," Lori argued.

"That could be hours," Jess rebutted. "They just got started. There will be questions, et cetera, et cetera." Lori still wasn't convinced. "His order was that you not let me out of your sight. So you won't." Jess put her hands up and shrugged. "We'll be together in your car. Armed and ready for whatever we encounter. *Together.*"

"If...," Lori ventured, "we go, you have to...follow—"

"Your orders," Jess finished for her. She stood. "Done. Let's go."

Lori closed her laptop. "We can use the rear exit. Miss the crowds outside." She managed a smile that didn't reach her eyes.

She was worried. Jess could understand that. The innuendos flying about her being a maverick were enough to make any smart cop nervous.

If Jess looked past her own denial, she was damned worried, too.

What if she was wrong about this? She could be wasting time...making mistakes.

Like before.

Warrior, 12:22 p.m.

"That's definitely it."

"Looks like someone's home." Jess craned her neck to

count the vehicles. Two cars, one truck, and two SUVs. All older models. Nothing fancy or new. "You think they're having a party, maybe?"

"I guess we'll find out." Lori opened her door, then hesitated. "Let's take this slow and easy, Jess. We don't want any complaints filed against us."

Jess blew out a puff of frustrated air. "Those stories about me are more about hype than about truth."

"Hey, I wasn't talking about you." She nodded toward the house. "The Debarros filed several complaints against the investigators when their daughter went missing. I saw the notations. Everything from racism to plain old disrespect. There may be a few shoulders with big-ass chips on them in there."

Jess moistened her lips and smiled, even though she suddenly felt like crying. Had to be the lack of sleep and the frustration of getting nowhere on this case. Not to mention this damned smear campaign was getting to her. The exhaustion and frustration were making it way too easy.

"Come on." Lori flashed a real smile. "Let's find that big break we've been praying for."

Jess followed the detective across the yard. There was no sidewalk in front of the small box of a house. No porch. Just a set of steps that led to the front door. No shrubbery or flowers. Just grass and ruts where as much of the lawn was used as driveway as not.

Lori stood on the top step and rapped on the door. She really was a good detective and a nice woman. Friend material. Jess hadn't had time for friends in a long time. The detective was attractive, too. Tall and slender, with long brown hair. Chet had better sharpen his game; this lady was a catch.

And the perfect example of the Player's type.

Jess shuddered and instinctively surveyed the narrow paved road that had brought them here. Five or six other small houses dotted the road, woods crowded up behind them.

Another knock brought someone to the door. Lively music greeted them as it opened. It was Saturday afternoon. Rest and relaxation time for lots of hardworking folks.

A Hispanic man filled the doorway. He looked from Lori to Jess, out to the red 1967 Mustang they had arrived in, and then back. "You lost, ladies?"

"Are you Jorge Debarros?" Lori asked.

"Depends." He leaned on the door frame. "Are you Megan Fox?"

Lori showed her badge. "We need to speak with Mr. Debarros, please."

The man stared at her for a moment longer, blatantly enjoying the frame he imagined lay beneath her reserved slacks and blouse. "Jorge!" he shouted over his shoulder. He shifted his attention back to the unexpected visitors. "Come on in, ladies."

Her right hand instinctively going to the center of her back where her holstered weapon was nestled, Lori followed him inside.

Jess was right behind her, studying the living room, with its worn but clean furnishings and bare wood floors. The pale green walls were heavy with rows of framed photographs. One of the larger ones drew her across the room. *Christina*. Probably a school photo. Her dark features and big smile made for a very photogenic face. Though Jess had seen the case photo, this one showed the mere child that Christina had been. Far too young, in Jess's opinion, to have been engaged in sexual activity.

The music shut off and the voices in the next room hushed.

Another man came into the room. He stopped several feet away. "What do you want?"

Jorge Debarros spoke near perfect English with scarcely a hint of an accent. He was neatly dressed and clean-shaven.

"Mr. Debarros, I'm Detective Wells from the Birmingham Police and this is Agent Harris of the FBI."

He glanced at Jess. "What do you want?" he repeated.

Jess reserved judgment. The gentleman appeared to have had some trouble with the investigation of his missing daughter. It was doubtful that he would be disposed to cooperation.

"Mr. Debarros"—Jess approached him and extended her hand—"I'm here to follow up on your daughter Christina's disappearance."

He snorted a laugh, didn't bother to take her hand. "Right, after almost six years? I came to you people"—he directed this at Lori—"over and over again the first two years my Christina was missing and nothing changed. Why should I believe anything has changed now?"

"What is this, Jorge?"

Jess looked past Mr. Debarros to the woman who hovered at the doorway between the living room and what might be the kitchen, since that was where it sounded like all the other folks in the house were gathered. Her accent was heavy, the trepidation in her voice even heavier.

"Nothing. Stay in the kitchen!"

The woman backed away from the doorway. Mr. Debarros's attention swung back to Jess.

"I don't want to disturb your family and your guests. Can we talk outside, sir?"

He didn't answer, didn't move for several seconds. Then he walked out the door without a glance at either of them.

Jess shared a look with Lori before exiting the house. Whatever happened during the investigation all those years ago, the Debarros family felt wronged. Giving the BPD grace, it was difficult to persuade a family that everything possible had been done when their child remained missing.

They stood in the neglected front yard in a wary triangle. There was nothing Jess could say to ease the loss he had suffered. But if anything this man told her helped find the missing girls, perhaps it would be worth the pain that her questions would no doubt awaken.

"Have you found my Christina?"

"No, sir. I'm sorry. We haven't found her."

Devastation lined his face. "Then why are you here?"

"We need to ask you a few questions about your daughter's disappearance."

"Because of the missing white girls?"

Jess didn't blink. She held his relentless stare. "Yes, sir."

One, two, three, four seconds elapsed. "So ask."

"Would you tell me about Christina? What was going on in her life those last few days and weeks before she disappeared?"

"She was a very good student." His deep voice trembled. "We believed she would be the first in our family to go to college." He took another stretch of time to compose himself. "She started staying late after school to work on a special project. After that project it was another and then another. One day it was almost dark and she still wasn't home. I was worried and I went to the school to pick her up."

His tension visibly built as he spoke. "She was already halfway home. Walking. I noticed something on her neck." He touched his throat. "A red mark. When we got home I demanded answers. She swore it was from a fight she'd had with a friend, but I knew it wasn't true. It was a lover's mark, but I didn't want to believe that." He shrugged, the gesture listless. "My Christina had never been in trouble, so I let it go with a warning."

He fell silent, his head bowed.

Jess exchanged another look with Lori.

"Mr. Debarros, what happened after that?"

His entire being shuddered. "Three weeks later she vanished. She went to school one day and she never came back." He lifted his head, eyes red, tears on his cheeks. "They said she never came to school that day."

Her pulse hammering, Jess moistened her lips. "Sir, what did you do after that?"

"We called the police. Started to look for her. Called all her friends. Her teachers. No one knew anything." A sort of calmness settled over him. "Then my wife confessed what she knew. Christina had a boyfriend. She told her mother she had stopped having her monthly. Her mother was afraid to tell me."

"When your wife admitted this to you, what did you do?"

"I told the police. They questioned the boy but he denied knowing Christina. His friends backed him up. The only proof I had was Christina and she was gone. They wouldn't believe my wife. She spoke little English so that made her nothing in their eyes."

"Did you confront the boy?"

He nodded. "I followed him home from school and confronted him and his father. They both denied what my Christina had said and they called the police. The cops said if I bothered the Murrays again I would go to jail." He shook his head. "Every week I called and nothing. I stopped calling three years ago when I heard of his death. My Christina was still lost to me but at least he was in hell."

Jess struggled to draw in a breath. "Warrior is a small town. Have you run into his parents since this happened?"

"Once."

Jess waited for him to go on.

"I stopped for gas and he was there for the same thing. He looked at me and I looked at him. I told him that now he knew how I felt, then I got back in my truck and drove away."

"Your wife," Jess said, "she's certain Tate Murray was the boy your Christina said got her pregnant?"

He nodded. "It was him. I saw it in his eyes when I confronted him after my Christina disappeared. *It was him.*"

"Sir, you filed complaints about the investigators in your daughter's case. Will you tell me what happened?"

"My wife was not a citizen. But I and my daughter were…are. It was my wife's word against the Murrays'. There was no other proof. Christina had not told any of her friends. If she did, none would say. Last year the man in charge of the investigation died of a heart attack. I felt no sympathy for him or his family. He did not care if he found my Christina."

"Mr. Debarros, I am so sorry your daughter has not been found. I promise you, sir, that I'll personally see to it that her case is reopened." Jess extended her hand once more. "Thank you for your time, sir."

This time he closed his hand around hers and shook it.

He didn't say thank you or ask her any questions. He went back into his home and rejoined his family.

Lori looked as if she'd eaten a bad burger. "What's wrong, Detect—Lori?"

She headed for the car, prompting Jess to do the same.

"Now that was creepy," Lori said over the roof of the car to Jess.

"How so?"

"That detective he was talking about who had the heart attack? That was Joe Newberry." Lori opened her door. "His heart attack opened up a detective's spot for me."

"And here you are," Jess suggested, "picking up the ball it appears he dropped."

Jess looked back at the Debarros's home as Lori backed out onto the road. A face was pressed to the glass of one of the front windows. Looked like the woman who had been ordered back into the kitchen.

Christina's mother.

Jess stared at the window until she could no longer see the house. She faced forward and made up her mind what had to be done next. Burnett would be livid when he found out. He was going to be hell-raising, fire-spitting mad anyway. What was another degree or two?

"Are we going back to the office?"

Now for the next hurdle. "Eventually. First, we're paying a visit to the Murrays."

Lori glanced at her. "You have a plan?"

"I don't need a plan." The sudden urgency nudging at her wouldn't wait. She wanted to go now.

"Because . . . ," Lori prodded.

"Because we just reopened a cold case in which the Murray family are persons of interest."

"We did," Lori agreed. "The Murrays don't have to talk to us, but making the attempt to question them is not only appropriate, it's our job."

Oh, yes. Detective Wells had the right stuff.

"I don't get it," Lori said. "If the Murrays are involved, why would they do this? There's nothing in their backgrounds to indicate trouble."

Jess didn't have to consider the question. She had already formed a basic profile on the couple, even though she had met only the husband. "Denial. Their only child died suddenly. They appear to be common, salt-of-the-earth people. Probably no education above high school. Hardworking. Family is everything. Their son was their whole life."

"They sure wouldn't want his future ruined with an unexpected pregnancy before he'd even finished high school," Lori suggested.

"Absolutely not." Jess understood the human psyche and its fragility. "If our theory is correct, whatever happened to Christina was the first act of evil. Their consciences were bruised, but denial helped them rationalize their actions. When their son died, the loss was so profound, denial took over again. It was their only hope to survive the emotional devastation. The only safe place they could escape to."

"Denial can be that powerful?"

That was something Jess knew a little something about from personal experience. "In extreme cases, denial can be immensely powerful. Couple it with something like obsession and you have a recipe for tragedy."

"Okay, I guess I can see that," Lori said. "But why abduct these girls now? All these years later? What's the motive?"

"That depends on the need that has been nurtured by the denial." That was also the part Jess had the least insight into at this point. "Are they looking to replace his absence with a daughter? A son would be too painful, almost as if they were trying to replace *him*. The other possibility is that they are in complete denial and are looking for a companion for him. If their son had lived he would have perhaps graduated from college. Maybe be engaged."

"That's sick." Lori shook herself.

Jess shrugged. "There are far worse scenarios."

Lori glanced at her, dread in her eyes. "You mean like Spears."

"Evil comes in all shapes and sizes," Jess explained. She had spent years studying the levels and faces of evil. "You have sociopaths like Eric Spears who rank at the very highest level of the scale, tormenters. His singular motive is pleasure. The only way he can feel it is to torture his victims in the most depraved ways. He feeds on the fear. The murder itself is actually secondary. It's all about the pain he can inflict before he takes their lives. The longer they pleasure him, the longer he keeps them alive. He plays the game."

"By pleasure him," Lori questioned, "you mean entertain him?"

"That's right. Their reactions give him pleasure. Excite him."

"How do you analyze freaks like that with any kind of objectivity?"

"You set all emotions aside and focus on the facts." The memory of staring into Spears's cold eyes twisted in her belly. "Then you hope the bastard gets what's coming to him when the courts are finished."

"Do you think the girls are being tortured? Could the Murrays be that twisted?"

"I can't assess that just yet. The fact that we don't have any bodies may indicate that the girls are alive. Or it could simply be that we haven't found them yet. The only aspect of this case that lends itself to the option of revenge is Dana Sawyer. She was his girlfriend who went on with her life without him."

There were too many missing details for her to build a comprehensive profile. "My guess is they're shopping for a daughter or a daughter-in-law."

"That could mean the girls are alive," Lori offered with another quick look in Jess's direction.

"Don't mistake a lesser ranking when it comes to depravity with a lack of proclivity toward violence. Even a simple obsession can turn deadly. Particularly if the plan goes wrong."

Burnett had insisted Andrea was strong and smart. Jess hoped he was right. "If, as I suspect, these people have planned this for a long time, then, in their minds, their entire existence depends on this—whatever it is—going as planned. Failure would destroy the world they've built to escape reality."

"We have to approach with caution."

"We do." Speaking of caution, Jess dared to check her cell. Two missed calls from Burnett, one from Lily. "Damn." She'd set it to vibrate. Good thing.

"Me, too," Lori said. "Two calls from the chief, three from Harper."

"The reception isn't very good out here." The woods,

the mountains. They were miles and miles off the main road.

"Not very good at all," Lori agreed.

They rode in silence for a few minutes, anticipation thumping inside Jess. It had to mean something that the Murray family kept popping back into the mix. She needed just one suspicious word or deed out of the father. He'd been happy to talk when she and Burnett stopped by. All she had to do was keep Lori cooperative.

"You and Harper serious?" Jess asked. Time to lower the tension. Calm. Focus. By the time they reached the Murray place, they both needed to be at the very top of their game.

Lori sent her a questioning glance. "About work, yes."

Jess laughed. "I see the way he looks at you." She also saw the way Lori looked at him.

"He doesn't fit into my plan outside work." She didn't sound convinced.

"Sometimes we have to revise our plans." Jess relaxed into the headrest. Sleep had eluded her last night. With them no closer to finding the girls and her professional reputation being ripped to shreds on the news, it was no wonder. Being stuck under the same roof with Burnett hadn't helped.

"What about you and the chief?"

"What about us?"

"I see the way he looks at you."

She'd asked for that. Jess shook her head. "What you're seeing is familiarity. Our relationship was over a long time ago."

"If you say so."

Before Jess could set her straight, Lori asked, "You

mind if I stop at that convenience store on 31? I need a restroom."

"I could use something to drink." They had skipped lunch and the lack of fuel was catching up with her now.

Jess watched the wooded landscape evolve into the small town of Warrior. It still rattled her that evil could happen in such a serene natural setting. But it did. Every minute of every day.

"Did you restore this yourself?" Jess didn't know that much about cars but she had been raised in the south. A Shelby Cobra Mustang of this era was a highly sought after vehicle.

"It was my father's." Lori smiled as her hands caressed the steering wheel. "When I turned sixteen, my mother gave it to me." She released a big breath. "He died when I was a kid. She'd kept it in the garage for me all that time."

"Sorry." Something else they had in common. "I lost my parents when I was a kid, too."

"That's one reason my career is so important." Lori glanced at her. "My mother and younger sister depend on me financially."

That was a heavy burden. "I have a sister, too. She's older. Married. Kids. The whole nine yards."

"Does that make us the bad guys?" Lori eased into the turning lane. "Because we don't want it all right now? That we're more focused on ourselves?"

"Maybe." Jess attempted a laugh. "Or maybe we're just the smart guys."

There were always two sides to every coin.

At the convenience store, Lori hit the ladies' room and Jess grabbed a couple of Pepsis. She paid and returned to the car. She'd just settled into the passenger seat when her phone vibrated again. No doubt Burnett burning up the towers.

Text message.

Tormenter.

Ice slowed her blood.

I like your friend.

Son of a bitch!

Movement snatched Jess's gaze forward. Lori bounded from the store. She jerked her door open and dropped behind the steering wheel

"We have to get back downtown." She sounded breathless...upset. She couldn't know about the text Jess had just received.

Jess shook off the distraction. "Has another girl gone missing?"

Wells backed up the Mustang, pulled forward, but then braked before pulling out onto the road. "The chief got a text asking him why he wasn't watching you more closely."

Jess's throat tightened.

Spears was here.

Andrea fought to stay focused.

She didn't want to be carried out of the kitchen by that man.

Callie and Macy were gone now. To wherever he had taken Reanne.

The only girl left besides her was the new girl, Dana. The one the woman had said she didn't like. The man liked her, though. Andrea watched the way he cheered her on and smiled when the woman wasn't looking.

Andrea didn't know what happened to the winner in this competition but she knew one thing for certain, she didn't want to be one of the losers. She already knew what happened to them...yet if she won, all the others would die like the girl in the basement.

"Answer the question, Dana!" the woman screamed.

Andrea jumped.

Dana sat perfectly still. She didn't even blink, like she was in a coma even without the pills.

The woman stuck her face close to Dana's ear and

shouted, "Who will you love and respect most besides your Lord and your husband?"

Dana turned slowly and lifted her face to the woman glaring at her.

Andrea held her breath.

"You...are...insane," Dana said in a voice so low, so terrifyingly anger-filled, that Andrea flinched.

The fury that erupted across the woman's face almost made Andrea's heart stop. She tried to control the trembling but it would not be stopped.

Her eyes still bulging with anger, the woman hurried around the table to Andrea. She stared down at her. Andrea was afraid to look up or to say anything.

"Andrea, can you answer the question?"

The woman asked so sweetly and softly that the difference was as startling as it was stunning. Andrea feared anything she said would turn the woman back into that raging monster.

But if she didn't answer...

"You." The word was rusty and shaky. Andrea prayed that was the right answer. She was pretty sure it was. But there had been so many lessons. So many rules and Bible verses.

"Who else?" the woman prompted in that same sweet tone.

Andrea struggled to drag in a breath. She managed a brittle smile. "Him." She looked to the man. Something the woman had said to her climbed out of the fog in Andrea's brain. "I like it here. I want to be your daughter."

"We have a winner!" The woman threw her arms up in the air and skipped around the table. "Andrea's a winner!" she repeated over and over.

Andrea's gaze locked with Dana's. There was something in her eyes... *relief.* Tears burned Andrea's eyes. What was wrong with these people? Why were they doing this?

The man lifted Dana from her chair and hoisted her over his shoulder. Andrea thought his cheeks looked wet as he glanced back at the dancing woman, then turned and carried Dana out of the kitchen.

Andrea felt the hot tears slipping down her own cheeks. She didn't want to cry for fear of angering the woman. She wanted to be strong. The woman stopped long enough to kiss Andrea on the head.

Please, God, she prayed. *Help me!*

"Come on," the woman urged. "It's almost time."

She dragged Andrea out of the chair.

"Come on, come on." She ushered her from the room. "I think you'll like the dress I bought you. I knew it would be you. Mothers know these things."

At the stairs, she gestured for Andrea to go first. Lightheaded and with weak knees, Andrea climbed the first step, then the next. She couldn't hold on to the banister, since her hands were still tied behind her back.

At the top of the stairs, the woman led Andrea to a door on the right. She opened the door and motioned inside. "Do you like it?"

Unable to breathe much less speak, Andrea nodded.

"Oh good!" She pulled her into the room. "I picked out everything myself. You told me you like pink. So I painted it pink. I didn't care if the others liked it or not. I wanted you to win and you did!"

When had Andrea told her that? She couldn't remember. All those Bible verses and rules and names kept rolling through her mind.

"I watched you for a long time before we bumped into each other at the store." She smiled. "You're so pretty and smart. Not like the other girls." She nodded knowingly. "I had watched them too and they weren't good girls like you." She laughed. "Daddy wanted Dana to win but I knew she didn't deserve to win." She leaned close to Andrea. "I played a trick on her. Made her think she was losing her mind." The woman snorted. "She deserved it. She broke his heart. But that's behind us now. Come on!"

She guided Andrea to the bed to sit down. Then she went over to the closet and pulled out a white dress with small pink flowers on the sash. "You like it?"

Andrea licked her dry lips and nodded. "It's very pretty." Say something else, Andrea! Be smart! "Thank you."

The woman carefully laid the dress across the bed next to Andrea. Then she rushed to the chest of drawers and gathered up panties and a bra. She placed them on the bed, too.

Footsteps outside the room drew Andrea's attention to the door. The man walked in. He wasn't crying anymore but he looked sad and tired. Why was he letting the woman do this? Why didn't he stop her?

What had he done to the others?

"Wait outside, Daddy! She has to change. She has to be ready. This is the most important day of her life."

He stepped outside the room, pulling the door closed.

"Now, I'm going to untie you, but if you do anything stupid you'll be a loser like the others." She sighed. "Then we'd have to start over." She patted Andrea on the shoulder. "So you be good, okay?"

Andrea nodded.

She held her tears and fear inside and stood while the

woman untied her hands. She rubbed her wrists and wrestled back the urge to run. The man was right outside the door. She didn't want to be a loser.

"Take off your clothes and I'll help you with the dress."

Her hands shaking, Andrea pulled her blouse over her head. She unbuttoned her jeans and peeled them down her legs, kicked them off her bare feet. Her bra and panties came off next. Her arms covering herself, she waited for what the woman would tell her to do next.

One item at a time, the woman helped Andrea dress. The new fabric felt scratchy. Andrea didn't care. She had to keep this woman happy until she saw a chance to escape.

What if they were dressing her up to put her in one of those boxes like the girl in the basement?

The tears burned her cheeks before she realized she was crying. Why had this happened to her? To the others?

The woman guided her to the mirror over the dresser. "Don't you look pretty?"

Andrea smiled but her lips trembled.

"Let's brush your hair and you'll be ready."

Andrea closed her eyes while the woman brushed her hair. She prayed again but she wasn't sure help would come in time. Something big was about to happen and she just wanted to live through it. If she died in this awful place, would they ever find her? No one had found the girl or the baby in the basement.

"You are so pretty, Andrea." The woman smiled at her in the mirror. "From the day my son was born, even though they told me I couldn't have any more children, I knew one day I would have a daughter." She laid down the brush and squeezed Andrea's arms. "And now I do."

Andrea's heart threatened to burst out of her chest.

Since she didn't know what to say, she stretched her lips into a smile and nodded.

The woman guided Andrea into the hall outside the room. "Doesn't she look pretty, Daddy?"

"She sure does, Momma."

"Hold her hand," the woman ordered.

The two led Andrea to another room, farther down the hall. Outside the door, they hesitated.

"We've waited a long time to find the perfect daughter." The woman reached for the door. "Now you'll see why we're so excited."

The door swung inward. The room was a light blue, trophies stood on the dresser. Sports posters lined the wall. The curtains were closed over the window, but next to it a pale glow from the table lamp spilled over a young man seated in a chair. At first Andrea thought he was asleep, since his eyes were closed, maybe drugged like she had been. But he didn't move at all. His chest didn't rise and fall. His face was pasty and pale. He wore jeans and a dark blue polo shirt. His arms and hands rested on the arms of the chair.

Andrea's heart stumbled, then pounded erratically.

"Andrea," the woman said, "this is our son, Tate." She smiled at the boy in the chair. "Tate, this is Andrea. The one I've been telling you about." The woman laughed. "Yes, she is beautiful." She looked at Andrea with approval. "She's perfect. She passed all the tests."

Andrea swayed. She tried to steady herself. *Don't mess up. Don't mess up!* She had to be strong.

"Tate and Andrea," the woman singsonged. "It's just perfect."

Andrea fought the blackness trying to drag her down.

She had to hold it together. She wasn't tied up anymore. Maybe she would get a chance to run before it was too late.

"Daddy, you help Tate get ready. He can't get married wearing that lucky polo shirt of his."

Andrea's knees buckled.

The woman steadied her. "You're all right, hon, it's normal to be nervous before your wedding." She hugged Andrea. "I'm so proud of you. You're the perfect wife for my son."

But her son was . . . *dead*.

BPD, 2:51 p.m.

Dan took another breath in hopes of remaining calm. "I have a unit watching your sister and her family," he said to Jess. "Lily knows that since the media brought her into public focus, that she and her family may end up in Spears's crosshairs."

"I tried—"

He held up his hand to stop whatever excuse Jess intended to offer. "I've contacted my bureau liaison to see what they intend to do in the way of protection. I'm certain after hearing about the text messages from Spears they'll have no problem stepping in." Dan had had some time to come to terms with the situation and still it twisted his gut into knots.

"At this point," he went on before Jess could try taking charge of the conversation again, "we have to assume he's here and watching you." Fury whipped to a new frenzy when he considered how that bastard had taunted him about Jess. "For now, I'm responsible for your protection, Jess. You will do exactly as I say." He glared at his detective. "That goes for you, too, Wells. When I give an order, I expect it to be followed."

She and Jess started talking at the same time.

He held up both hands this time. The two fell silent. "I have just one question." He reached for calm again, didn't exactly find it. "What the hell were you thinking?" He stood behind his desk, Wells and Jess at attention on the other side, both rigid with guilt. He figured he needed something between him and the two of them to prevent shaking the hell out of one or both.

"I'm sorry, Chief," Wells said respectfully. "The urgency of the situation got the better of my judgment."

"That's not true," Jess argued. She looked from Wells to Dan. "She followed my direct orders. Detective Wells had no choice."

Now that, he didn't doubt.

"That's not the way it happened, sir," Wells countered. "I made the decision on my own to follow up on the Debarros case in connection with our current case. Anything Agent Harris said or did not say was not the deciding factor."

Dan shook his head. "That's all you have to say for yourself?" This he directed at his detective.

"No, sir." Wells squared her shoulders. "I respectfully request that I be dismissed so that I can get back to work. I'm hopeful that any disciplinary action can wait until we find those missing girls."

If she hadn't been right Dan would have given her the dressing down she deserved. "Go. The others are in the conference room going over the possible link between the Debarros case and this one."

"Thank you, sir."

She and Jess exchanged a look before Wells left his office, closing the door behind her. Dan rested the full weight of his unhappiness on the last woman standing.

"Detective Wells did what I asked her to do," Jess told him without a hint of remorse. "She argued that we should wait until after the press conference. I pushed the issue. She reluctantly agreed." Jess bracketed her waist with her hands. "She doesn't deserve any sort of disciplinary action. Besides, this investigation is more important than a stupid press conference. Waiting would have wasted precious time, just like what we're doing right now is gobbling up time that should be focused on finding those girls. The Murrays—"

"You got your point across about Wells." He tamped back the rising frustration. "But you had to throw out a smart-ass remark about the press conference. That was outside my control."

"You know I'm right."

"You're right, Jess." He threw his hands up. "You're right. But I can't help these girls or anyone else if I'm fired. I, for one, would like to keep my job."

She looked as if he had slapped her in the face. Oh hell. "Jess, I wasn't implying—"

"Yes, you were. And you're right." She glanced around for someplace to focus her attention besides on him.

Well, hell. He rounded the desk and took her by the shoulders. "You don't understand."

Reluctantly she met his gaze. "I should have gotten word to Sergeant Harper to provide backup in case we ran into trouble. I screwed up. Again. Shit. Shit. Shit!"

"Jess, your instincts were right on target. I'm the one

who freaked out. Instead of rushing to provide the two of you backup, all I could think about was the fact that the text messages that bastard sent might mean he was watching you. That he was close to you."

Anger flared in her eyes. "I am not twenty-two years old anymore. I can take care of myself. Wells and I had the situation under control." She shrugged away from his touch. "We should be talking to the Murrays right now instead of playing these ridiculous power games."

Dan once more restrained the need to shake her. Resisting was a hell of a lot harder this time. "What you and Wells found is damned interesting. But I knew Detective Newberry. He was a good man and a damned good detective. If he couldn't find a connection between the Murray boy and the missing girl, then one didn't exist."

Jess rolled her eyes. "Are you sure about that, Burnett? Or are you just assuming he couldn't find a link because he belonged to the same club as you? I know how you good old boys stick up for one another."

That flame of frustration he'd kept at a low burn blazed higher. "You have to be right, don't you? No matter the cost to yourself or anyone around you. You just can't see past your vision of how things are."

"Don't be absurd." She lifted her chin. "My vision and the facts are one in the same in this case. That is what we're talking about, isn't it? The case? Five missing girls?"

The blaze roared into an inferno. "It's just like that last summer we were together." He was barely hanging on to reason. He knew it but, at this point, he could do nothing but embrace the concept that he was losing control. "You refused to see any other route to our future together except the one you had planned. It didn't matter that I might have slightly different priorities."

She laughed, a dry, aching sound. "We had lived together for four years. I think I understood your priorities as well as anyone could. At least until your ego got the better of you."

The emotional impact of that statement stunned him, obliterated the last of his reason and any lick of his self-control. "Okay, yes." He steadied himself against the tremors rocking his insides. "I was disappointed and my ego was bruised when I didn't get the internship. Is that what you want to hear?"

"I didn't need to hear you say it. I've known it for twenty years!"

His jaw ached from clenching. "I was also struggling with the fact that my family was here. I wasn't so sure at that point that I wanted the rest of my life to play out in a whole other region of the country." He grappled for calm. Couldn't find it.

"I guess you forgot to mention that part to me."

He took a moment, fought for some semblance of composure. "I didn't want to be the reason you didn't follow *your* dream."

"How noble of you."

"You had no one holding you back. Your sister is here but that's different. My parents weren't getting any younger. I knew there would come a time when they needed me. I realized this was where I was supposed to be."

"Like Katherine Burnett would ever need anyone." Jess scoffed. "She probably talked you into coming back. She never liked me any way."

Jess and his mother had started off on the wrong foot and time hadn't altered that path. His mother's opinion of Jess had been irrelevant to Dan. "She didn't talk me into anything. I talked myself into taking the step that was best for you and for me. You wanted to be free of entangling commitments with family. I didn't. It just took me a while to be able to grasp it, accept it, and do the right thing. It was the right thing, Jess. It was right for both of us."

Her own fury tightened her lips, glistened in her dark eyes. "You think so? I mean, after all, the only thing you had to do was turn your back on me."

"You had already turned your back on me."

"Wow. We really are fucked up, aren't we?" She shook her head. "You came back here and married three times, ending up divorced every time. I ignored my personal life until someone barged in and made me pay attention. And look how that worked out."

"Your husband made a bad decision." The man had hurt Jess, whether she wanted to admit it or not. Dan felt her pain, saw it in her eyes.

"Yeah"—she nodded—"he did. But I wasn't referring to him."

Confusion furrowed his brow. "Someone else barged into your life?" He didn't know why he was surprised. Jess was a beautiful woman. Smart and ambitious. What man wouldn't fall in love with her?

"It was you, you idiot," she accused. "In that damned Publix on Christmas Eve. You just appeared"—she made a *poof* sound—"and I fell into bed with you as if ten years hadn't passed since you broke my heart completely in two."

He couldn't stop himself. He had to touch her. He took her face in his hands, made her look at him when she tried to look away. "I'm sorry, Jess. I didn't set out to hurt you. I missed you so much."

"At least you had your family and friends." Her lips trembled. "You were here. Surrounded by all those people who care about you. I had nobody."

"Why didn't you come home?" God Almighty, he had hoped and prayed a thousand times that she would come back. But he hadn't asked her to come back. Not once.

"What?" Her voice trembled. "And look like a failure?" She shook her head. "No way."

"You graduated summa cum laude, Jess. You were chosen for an internship with the bureau, not once but twice. How could anyone look at you and see failure?"

"Are you kidding me? You and your family had it all. My sister and I had nothing. We barely survived after our parents died. Four different foster homes in eight years, Dan. Four. As soon as I was out of high school, I was out of *here*. My sister had already married her high school sweetheart and was expecting her first child. I needed to find my life. Anywhere but here."

"And you did," he said softly. "You reached a career pinnacle few can ever hope to accomplish. You did good, Jess."

She shook her head. "Yeah, right up until the time I screwed up. I screwed everything up. My life. My career. Everything. Now look at me. I don't even know who I am anymore! I'm back here a day or two and suddenly all that I thought I was just disintegrates!"

"I think maybe you had a little help. Me, for one, and this bastard Eric Spears for another. Not to mention a superior who prefers to make you look bad rather than to simply go public with the facts."

A tear rolled down her cheek. "It's more than the job or a case. It's me. The person I worked so hard for years to become. She's . . ."—she shook her head—"gone. I don't know who I am anymore. It all went to hell in a matter of days and I can't catch up. Not to mention that sick bastard followed me here. Now my sister and her family are in danger. You're in danger."

Dan laughed softly, not because her feelings were funny but her worry for him was amusing. "Why the hell would you think I'm in danger?" Truth was, he would rather Spears be after him than after Jess.

"He's been watching us, Dan. At Katherine's house. He's probably been following us or had someone following us. I thought when he sent me that text saying he liked my friend that he was talking about Lori. But after the way you two sparred, I'm thinking he has his eye on you." More of those uncharacteristic tears fell. "This is all my fault."

Dan wished he knew the right words to say, but there were none. He could only offer his understanding. "This isn't your fault. Your world has been turned upside down, Jess," he said gently. "Give yourself a break. You need time to adjust to all these changes. The bureau will take care of Spears."

"Maybe you're right." She scrubbed at the tears. "All I know is that right now I need to think about anything but that." She searched his eyes, desperation in hers. "We have to find these girls. I can feel the connection to the Murrays, but I have no proof, just like with Spears. We can use the Debarros case as a way to question them further. It can work, Dan. We won't be crossing any lines. We'll be doing our jobs."

"We are going out there. And we will get the truth."

"We have to hurry," she urged. "I'm terrified it's too late already."

He nodded, dropped his hands to his side. "All right. Let's get this done."

"You did the right thing, you know. Back then."

Her statement surprised him, but her eyes backed up the words. "Sometimes I wonder."

"I was on a mission to prove something," she confessed. "Whether it was that summer or the next, we would have fallen apart. I couldn't see past what I wanted for my future to notice what was happening to us. We were drifting apart."

He felt weak with relief. All this time he'd carried that guilt. He'd walked away from her…left her, and somehow she'd made it all by herself. Had he been carrying guilt all this time or had it been resentment? He hadn't meant to resent that she hadn't needed him. Whatever it was, he didn't want that to stand between them anymore.

"Thank you for telling me." The liberation he'd expected to feel if this moment ever came—this clearing of the air—didn't show. He still felt—

"Just one more thing."

He looked at her expectantly.

She reached up, took his face in her hands, rose on her tiptoes, and kissed him. His arms went around her and he kissed her back. She felt good in his arms.

God help him, *this* was what he'd carried all these years. He still wanted her. He wanted to hold her like this…to kiss her like this.

She drew back first, pressed her forehead to his cheek. "I don't know what's wrong with me."

A rap at his door forced them apart.

Jess's eyes were wide with mortification but her face was flushed with the same desire he felt.

The door opened and Harper stuck his head into the room. "I think you two should come to the conference room. We found something you'll want to hear."

"We'll be right there," Dan assured him.

The door closed.

"I'm sorry," they said in unison.

The flush on Jess's cheeks deepened. She pressed her fingers to her lips. "I didn't mean to do that. So, if we can just act like it didn't happen, I think that would be best."

"It did happen, Jess. Frankly, I don't want to pretend it didn't. Just like when I kissed you night before last. It happened and I'm glad it did."

He reached across his desk for his cell, tucked it into the holster at his waist. "Let's find these girls and then we'll finish this... conversation."

He crossed the room, opened the door, and waited for her to exit before him. She hesitated. Clearly shaken and uncertain.

She took a breath. "Whatever you say, Chief."

Jess wanted to crawl into a hole. Instead, she matched her stride to Burnett's and headed to the conference room. Griggs and Patterson were already seated at the long, cluttered table. Chet and Lori were huddled near the window.

Another wave of mortification washed over Jess at the idea that she and Burnett must have looked like that when Chet poked his head into Burnett's office. She had ten years' experience, at least, on those two. There was no excuse for her unprofessional behavior.

What in the hell had gotten into her?

Stress. Frustration. Temporary insanity. Pick one. Hell, pick all three, she thought in disgust.

And Lily. Her sister was terrified for her family and for Jess.

What a mess.

Dan moved to the head of the table and waited for everyone to be seated.

Jess settled into a chair at the opposite end. She had to pull herself back together. She needed to focus.

"You okay?" Lori murmured as she took the seat next to Jess.

"I will be," she muttered, "as soon as we find these girls." *And I give Spears what he deserves*, she kept to herself, *and then run as far away from here as possible.*

"Sergeant Harper," Burnett said, "give us a rundown on this new development."

"As Agent Harris and Detective Wells learned earlier today, the Debarros case, one that involved a missing girl with similar circumstances, has a vague link to one of the girls in our current case. Christina Debarros's mother claimed her daughter's secret boyfriend was Tate Murray. Dana Sawyer was the longtime girlfriend of this same young man through his high school years."

"The problem is," Griggs interjected, "Tate Murray has been dead for over three years."

"Yes, sir," Chet agreed. "We have considered the possibilities of some sort of revenge for his death, either from the parents or a close friend, but we feel that revenge isn't the motive, since none of the missing girls had anything to do with his death. His and Dana Sawyer's relationship had ended several months prior to the accident that took his life."

"Then what is the motive and what do you have to substantiate it?" Patterson demanded, his impatience vibrating in the room.

"What we have," Chet answered, "is the fact that suddenly, after all these years, five young women have gone missing under similar circumstances. Christina Debarros's disappearance can be characterized in this same manner. Sudden disappearance with no forewarning to friends or family."

Jess silently urged him to get to the part she didn't know yet.

As if Griggs had read her mind, he said as much. "Is there an echo in the room? We got that part already."

"Please continue, Sergeant," Burnett said, with a sharp look in Griggs's direction.

Jess leaned back in her seat and put her hand over her mouth to hide a smile. It was about time Burnett stopped letting these old coots throw their weight around. She was glad one of them had let his impatience show rather than her for a change.

"Detective Wells and I have been running various searches on the name Tate Murray. We didn't find any relevant to our case, until we considered the name Tim. Reanne Parsons received text messages from someone named Tim, as we all know."

Jess held her breath. She looked to Lori, who nodded.

"Tate Murray's full name is Tate Isaac Murray. T. I. M."

The tension in the room thickened. Jess's heart thudded harder.

"We searched the name Tim Murray," Chet explained. "And we got a hit. Tim Murray has been enrolled in an online university for the past two years. The kind that doesn't require any actual classroom attendance or even any face-to-face interviews. He received his associate's degree in agricultural management in early June, just a few days before our first girl went missing."

Her preliminary conclusion had been right. Jess had to hold herself down in her chair. She wanted to act!

"How can you be certain Tate Murray and Tim Murray are one in the same?" Patterson shook his head. "The boy's dead for Christ's sake."

"The school website displays photos of its most recent graduates. Most of the photos look like the senior photos taken for high school graduation. Tim Murray's photo matched the one of Tate Murray in the Warrior year book his senior year. Tim and Tate *are* the same person. And," Chet said before anyone could start throwing out theories in an attempt to counter his obvious conclusion, "according to what I just learned from the search of the archived vehicle registrations I ordered yesterday, Tate Murray owned a truck when he died. A 1972 blue *Ford* truck."

Good God. Jess felt the air leave her lungs in a rush. It *was* him.

"That's quite a story, Sergeant. However, one thing is certain," Griggs tossed in, his tone reflecting his disbelief, "Tate Murray didn't text anybody or abduct a single one of these girls. Who are you theorizing is the unsub?"

My Tate. Mr. Murray had shown no sadness when he spoke of his son.

Jess launched to her feet, almost sending her chair tumbling to the floor. "Sergeant Harper is right. Mr. and Mrs. Murray have been living in denial for years. They haven't accepted their son's death."

Words and images flooded Jess. The grief those people

must have suffered at losing their only child. The sheer agony. Bitterness and resentment as they watched the other children in their community grow up. The infinite need to simply love their son. Wrestling back control, she set aside the overpowering emotions.

"We can all sympathize with the loss of a child," Patterson offered, "but what you're suggesting is—"

"They've carried on as if he's still alive," Jess said, the realization settling firmly. "They enrolled him in an online university that didn't require a physical presence. The longer they lingered in denial the more obsessed they became. They couldn't let their son be dead so they went on with his life for him." Jess turned to Chet. "Find a judge who will sign a warrant to exhume his body. I'll wager Tate Murray hasn't been a resident of the cemetery where he was buried since shortly after the graveside service."

"We can't go digging up someone's dead son based on speculation," Griggs argued.

Patterson agreed, "The press will eat us alive."

Lori had opened her laptop and her fingers raced across the keys. Jess didn't know what she was looking for but she hoped it would be something to win this unreasonable standoff. They had to act now.

But what if she was wrong... about part or all of this?

"Gentlemen"—Burnett stood—"we've run out of time and excuses. The gloves have to come off. Detective Wells, call Judge Schmale, tell him I'm calling in that marker he owes me."

"An exhumation may not be necessary, Chief," Lori spoke up. "Tate Murray was buried in the family cemetery on the Murray farm."

"That's even better," Burnett said. "We need a search warrant for the Murray property. List the girls' names. And don't forget Christina Debarros."

"Make it fast," Jess urged. "Tate Murray graduated college recently. His family is ready for him to take the next step."

Dan's eyes met hers as if he'd just realized the same thing.

A new kind of terror flooded Jess. "I believe the Murrays have been searching for their son's bride."

Andrea sat in the chair next to the dead boy. The trembling wouldn't stop. She worked hard to keep it from showing. Her fingers tightened around the bouquet of flowers she held.

The man and woman had decorated the living room with flowers and ribbons. A two-tier white cake with a topper featuring a bride and groom sat on a table. They had both read from the Bible. Hugged and kissed each other, Andrea and the boy.

This was crazy. Andrea wanted to go home. What had they done with the other girls? Hours had passed and neither the man nor the woman had mentioned the others. She hadn't heard any screaming.

Tears burned Andrea's eyes. Don't cry! *Don't cry.* She had to be strong. She could escape if she stayed strong and calm. Dan wasn't coming in time. She had to stay alert for an opportunity. She hadn't seen a gun, which meant all she had to do was be faster and stronger and smarter. If they caught her...they would do to her whatever they had done to the others... to that girl and baby in the basement.

"Andrea," the woman said, "do you take Tate for your lawful wedded husband? To have and to hold until death do you part?"

He's already dead! "I..." Andrea swallowed back the terror. "I do."

"Do you, Tate," the man asked, "take Andrea for your lawful wedded wife? To have and to hold until death do you part?"

A moment of silence passed.

The man and woman smiled. "That's my boy," the woman said.

"We now pronounce you man and wife," he said.

The woman snapped another photo. "Now the kiss!"

The man hurried over and scooted the boy's chair around until he was facing Andrea. "Tate," he said gently, "you may kiss your bride."

"Get out of the way, Daddy!" the woman shouted. "You're blocking my shot."

Andrea couldn't move for a moment. She stared at the pitiful face that, though not decomposed completely, was showing signs of deteriorating. They were waiting, the camera poised to capture the next shot.

She had to do this. Her life depended upon it. God only knew what they had done to the others already.

Andrea leaned forward. Her breath caught at the smell, something pungent like disinfectant, as she grew closer and closer. She pressed her lips to his cold, hard mouth.

The camera flashed. Cheering and clapping filled the room.

"Get the champagne, Daddy. I'll cut the cake."

Andrea stared at the corpse. What had happened to this boy? Were these people really his parents? What about the bodies in the basement? Were there others?

A small china plate filled with cake was shoved in front of her. Andrea forced her lips into a smile. "Thank you." She tried to keep her fingers from shaking as she held the plate. If she dropped it, they would probably punish her.

Another plate with a big slice of cake was placed on a table and dragged over to the boy's chair.

A pop startled Andrea. She almost dropped the cake. Her fork rattled against her plate.

The bottle of champagne bubbled over. Two stemmed glasses were filled. One thrust at Andrea. The other placed on the table next to the boy.

The man and woman drank champagne and danced around the room. They toasted their son and talked about what a perfect birthday present his new bride was. They sang "Happy Birthday" to him.

Today was his birthday.

Andrea sat watching them. She couldn't move. She felt sorry for the dead boy. If these people were really his parents, they shouldn't be doing this to him.

She decided he had been handsome when he was alive. Young, too. Probably only seventeen or eighteen. The suit he wore looked new. Had they preserved him like this? Had they killed him? Maybe he died of some illness and they just couldn't accept that awful truth.

Andrea sipped the champagne. Sip after sip, she watched the boy and drank, praying the alcohol would numb her to this nightmare. Then she remembered what Dan had told her. *Be smart. Don't drink yourself into stupidity.*

"Eat your cake, Andrea." The woman took Andrea's empty glass and set it aside.

Andrea ate the cake, forcing forkful after forkful into her mouth. She chewed just enough to swallow the lump.

"Isn't that cute?" the woman said to her husband. "See the way she looks at him? Now that's love."

Andrea kept ramming the cake into her mouth until it was gone.

"Good girl!" The plate and fork were taken away. "Tomorrow we'll start your cooking lessons. But tonight is all yours and Tate's."

Andrea felt the cake scaling back up into her throat. She swallowed harder to keep it down.

"First," the man said, "there's that one other thing we need to get done."

Another urge to vomit contracted Andrea's muscles. She struggled to contain the compulsion.

The woman nodded. "I almost forgot about that. Get her some gloves, Daddy. We don't want her hands all blistered up. Tate wouldn't like that."

"Come along, daughter." The man took her by the arm and hauled her out of the chair.

"Tate and I will keep celebrating!" the woman said. "Tate and Andrea sitting in a tree," the woman sang, "k-i-s-s-i-n-g . . . first comes marriage . . ."

The crazy song faded as the man led Andrea through the kitchen and out the back door. It was still daylight outside. The urge to run slammed into her. *Not yet!* He would catch her.

She blinked at the sun, tried to look around without drawing his attention. The house was big and old. The yard surrounded by woods. Not in the city, she realized.

She needed to turn around to look for the road. *Just do it!* She twisted her head around and stared beyond the house. The road was far away but she could see it!

"Now come on, darling." He hustled her forward. "I'll get you back to your new husband soon."

He led her to a big old barn. While he heaved the large sliding door open, she scanned the woods. Thick and dark. When she got away, she could run into those woods and hide.

The barn was creepy and dark. He slammed the big door shut, leaving them in total blackness. Fear twisted inside her. A light switched on. Andrea blinked, looked around. What looked like a truck and maybe a car were covered with big green tarps. Shelves and a workbench lined one wall. But at the far side of the barn was a big pile of dirt. He ushered her closer to the pile. Her heart nearly stopped when she saw the hole.

The other girls were in the hole. Bound and gagged and too still. *Breathe*, she told herself.

There were five bodies, not four. She couldn't see the other one's face. The hole wasn't wide enough. They were piled on top of one another. Some had fallen to the side. She could see the profiles of those two. Dana and Callie.

They were dead! Oh God!

Don't scream!

"Here's the gloves, little girl."

Hands shaking, Andrea pulled on the gloves. That he held a shovel in his other hand terrified her. What was he going to make her do?

"This won't be an easy chore, but it will bind us as a family." He held the shovel out to her. "We'll have no secrets in this family. We will all take equal responsibility for making sure Tate has a happy future. We cannot allow anyone to get in the way. This is your responsibility, Andrea. You won the right to be Tate's bride. Now you must ensure the losers never cause us any trouble."

Andrea wrapped the gloved fingers of one hand around the wooden handle. "I understand."

"Good girl. I guess Mamma was right about you."

Andrea stared at the stack of bodies in the hole. They were all dead. She was alone and no one was coming to save her. She had to do this. Putting the dirt on top of them wouldn't hurt them any worse. She scooped up a shovelful of dirt and tossed it as gently as she could into the hole.

Callie's body quaked.

Andrea stared at her. Squeezed her eyes shut and then opened them to clear her vision. Had she imagined it? Could any of them still be alive?

Callie twitched.

Andrea's breath stalled. *She was alive!*

She bit her lips together to prevent calling out to Callie.

"Hurry up now," the man said. "You don't want to keep Tate waiting for your wedding night."

Andrea nodded.

She scooped up another shovelful of dirt and tossed it into the hole. The sound of it scattering over the bodies made her jerk.

"You get tired, I'll help you," he offered.

Andrea turned to him and smiled. Her fingers tightened on the wooden handle. "Thank you, Daddy."

He smiled back at her.

She lifted the shovel, dumped the next scoop. She steeled herself. Then she drew a deep breath, tightened her grip on the wooden handle, and swung the shovel at him with every ounce of strength in her body.

She hit him in the gut. He doubled over.

Andrea stumbled back from the impact.

He straightened. Charged her. She swung again. The metal of the shovel connected with his skull. He staggered. She swung again. Hit his head a second time. He fell to his knees.

Andrea threw the shovel and ran. She shoved hard at the door to open it far enough to slide out sideways.

She couldn't run for the road. The woman might see her.

The woods?

Something slammed into her back.

Andrea hit the ground face-first.

"Liar! Liar!"

Andrea tried to move. The woman was on top of her. Fear detonated in her veins. She had to get away!

Andrea bucked. The woman toppled off.

Scrambling forward on her hands and knees, Andrea clambered to her feet. Started to run.

Fingers manacled her ankle.

Too strong to be the woman.

Her foot was yanked out from under her and she went down.

The man towered over her, his face twisted with rage.

Andrea tried to crawl away.

He snatched her back.

The woman grabbed Andrea by the hair. "Where do you think you're going, you stupid little liar?"

"I told you Dana was the best."

The woman scoffed. "They're all *losers*."

The man jerked Andrea to her feet. “Maybe we should just start over.”

“We don’t want to disappoint Tate,” the woman argued. “It’s his wedding night. Can’t have a wedding night without a bride. We’ll punish her until she learns her lesson.” The woman looked to the man. “Take her to him. He might need some help from you. I’ll take care of the mess in the barn.”

“Come on, daughter.” The man jerked her forward. “It’s time you did your first wifely duty.”

5:49 p.m.

I thought that judge owed you a favor." Frustration and anticipation gnawed at Jess. They were wasting time!

"We're in position," Burnett offered, his own patience audibly wearing thin. "The moment we have the word, we're moving in."

Jess tugged at the bulletproof vest she wore over her suit. She curled her toes. This was a hell of a time to be wearing heels. Talk about being ill prepared. Prepared or not, what the devil was taking so long with that warrant?

Griggs's voice rattled across the earpiece she wore demanding a status. Jess wasn't the only one out of patience.

Burnett touched the tiny mike at the neck of his Kevlar vest. "Detective Wells has arrived at Judge Schmale's residence," he told Griggs. "We should be hearing from her any minute."

Silence echoed across the communications link. Everyone involved understood that there was nothing they could do until the judge had inked the warrant. At least not legally. Jess had been scorched already by that hot-button rule

In her opinion they had exigent circumstances and should move in without the warrant.

Burnett didn't see it that way. *No clear evidence*, he insisted. No way to prove imminent threat to anyone . . . no way to prove evidence was being or about to be destroyed.

They were wasting time!

Jess forced herself to calm down. She picked up the binoculars hanging around her neck and peered toward the Murray home. Nothing moving. The shades on all the rear windows were lowered. Chet had reported the same about the front. He and two of Griggs's deputies were hidden in the knee-deep grass in the pasture across the road.

"Damn it," Dan muttered, his frustration mounting. "What the hell is taking so long?"

Jess couldn't believe he'd driven his Mercedes through that pasture and as far into the woods as was possible. The farm owner at the end of Jasper Lane had agreed to allow them access to his property. Burnett had explained that one of the missing girls had been spotted in the area and they were attempting a methodical search. Jess was shocked he'd embellished that much.

After driving as far as possible, he and Jess had then walked the remaining distance until the rear of the Murray house and the front of the barn were in view. The minivan sat between the house and the barn. The truck was parked behind the van. With both vehicles at home, there was every reason to believe the owners were as well.

Griggs, Patterson, and four more deputies had fanned out in the woods on the east and west sides of the house. As soon as the warrant was en route with Lori, two deputies would assume Jess and Burnett's positions while they approached the house. By the time they had the Murrays questioned, the warrant would be here.

One wrong word, one wrong move, and maybe they wouldn't even have to wait for the warrant.

But no one or nothing was moving!

Jess tried Lori's cell again. Straight to voice mail.

Why wasn't she answering?

Burnett said something. Jess glanced back at him. His cell phone was pressed to his ear. Thank God. Maybe that was Lori with word on the warrant.

The barn door slid open. Mrs. Murray wiped her forehead with the back of her hand, then scrubbed both palms down the front of her Sunday-go-to-meeting dress. Maybe she and her husband were planning an outing. Jess scanned down to her white pumps. The short heels were caked with dirt. Mrs. Murray shoved at the door hard enough to give the impression of being angry, then marched toward the rear entrance of the house. The sliding barn door had closed but bounced back open maybe a foot and a half or so.

Where the hell was that warrant?

Burnett was still on his phone. The Murray woman was angry. She had dirt caked on her heels. Something had happened... maybe in the barn.

Jess glanced at Burnett again, then at the back of the house as Mrs. Murray disappeared inside.

She wasn't waiting.

While Burnett was focused on his call, she rushed forward. No one on their team was going to shoot at her with POLICE emblazoned across the front and back of her vest. She cleared the tree line and slid to the ground next to the minivan.

"Harris! What the hell are you doing?" Patterson demanded.

Jess ignored his voice in her ear.

She wanted in that barn. Now.

"Jess."

She braced for Burnett's rant.

"Judge Schmale had a heart attack. Wells had to attend him until the paramedics arrived. She's en route to Judge Benford's residence. He has agreed to sign off on the warrant since Schmale is out of commission. Do *not* move until we have that warrant signed."

Jess leaned her head against the van. Damn it! She gave Burnett a nod. He would be watching her through the binoculars. Her position was not visible from the house if anyone were to look out the windows. She was safe.

She also understood that his hesitation was about her. Her fuckup in Virginia had him running scared.

If those girls were here, and Jess would bet her life they were, this bullshit waiting could cost their lives. Or, at the least, more pain and suffering. That was on her and she didn't like it.

She eased her binoculars into place and tightened the view on that narrow opening into the barn. It was as dark as hell in there. She swore under her breath.

"Mrs. Murray is coming back outside," Burnett warned.

Jess froze.

"Headed to the barn. Don't move, Jess."

She kept her attention on that door... waiting for it to open wider.

The woman's image filled her view. Jess held her breath. Waited for her to move out of the damned way.

Mrs. Murray continued into the barn. Jess scanned as far as the open door and the sunlight that poured in would allow. Shelves... tools.

Something big and green drew her attention back to the left... a tarp or something.

Damn it!

"There's something big under a tarp in there," she whispered. "Could be a car."

"Do not move, Jess," Burnett repeated.

Dr. Sullivan had been driving a white Taurus when she disappeared. Mr. Murray said she had shown up here. No one had seen her since. That could be her car hidden in there. When would these guys see that all these little coincidences added up to evidence? At least in Jess's mind.

She had to get in there.

Mrs. Murray stamped out of the barn and slid the door closed. The door's metal-on-metal squeak pierced the air.

With every step the woman took, something clinked.

What was she carrying?

The sun glinted against the object in her hands. A pile of something silver. Shiny links spilled out of her hold.

A chain?

"She's going back in the house," Burnett said, his voice whispering in Jess's earpiece.

Jess touched her mike. "Did you see what she was carrying?"

"I saw it."

"We can't keep waiting." Jess was going in that barn. "If the chain doesn't do it for you, I don't know what will."

Why the hell would a woman take a chain into her house? Unless to bind a hostage. She didn't look like the type to be into sexual bondage.

"Do not move, Jess, that's an order."

She studied the barn door. It would make that awful screeching noise when she opened it. The windows on the house were closed. Surely the sound wouldn't be heard beyond those closed windows and doors.

The shades were all drawn...the chances of her being seen were unlikely.

Lori would have the search warrant signed any minute now. So what if Jess was a few seconds ahead of her? It wasn't like last time when she'd gone out on her own, without authorization or backup period, much less en route.

The chain did it for her.

Keeping low, Jess crept to the front of the minivan. Burnett shouted in her earpiece, but he was easy to ignore with the goal of getting a closer look at what was under that green tarp on her mind.

Staying low, she eased from the front of the vehicle to the barn door. She leaned one shoulder against the board and batten wall and pushed the door with both hands. It slid a few inches, squealed in protest.

"Damn it, Jess!"

She hesitated, glanced at the back of the house. She was in plain sight of anyone who peeked out a window.

Fuck it. She shoved the door hard, moved inside, and slid the door closed, flinching at the squeal.

The interior of the barn was black and silent.

Jess reached for the flashlight on the utility belt at her waist. No one yelled a warning, so she assumed she hadn't been spotted by the Murrays. She clicked on the light and surveyed the space.

There were two vehicles covered with green tarps, one larger than the other... like a truck.

Pulse skittering, Jess eased in that direction. She tried to find the end of the trap to move it away from the first vehicle. She tripped. Bumped her head. She needed more light.

"Jess, what're you doing in there?"

"Hold on," she murmured. "I need more light."

Jess scanned the interior of the barn with her puny light. There was a switch near the door. With the flashlight's beam, she followed the exposed wiring from the switch to an overhead light fixture. She headed that way. Struggled to get a deeper breath. Her heart thundered with the burn of adrenaline.

Her left foot mired into the dirt floor. "Shit." She jerked her foot upward, her shoe almost coming off. Not mud. Dry, loose dirt. Shining the flashlight on her shoe, she shook the dirt free and tugged the sling-back strap over her heel. What the hell? The barn floor had been hard packed dirt until she reached this point. The image of the dirt on Mrs. Murray's heel flashed through her mind.

For six or seven feet from where she stood on firm ground to the back of the barn the dirt looked loose. She used the flashlight to study the loose ground. About four feet wide.

Grave?

The dirt shifted.

Jess stumbled back, almost dropped the flashlight.

She eased back to the door and felt for the switch, since taking her eyes off the loose dirt was out of the question.

"Jess?"

The overhead light chased away the darkness.

The dirt moved again. Shifted like a tiny earthquake had shaken that small section of the ground.

Jess eased closer. She dropped to her knees and reached down to touch the dirt. It moved. She jumped.

The blood roaring in her ears along with Burnett's demands, she dropped the flashlight and started to dig with both hands. Her fingers dragged through something long and stringy. *Hair.*

"Oh God." She scraped the dirt away from the lump she'd touched.

A face. Her insides went deathly quiet. Jess hurried to uncover more. Female. Blond hair.

Macy York.

Her eyes were closed and she wasn't moving. Jess ripped the duct tape off her mouth and leaned her cheek close to the girl's nose.

She was alive! Barely breathing but alive.

Trembling, Jess touched her mike. "I found Macy York. We need paramedics. By God, we have exigent circumstances." Screw the search warrant.

Jess pulled the girl from the dirt. Started digging again. This time the lump she encountered was moving. *Callie Fanning.*

Burnett announced, "Move in."

"Callie Fanning is here, too," Jess reported. "Both are alive." She studied the other forms emerging from where she had removed dirt. "We need at least four ambulances."

Jess pulled the tape from Callie's mouth and the girl started to sob. "Shhh." Jess glanced at the door. Then quickly ripped the tape from her hands. "Help me, Callie. You check on Macy while I keep digging."

As if the mention of the other girl's name flipped a switch, Callie stopped crying and turned to Macy.

Jess was digging again when the barn door slid open.

Burnett was suddenly on his knees next to her. "Oh my God."

With them both digging, they uncovered Dana and Reanne. At the bottom was Dr. Sullivan. Jess dragged her out of the hole.

"Sullivan's not breathing." Jess assumed a position for executing CPR.

"Where's Andrea?"

Jess hadn't realized until he spoke that all the girls except Andrea had been found and they had reached the bottom of the makeshift grave.

"She's in the house," Callie croaked, then coughed. "They're doing something to her. They're crazy."

Burnett rushed out of the barn.

Jess focused on Sullivan. "Come on, Maureen, breathe." She forced more air into the woman's lungs. Her skin felt warm. There was still a chance.

"Agent Harris!"

Chet. Thank God.

He got down in the dirt next to Jess. "Take care of the girls. I've got this." Chet assumed Sullivan's CPR. "Paramedics are en route."

Jess stood, her legs shaking, and went to the girls. They were alive. Dana and Reanne were coming around. All were sobbing.

Jess blinked back the tears and managed a smile. "It's okay, girls. You're safe now."

She prayed Andrea was still alive.

Sheriff Griggs and two of his deputies were already in the house when Dan burst through the back door. Mr. and Mrs. Murray were seated at the kitchen table having what appeared to be dinner.

"If I'd known we were having company," Mrs. Murray announced, "I would have baked a bigger cake."

A white cake sat in the middle of the table. Several slices were missing. A wedding cake topper leaned precariously from the top layer.

"Where is Andrea?" Dan demanded.

Mr. Murray started to push back his chair. "Don't move, sir," a deputy warned.

"Now, see here," Murray said, "you barge into my home and disrupt the supper my wife worked hard to prepare. What is it you want?"

"Where is the other girl?" Dan repeated. One side of the man's face was red and puffy as if someone had broadsided him with an oar.

"She can't be disturbed," Mrs. Murray said with far more cheer than a woman with no less than four armed men surrounding her should. "It's her wedding night."

A new kind of terror lashed through Dan. "Griggs, help me find her," he said as he headed deeper into the house. He heard the sheriff order his deputies to keep the Murrays seated.

Griggs and Dan spread out, searching each room.

Dan headed up the stairs first.

The absolute silence terrified him. In his ear he could

hear the coordinating going on between Jess and the others. Sullivan wasn't going to make it.

What the hell had happened here?

Four doors upstairs.

Griggs took the ones on the left, Dan the ones on the right.

The first room Dan entered was painted pink. *Andrea's favorite color.*

Nothing under the bed or in the closet. He hesitated, reached down to pick up a pair of discarded jeans and a blouse. Andrea's? His heart slammed against his sternum.

He moved on to the next room.

Dan listened at the closed door. No noise. Wait. He listened again. Heavy breathing...no...sobbing.

His weapon readied, he burst through the door and scanned the room down the barrel of his service revolver.

At first his brain refused to acknowledge what his eyes saw.

Andrea lay on the bed. A male on top of her.

Her scream yanked Dan from the haze of disbelief.

"Get off her!" Dan rushed to the bed. Shoved the muzzle to the bastard's temple. "Get off her," he roared.

The discoloration of the skin along the man's bare back...that he was not moving and hadn't even looked up sent a shock through Dan.

"Get him off me!" Andrea cried.

Griggs rushed in. He stalled next to Dan. "Sweet Jesus."

Dan holstered his weapon. "Help me, Roy."

Together they lifted the male corpse off Andrea. Dan quickly swept the sheet over Andrea's nude body and attempted to lift her into his arms. Chain rattled.

Andrea screamed, "Get me loose! Get me loose!"

"I'll get the bolt cutters." Griggs rushed from the room.

"You okay?" Dan searched her face, throat, and arms. He didn't see any blood or injuries.

She nodded, her face wet against his jaw. "Just get me out of here! Please!"

"Sheriff Griggs will be right back and we'll get you out of here."

"I wa...I want...my mom." Andrea buried her face in his vest and Dan felt the hot tears crawling down his cheeks. Andrea was alive. Thank God. She was alive.

Griggs rushed back into the room. He snapped the short length of chain close to Andrea's ankle.

Dan made sure the sheet covered her and adjusted his hold before taking her the hell out of here.

"Lord, have mercy," Griggs murmured. "What have these people done?" He dragged the bedspread from the foot of the bed and covered the boy's naked, partially decomposed body.

The wail of sirens announced the arrival of backup and emergency medical services. Dan carried Andrea downstairs and out the front door so she wouldn't have to see the Murrays.

Once he had her under the care of the first paramedics on the scene, he kissed her forehead and promised to be right back.

Dan led the other teams of paramedics to the barn.

Jess was huddled with the sobbing girls. Harper stayed with Dr. Sullivan. He motioned one of the paramedics over. Harper met Dan's gaze and shook his head. Dr. Sullivan was dead.

Harper had pulled aside the green tarps Jess had seen

before entering the barn. The white Taurus and blue truck sat side by side.

Dan moved toward the girls and Jess. He watched her softly reassuring them as the paramedics filtered into the group.

The girls had been buried alive. If Jess had waited for word the warrant was en route, would all those girls still be breathing?

Her instincts had found them and saved their lives.

How could anyone see her as anything other than the hero she was?

"Burnett?"

Griggs's voice crackled over the communications link. Dan touched his mike. "I'm in the barn."

"I think you're going to want to come to the basement."

Dear God. What else?

9:41 p.m.

Lori parked behind the truck and shut off the engine. It was almost dark now, but Jess wanted to do this in person. Tonight.

They emerged from the car. The light above the front door came on as they approached the steps.

The door opened and Mr. Debarros stepped out onto the top step and waited beneath the light.

"Mr. Debarros," Jess acknowledged as she stopped at the bottom of the steps. Lori waited next to her. "I'm sorry to bother you so late."

"You found her." His voice as he uttered the three simple words carried the weight of many long years of agony.

Jess nodded. "Yes, sir. We believe we have. There are tests we need to conduct before we can confirm that she is your daughter, but she was wearing this."

Lori handed him the delicate silver charm bracelet. In the original report when Christina had gone missing her father had reported that his daughter always wore the charm bracelet her grandmother had given her. Mr. Murray had admitted that the skeletal remains in the basement were Christina's. Still an official ID was necessary.

Debarros's hand shook as the bracelet slipped into his palm. He studied the tiny charms one by one and then nodded. "This is Christina's."

Andrea had told Dan about the remains of an infant, which the forensic techs had found right where she told them to look. Jess suspected this was the child Christina had been carrying when she went missing. But she would not pass along this information until she was certain. She also would never tell this poor man that the day he confronted Raymond and Tate Murray at their farm, his dear Christina had been alive and probably only a few yards from him in that dark, dank basement. There were some things he did not need to know. Whatever conclusions he came to later were his to make.

"As soon as dental records have confirmed her identity, we can release her to you so that your family can make the final arrangements. I am truly sorry for your loss, Mr. Debarros."

Jess started to turn away, but there was more she needed to say. "Mr. Debarros, I wish there had been more we could have done sooner." If that baby was Christina's then she had been alive for months after her abduction. Dear God, the idea was unthinkable. "You have my word that the people who did this will be prosecuted to the fullest extent the law allows."

The Murrays had a lot to answer for. Kidnapping and attempted murder. At least three deaths. Like Christina's, the infant's cause of death was not readily apparent. Whether by their hands or not, the Murrays were responsible in that they had abducted the girl and most assuredly abused and neglected her and, possibly, the infant. Dr. Sullivan's death was murder, cut and dried. Then there was the issue of abusing a corpse.

Jess shuddered inside when she considered what they had done to their son. Unable to accept his death, they had exhumed his body and brought him home, and each passing day had accelerated their obsession and incited more and more unstable and erratic actions. The efforts they had gone to in an attempt to keep his body preserved were incredible. Any decent defense attorney would go for an insanity plea. Jess suspected that argument would be won.

Mr. Debarros said nothing. He stared at the piece of jewelry that provided a bittersweet sense of relief.

She and Lori started back to the car. They had done all they could for now.

"Agent Harris."

Jess paused and turned back to him.

"Thank you." He nodded to Lori. "Both of you."

Jess nodded. She couldn't have spoken had her life depended upon it.

Back in the Mustang, Lori started the engine and backed out onto the road. "We should head to the hospital so we don't miss the reunions."

Chet was back at the Murray farm overseeing the evidence collection. The Murrays were in custody. Burnett, Griggs, and Patterson were at the hospital overseeing the collection of statements from the victims as well as the reunions with their families.

"I'm sure the guys have it under control."

"No doubt," Lori agreed. "Reporters are already all over the place." She shrugged. "I was thinking this would be a good time to show your face. We might not have found those girls in time if not for you."

Jess appreciated the sentiment. "Speaking of time. You took your sweet time getting that warrant signed," she teased. "We all were on the verge of strokes waiting."

"He had the pen in his hand when the cardiac episode occurred," Lori explained. "It was a rough go for a minute or two. Don't think that after I called 9-1-1 I didn't consider signing his name myself just in case he didn't make it and I couldn't get anyone else. I had two choices. CPR or search his desk for a signature to copy."

Jess laughed. Lori was definitely a kindred soul. "You did the right thing. Particularly since he's going to recover. I'm not sure you could have convinced him that he'd signed the warrant and didn't remember." Jess was glad this was over. "I think I'll skip the reunions and the press. Just drop me off at my car. I need a long bath and a deep glass of wine."

"I don't think so," Lori said with a shake of her head. "The last orders I got from the chief included not letting you out of my sight."

Spears. "I would argue with you, but I'm too damned tired."

"Off to the circus, then," Lori suggested.

Jess twirled her hand in the air. "Whoopee!"

It was over. The case was solved. The girls were safe.

The end.

Jess figured it was the end for her, too. Not a problem. She had her next move all planned out.

Funny thing was, running away no longer held any appeal.

Monday, July 19, 9:10 a.m.

The bag Jess had hastily packed before coming here had once again been hastily packed and was loaded into the Audi. Thirty-six hours with her sister had fulfilled Jess's family obligations for the remainder of the century.

It had also given her some distance from Burnett and the case and the crap with the bureau. She had shut off her cell phone and turned it back on only this morning. Thankfully she had no more text messages from Spears.

Jess had to go. Uncertainty plagued her all over again. She didn't have a choice. She hoped if Spears had indeed been watching her, he would follow her when she left. Then Lily and her family would be safe.

Dan would be safe.

Jess inhaled deeply, pushing aside the emotions warring inside her. She knew what she had to do.

Speaking of Burnett, he had left her a voice mail asking

her to be at his office at nine this morning for a post-mortem.

And he wasn't here.

She blew out another big breath of impatience.

A long drive lay ahead of her and the daunting task of clearing out her office. Packing up her house and putting it on the market. Since she was about to be officially unemployed, there would be no paying that enormous mortgage payment with unemployment benefits. Her savings wouldn't last more than a few months.

Her sister had begged her to stay at least until Jess decided her next step. Lily had even gone as far as having her friend and real estate agent show up for dinner last night with property listings for Jess to peruse. Lily was a wonderful sister, the perfect wife and mother. Her son was in his senior year at UA. Her daughter would be going there herself this fall. Jess suspected her sister was feeling empty-nest syndrome descending. Jess couldn't deny feeling an emptiness coming herself.

Mainly, she just didn't know where she went from here.

As much as she loved her sister, Jess could take her perfect, careful world only in small doses.

And drawing Spears away from Birmingham had to be her top priority.

She checked the time on her cell. 9:15. Where the hell was Burnett?

The door opened and in breezed the handsome but tardy chief. Jess mentally rolled her eyes at her own foolishness. The handsome part was irrelevant and formed in her head far too effortlessly.

"Jess, I'm sorry."

Sheriff Griggs marched in right behind him.

"Morning, Agent Harris," the Jefferson County sheriff offered.

"Morning, gentlemen." She presented a perfunctory smile.

What was this about? She had said her good-byes to Lori and Chet Saturday night. This morning she had expected a similar hit and run with Burnett. A quick review of the final details of the case. A good-bye handshake—okay, maybe she had hoped for something more than a handshake—and then she would be on her way. She had dressed in the ivory dress that was her favorite. Whenever she wore it she always got lots of compliments. And the matching ivory stilettoes were sexy. At least they made her feel that way. A woman needed her armor when facing such an uncertain future.

She ordered the trivial thoughts from her head and focused on the here and now. Maybe Griggs had opted in for the postmortem. Burnett stood behind his desk. The sheriff had settled in the chair next to her. Then again, maybe she needed more than armor. The mood in the room carried the distinct feel of a setup.

"Has there been a new development with the case?"

"Nothing you don't already know." Burnett took his seat. "The sheriff and I spent most of the afternoon yesterday discussing certain other issues we have in common. But first things first."

She braced for unpleasantness. Burnett hadn't even bothered with good morning. Besides, she wasn't sure what their discussions had to do with her unless the two felt she was the issue. That would certainly put the icing on the farewell cake.

"Your conclusions about the Murrays were spot-on," Griggs commented, drawing her attention to him. "The denial about their son's death, all of it."

Jess nodded. She would never say as much out loud but after the debacle with Spears, she had, on some level, doubted herself several times over the past few days. It felt good to know she could still get the job done. With some outstanding help, admittedly.

"Did either of them reveal how they chose the girls?" Jess had drawn her own conclusions, but the Murrays were unique, as all humans were, and they would have their own individual methods for acting on the motives driving their obsession.

"Mrs. Murray skimmed the papers for academic accomplishments." Burnett's expression turned grim. "She made preliminary choices, then moved in closer to watch the girls. Once she had ruled out those she perceived as unfit, she found a way to get close to each of her approved candidates."

Jess understood that reality was difficult for him, considering Andrea had been one of her choices. Though all the girls had come away from this nightmare basically unharmed physically, months, maybe years, of counseling were in order.

"The exception, of course," Griggs chimed in, "was Reanne. Mrs. Murray saw her for the first time at a church revival shortly after Tate's death. She never forgot how spiritual Reanne and her family appeared. That appealed to the woman somehow."

"And Dana," Jess pointed out. "She was chosen for different reasons than the others and approached differently as well."

"That's right," Burnett said with a shake of his head. "Mrs. Murray wanted her to suffer."

"But Dana took a step the Murrays didn't expect. She reached out to Dr. Sullivan." Jess hoped the girl understood how smart she had been to reach out to someone.

"Her actions provided a major break for our investigation," Griggs allowed. "We might still be wondering what the hell was going on."

Jess couldn't argue with his assessment. The Murrays had certainly covered their tracks. Still, no matter how well thought out the plan, there was always a deviation. A mistake or an oversight. There were no flawless crimes.

Spears attempted to intrude. She pushed him aside. His crimes were not flawless...she just hadn't found the imperfection yet.

That was someone else's job now.

"Mr. Murray has been quite forthcoming," Burnett said, drawing her from the troubling thoughts. "His wife, on the other hand, is a little too far over the edge to provide reliable details."

"Any word on the Debarros girl and the infant's remains?" Jess wished closure for that family. They had waited a long time. Too long.

"Officially no." Burnett's regret was palpable. "But Mr. Murray admitted that his wife had brought the girl home. He wanted to protect his wife and son, so they kept her in the basement until the baby was born. The girl died in childbirth and the baby died soon after. They never called a doctor, just let nature take its course."

The thought of how that little girl must have suffered emotionally and physically made Jess sick. "I suppose that made Christina even more of a loser than being the daughter of an illegal immigrant did." The Murray woman was one twisted lady. "Totally unfit for her son."

Griggs shook his head. "This is definitely a case for the textbooks. The Murrays were just everyday people without so much as a parking violation on their records. They weren't killers, yet three lives were lost."

Jess didn't bother reminding him that no one was exempt from the potential for evil. The Murrays had been good people but fear and tragedy had set their lives on a different course.

She wondered how much of the situation Dr. Sullivan had suspected when she dared to go to that farm looking for Dana. Whatever she knew or didn't know, looking for Dana rather than sharing her knowledge with the police had cost her her life.

"The Debarros case is a perfect example of what Sheriff Griggs and I discussed yesterday."

Jess shifted her attention back to Burnett.

"We're not happy with how a situation can so easily slip through the cracks for any number of reasons. Lack of manpower, language barrier, or, like the one we just solved, no clear-cut legal approach."

"We both have our various divisions," Griggs continued from there. "The usual suspects."

"Patrol, Support, Detectives," Burnett noted.

"Homeland Security, Criminal, Internal Affairs." Griggs made a rolling motion with his right hand. "On and on."

Jess nodded for lack of anything to say. These two were up to something.

"We need a new unit," Burnett announced. "One with a jurisdiction encompassing the entire county and whose resources are funded equally by the city and the county. We've run the proposal past the powers that be. That's why I was late this morning. We have an approval to reallocate the first year's funds."

"Have you outlined a mission statement for this unit?" Jess was glad to hear about their plan. Victims like Christina Debarros should never fall through the cracks. But, honestly, Jess didn't see what this had to do with her.

"We're hammering that out now," Griggs answered. "The unit will be classified as a Special Problems Unit. Numerous departments across the country have developed units like this and have seen a measurable drop in violent crimes. That's our goal. But we're expanding on the tried-and-true concept." He emphasized the last with his hands. "We're making it more like a special crimes or major crimes unit that encompasses the tactics of SPU. To have a unit devoted to the crimes that just don't fall into one of the usual categories. Devoted to the criminals who don't fit the usual profile."

"This would be a deputy chief's position," Burnett told her. "The pay and benefits are in line with that of a federal agent with eighteen to twenty years on the job."

Wait a minute. "What are you two up to?" Jess looked from Burnett to Griggs and back.

Griggs stood. "I'll leave you two to iron out the details." He thrust his hand at Jess. She accepted the enthusiastic shake. "Congratulations, Deputy Chief Harris. Glad to have you on board."

Before Jess could say what, thanks, or *shut up*, he nodded to Burnett and promptly exited the office.

The shaking started deep inside. Jess tried to stop it.

They were offering her a job. Since she didn't have one, she was flattered. But...

"Before you say no, Jess..." Burnett got up, came around to sit beside her. "Think about it for a day or two. We need you here."

No, no. She would not cry. She battled back the burn of tears. "I sincerely appreciate the offer. But I don't know if I can do that. Coming back here is..." She shook her head, didn't know how to explain. The Spears situation...

He leaned forward, braced his forearms on his thighs. "I'll make a deal with you. You stay here for six or so months and get this started for us and I'll make sure you have all the space you need. The past won't get in the way. You have my word."

Could she do this? Was she out of her mind? But how could she say no?

Definitely out of her mind.

"I need time to settle my affairs in Virginia."

"Take"—Burnett shrugged—"a whole week."

"A week?" Now who was out of their mind? "I need two."

"Two then."

"I'll need to find housing."

His gaze narrowed. "Speaking of houses, my parents got back from Vegas yesterday afternoon. My mother was up all night putting things back where they belonged. She's threatening to fire her housekeeper."

Oops. "Your mother is too good to clean her own house?" Jess didn't know why she was surprised. "What does she do all day?" He started to answer and she held up her hands. "Never mind. I don't want to know."

He grinned. "Don't worry, I smoothed it over."

Jess felt no remorse. The thought of Katherine in such a tizzy gave her a great deal of satisfaction. "Before I agree to this trial run, what kind of staff will I have?"

"Besides the necessary admin, we'll start with a couple of detectives, a forensics tech. Maybe a couple of uniforms."

"Sounds doable." She took a deep breath. "I have two conditions before I even consider your offer. One is that I get Lori and Chet. And that officer who helped out with Sullivan. Cook, I think his name is."

"I don't know about that, Jess. Wells and Harper are two of my best."

"You don't want this new prototype unit to have the best?"

"Okay. Fine."

For a guy who hated that word he sure used it a lot.

"What's your second condition?"

"That I have the full authority to conduct my investigations *my* way."

"As long as you don't break the law."

"I can't promise you I won't bend it from time to time."

"Deal. Anything else?"

Reality deflated the excitement she had allowed to build. "We can't anticipate what Spears will do."

"The bureau has assured me they will stay on top of that situation. *We* will stay on top of that situation. You have my word."

She could see that Lily and her family stayed safe if she was here... but if she left maybe their safety wouldn't be an issue.

Burnett held out his hand for a shake. "Welcome aboard, Deputy Chief Harris."

"Not so fast, Burnett," she cautioned. "I need a day or two to think about this." Jess understood that if she accepted this offer she would be taking a giant leap backward.

But *sometimes* a woman had to step back and take stock of her life before moving forward.

She placed her hand in his and gave it a shake. "I'll give you an answer tomorrow."

He held on to her hand. "I think we had a conversation to finish." He leaned in.

Jess held her breath. Told herself that this was not a smart idea. Especially if they were going to be working together.

His lips brushed hers, and her resolve melted. What the hell? She had twenty-four hours before she had to say yes. She leaned into his kiss.

A rap on the door drew them apart.

Jess touched her lips to quell the fire. Regretted her impulsiveness. If she were seriously going to accept this position, he couldn't be her boss and her lover. Not even for just today, before the boss part was official.

"Don't," he warned, as if he'd read her mind, "do that. We will take this part one day at a time."

His receptionist entered the room. "Chief, I'm sorry to intrude but this package was delivered for Agent Harris. It's labeled urgent."

"Thanks, Tara."

Jess sat at attention. Who would send a package to her? Gant? She couldn't think why. "Let me see that."

Burnett reviewed the information on the front. He shook his head. "It's a special courier delivery, Jess."

"Local?"

"Definitely."

"It got through security, so it isn't likely a bomb." Even as she said the words an icy cold replaced the heat he had stirred. Bombs weren't part of Spears's MO, she reminded herself.

Except that he thrived on eliciting fear and having the entire building in jeopardy would do exactly that.

"We're not taking any chances."

Eight minutes were required for the bomb squad to arrive, during which time the building was evacuated. Seven more to determine that the package contained no explosive devices. Two members of the squad opened the eight-by-eight-by-six-inch box on the small conference table in the chief's office.

Once the all clear was given, Jess and Burnett simultaneously approached the table and leaned forward to see inside the small package. Resting amid a mass of crumpled off-white padding paper was an envelope with her name scrawled across the front.

The evidence tech reached in with gloved hands and lifted the envelope from the box. A white card inside included three words that stabbed right into Jess's heart and twisted.

Congratulations. Let's play.

Stone-cold fear filled her lungs. This was the way he began. "What else is in there?"

There would be more... a clue to the first victim.

The tech slowly picked through the packing paper. His gaze collided with Jess's.

He had something.

With deft fingers he unfolded the paper and revealed a gold detective's badge.

"Jesus Christ," Burnett breathed the words. He yanked out his cell. "That's Wells's shield."

Jess stared at the gold shield. *I like your friend.*

Lori.

Oh, God. All sensation bled out of Jess's body. Spears hadn't been talking about Dan...he'd meant Lori.

Wait.

This couldn't be happening. It was too soon...Jess firmly believed Spears had been killing for years, his cycles annual. If he was escalating, what else about his MO would change?

There was no way to anticipate what those changes would be. And why send the message to Jess? He usually sent his little gifts to the victims' closest family member. Lori had a mother and a sister.

But he'd figured out that Jess felt a connection to Lori.

That cold hard realty slid over Jess. And this was, after all, about her.

"Harper, find Wells. She's not answering her cell." Burnett listened for an endless moment.

Defeat sagged Jess's shoulders. It would be too late. Lori wouldn't be at work or at home or at a friend's.

She would be with *him.*

"I'm on my way," Burnett said before putting his phone away. He turned to Jess. "Harper says he's been trying to reach her all morning." Burnett scrubbed a hand over his face. "He just got to her apartment. The door was ajar. There are signs of a struggle inside. Wells is gone."

Jess stared at him, unable to speak. She had brought this evil here...to the first person in a long time she had thought would make a good friend.

"What can we expect, Jess? What's his next move?"

The fear and worry haunting Burnett's eyes had once haunted hers, but Jess had learned not to expend energy on those emotions where Spears was concerned. He tortured and killed, no deviation, no exceptions.

She moistened her lips. "He'll torture her for however long he finds it amusing. Could be hours, could be days. Then he'll kill her and leave her for us to find."

"Sick son of a bitch." Burnett's face paled.

"The bureau has been trying to catch the Player for years. If he doesn't want to be found, he won't be. And once he's begun, until he has tortured, raped, and murdered five or six women, he won't stop."

"There's no variation?" Burnett asked, "No hope that she might survive?"

"He has never varied before." Jess looked deep into Burnett's eyes and gave him the one hope they might have. "But this time is different. He has jumped back into the game more quickly. For some reason his cycle has escalated. There may be other changes. And I think I know why."

She took a breath, steeled herself. "He's found something more titillating than the usual routine. His curiosity has incited that twisted need of his. He loves this new rush and he wants more."

Realization dawned and Burnett shook his head. "That is not going to happen."

"It's probably the only chance we've got of getting her back alive and even that's not a given."

No other cop had gotten close to Spears. Once she had uncovered his identity, which she still could not prove, she had let him draw closer. He was intrigued, curious, and obviously excited. If she could keep him excited about the chase, he wouldn't be as likely to turn to torturing Lori for his pleasure.

Burnett started for the door. "I'll call our bureau liaison en route."

Jess followed. She felt numb.

Daniel Burnett had no idea just how ugly this would get.

The sole advantage they had right this minute was Spears's most recently revealed desire. He wanted to play with Jess.

If there was any hope of saving Lori and the victims that would follow, Jess had to lure him closer. She had to play.

As Burnett issued orders via his cell, Jess withdrew her own. She pulled up the Tormenter contact info and tapped a few keys. She wasn't sure it would work. He could very well have tossed that phone days ago. Nonetheless, she hit send and prayed her words would reach the bastard.

I'm ready to play.

Before she and Burnett were out of the building, her cell vibrated. She checked the screen.

Your friend will be glad.

Fury swept through Jess, obliterating the fear. She quelled the trembling in her hands and entered the words she wanted this son of a bitch to read and understand.

I'm coming for you.

Whatever she had to do. She would get him this time. The vibration against her palm tightened her fingers around her phone as she lifted the screen once more.

I'm counting on it.

Jess tucked her cell phone into her bag and climbed into Burnett's SUV. She closed out all emotions that would encumber logical thought. Lori's life depended on what she did next.

Jess fastened her seat belt and stared forward.

This time when she had the son of a bitch face-to-face, there would be no worries about evidentiary or criminal procedure.

This time he was dead.

Agent Jess Harris's nightmare continues in this terrifying novel in the Faces of Evil series.

Please turn this page for a preview of

Impulse

Monday, July 19, 10:31 a.m.

Did you know that one drop of blood travels from the heart to the toes and back in under sixty seconds?"

Lori Wells tightened her fingers into fists, tugged futilely against the tape binding her to the chair, and forced herself to meet the son of a bitch's eyes. "Did *you* know all that blood rushing through my veins at this very moment is teeming with the urge to watch you die?"

Eric Spears smiled and made a breathy sound that wasn't quite a laugh. "You are such a brave girl, Detective Wells. I wonder if that's because your father committed suicide when you were so young." He inclined his head and stared at her as though memorizing each detail of her face like a lover intent on never forgetting the moment. "Did you have to help your mother clean up the blood afterward? Or did your neighbors jump in to help out? *Y'all do that down here in the South, don't y'all?*"

Lori turned away from him. *Bastard.* How could he

know so much about her? He hadn't known her name five days ago.

A long-suffering sigh hissed past his lips. "You're quite boring, Detective." He stood. "What should I do about that?"

Renewed fear trickled inside her. Lori snapped her head up and stared into those piercing blue eyes. *No.* She would not give him the pleasure. She hardened her expression, refused to let him see the fissure of terror widening inside her.

"What's wrong, *Eric*? Can't get it up if I'm not crying like a scared little girl?" *Don't let him gain control.*

Fury tightened his lips. He drew back his hand.

She braced for the blow.

He laughed at her instinctive reflex. Dropped his hand to his side. "See, you are a scared little girl. Frankly, I find all that feigned bravado quite tedious."

"Life sucks like that sometimes."

He made a sound of agreement. "It does indeed." For five or six seconds he deliberated as if undecided how he would proceed. "You know the reason you're here. Why make our time together more unpleasant than necessary? It'll be much easier for both of us if you cooperate, Lori *Doodle*."

How dare he call her that! Her father had given her that nickname...this scumbag had no right. She didn't need him or a GPS to show her where this was headed. "Go to hell."

She wasn't making this easy for him. He would kill her anyway.

Spears turned his back and strode across the room.

Lori quickly scanned the space now that the lights

were on, searching for any aspect of her surroundings that might provide some hint as to where the hell she was.

The sedative he'd injected when he'd held her at gunpoint and forced her into his SUV had prevented her from assessing the distance or the traffic sounds as he'd driven her here. She still felt a little groggy. Her mouth was dry. She squared her shoulders, focused on clearing her head. She had to pay attention, to be ready for whatever came next. *Let your training and instincts guide you.*

Focus, Lori.

A warehouse, she decided. An old one for sure. Smelled of neglect and vaguely of oil or grease. Brick walls soared some twenty or so feet to a ceiling where steel beams supported the roof. Naked fluorescent tubes glowed from metal fixtures suspended five or six feet overhead. The smell of disuse permeated the air. She tried to get a better look behind her. Couldn't. Wooden crates lined the wall to her right, suggesting the warehouse had been used recently in some capacity. She squinted to read the word stamped on some of the crates... GRIMES. She'd lived here all her life but that name didn't ring a bell.

Birmingham had its share of neglected and abandoned buildings...she'd been in a few but not this one. From her position in the middle of the large open room, she could see a door. Maybe an exit. Maybe just an office or bathroom.

One shot at that door was all she needed... if it wasn't a dead end.

Images of what this monster had done to his other victims, all women, rolled like an old-fashioned filmstrip through her mind. Defeat chiseled away at her courage.

Spears grabbed the one remaining chair in the place

and dragged it over to where she sat bound—wrists, ankles, and waist—with duct tape to a similar heavy metal chair. He scooted his chair close and straddled the seat, his spread knees flanking hers. She squeezed her legs more tightly together; she didn't want any part of him touching her. She didn't even want to draw his scent into her lungs.

Like his subtle aftershave, his wardrobe conveyed an understated elegance. The navy suit jacket hadn't come from a rack in any store where men she knew shopped. The white shirt was crisp and pristine, as if he'd just picked it up from the cleaners. The jeans fit as if they had been designed by his personal tailor. The perfect packaging for his classically attractive blond-haired, blue-eyed features.

If you want to know what evil looks like, look in the mirror.

Jess Harris had definitely gotten that right. Eric Spears, aka the Player, appeared nothing like the depraved killer Lori knew him to be. Why did he bother abducting women when he could easily charm them into his lair with that killer smile and deep, smooth voice?

The hunt. Somehow it fueled him... drove his heinous desires.

Lori wished she knew half what Jess did about him. Maybe then she could do more than be a damned victim.

Even before she'd met Jess, Lori remembered vividly hearing in the news that not a single one of the Player's victims had ever escaped alive.

Her chest ached. She didn't want to die. Her sister needed her. Her mother needed her. She took solace in the knowledge that at least they were safe. As soon as Chief

Burnett and Jess discovered Lori was missing, they would take steps to protect her family.

And Chet Harper. Lori thought of the detective, the man, who wanted so much more from her than she had given. Would she have continued to push him away if she had known this day was coming?

Spears chucked her under the chin, forcing her attention back to him. "Let's get one thing straight, Detective. However much you test me, this isn't about you," he explained in that calm, clever tone that belied his every action.

"All your hard work to reach the esteemed rank of detective earlier than most means nothing to me." He tugged at a lock of her hair, twirled it between his fingers. "That you are most attractive means nothing to me."

Lori waited, her heart thudding with apprehension, for him to spell out exactly what he wanted from her besides her life.

"I brought you here so Jess will pay attention," he whispered, leaning forward so that he lingered nose to nose with her. "You think I have her attention?"

Fear buffeting ever harder against her defenses, Lori steadied herself. She would not let him use her to get to Jess. No way.

I might be a victim, but I will not be his means of reaching Jess.

"She told me all about you." Lori forced a smile, inclined her head, and studied his face the way he had studied hers. "What happened? Did mommy fail to protect you when daddy decided he preferred you to her? Is that why you hate women so much?"

His hand went to her throat; strong fingers closed tightly, cutting off her airway. "Do not toy with me,

Detective. There are things you will never know, so don't waste your time and energy trying to analyze me. You'll fail just like all the rest."

There was nothing amiable about his tone now. The fear she fought to restrain dug its claws in deep even as he released her. She gasped for breath. Her thoughts raced in frantic circles. The things Jess had told her kept colliding with her own instincts.

Should she play his game or resist? What he did to her in the end wouldn't change either way, but could she slow him down or trip him up by choosing one avenue over the other?

"Do you think I have her attention?" he repeated.

"Yes." Lori cleared her throat, wishing she had a drink of water. "I'm certain you have her attention."

"That's better," he said softly. "Now, tell me about this Chief Daniel Burnett."

She filled her lungs with a jagged breath, refusing to let the fear maintain a stronghold. "What about him?"

"What's his interest in Agent Harris?"

Lori cleared her mind. *Careful what you say.* Don't give him any ammunition. "She's a top-notch profiler and investigator. We needed her help on a case. Because of you she's probably unemployed." Anger at what he had done to Jess chased away some of the fear. He had ruined Jess's career with the FBI.

"One does what one must. She created quite the commotion up in Richmond when she so kindly screwed up any chances of a conviction against me." He lifted his shoulders in a shrug that communicated more arrogance than indifference. "Diverting attention was essential. Now the world is focused on her inept methods rather than the precise work of a master artist." A smug chuckle rumbled from his throat. "Ironic, isn't it?"

"You think? Well, I have a newsflash for you, asshole." Mad as hell now, Lori looked straight into his eyes. His turned wary and she loved that single moment of triumph. "Jess Harris is way too smart, way too sharp, and far too in demand for a generic piece of shit like you to keep her down. If the bureau cuts her loose, Chief Burnett will offer her a top position here, just you wait and see."

That was pure conjecture, but Lori suspected there was no way the chief would let Jess get away again for reasons completely unrelated to her investigative skills. Whatever Spears did to her, Lori could not let him learn that she sensed the chief still had personal feelings for Jess. That could make him a target, too.

"That's right, *Eric*," she continued, capitalizing on his obvious need to analyze the idea of failure. "You can't stop her and if you think the bureau will stop trying to nail you just because you pulled a bait and switch, I'm afraid you're going to be incredibly disappointed. They will get you—with or without Jess on their team."

His gaze narrowed as if he worried she might be right, and then he laughed, the deep, guttural sound echoing all around her. "You're quite good, Detective." He leaned close again as if he intended to share a secret. "Here's something hot off the wire just for you. That game is over. They will *never* achieve their goal." He reached out, traced her cheek with his forefinger. She shuddered. "This is a new game and I need Jess to play."

"You *need* her?" she bit out in disgust.

He shrugged. "Want her then. Let's not quibble over semantics. Will you help me, Lori Doodle?"

"Do I have a choice?" The answer to that was a big, flashing neon sign in her brain. Whatever she did or didn't do he would somehow find a way to use it. Tears burned her eyes. She blinked them back. She would not cry for this scumbag's pleasure.

"You always have a choice, Detective." His lips lifted again in that charismatic expression that masked the house of horrors beneath. "You have one now. Live daringly or die quickly. You choose."

She laughed around the fear crowded in her throat. "Do you really expect me to believe that if I cooperate you'll let me live? Wow, Santa's here already and it's only July. Give me a break."

"Oh, I will. You have my word," he promised. "For a bit anyway."

That was what she thought.

"Consider your options carefully, Detective Lori Wells." He put his face in hers again. "The longer you stay alive, the more opportunity you'll have to perhaps see that urge of yours to fruition. Who knows?" He straightened and drew back to look her in the eyes. "You might just get that chance to watch me die. After all, no one lives forever."

He stood and hauled his chair away from hers. "While you weigh your options, I'm going to find someone to keep you company." He laughed. "Actually, I think I'm the one who needs company. You are b-o-r-i-n-g with a capital B."

Lori's heart rammed into her throat.

She had to do something...otherwise he was going hunting...

"Wait!"

He stopped.

"I can't... don't leave me here by myself. *Please*."

He turned around slowly. A grin spread across his lips. "Ah... so you're ready to play, are you?"

His singular motive is pleasure. Jess's voice whispered in her ears. *The only way he can feel it is by torturing his victims in the most depraved ways.*

"Yes." Lori moistened her lips, wrestled back the fear. "I'm ready to play."

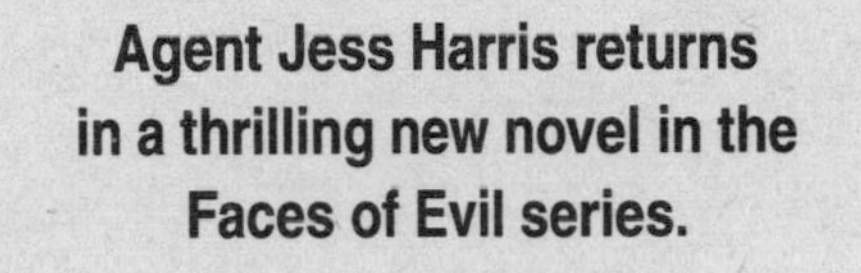

Please turn this page
for a preview of

Power

Cotton Avenue, Birmingham, Alabama
Monday, July 26, 2:45 p.m.

I need an estimate on time of death as soon as possible."

The young doctor whom Jess suspected was new to the Jefferson County Coroner's Office shot her a look from his kneeling position next to the victim. "Chief Harris, I just got here. There's an order to the steps I'm required to take."

Definitely new. Once he'd played his part at enough crime scenes he would understand that there was nothing orderly about murder.

Jess rearranged her lips into a smile that was as far from patient as the harried expression on the inexperienced ME's face. "I'm well aware of those steps, Doctor, but—" She glanced down the long center hall to ensure that Sergeant Harper was successfully keeping the potential witnesses away from the French doors and windows that opened to the mansion from the palatial gardens. "I have six little girls out back who are in various stages of hysteria and their mothers are chomping at the bit to take them home. I need time of death so I can question them with a reasonable grasp of the timeline we're dealing with here."

Before their mothers got any antsier and decided to lawyer up, Jess kept to herself.

The fact was she had heard enough rumors about the typical dance mom mentality to understand that once the shock of this tragedy wore off things would change. Not only would lawyers be called in but the ladies would close ranks to protect whatever secrets they felt compelled to keep, particularly if those secrets carried any ramifications whatsoever for their daughters' placement on the studio food chain.

Technically, Jess was supposed to ask if they wanted to have their attorneys present during questioning, but mere technicalities had never hampered her before. She might have failed to ask whether anyone wanted an attorney when she first arrived. With the level of panic among the girls, who would be surprised?

Doctor What's-his-name shifted his attention back to the victim sprawled in an unnatural manner on the unforgiving marble floor. "Like I said, there are steps. I'll get to that one momentarily."

Jess pressed her lips together to prevent saying something she would regret. What was it about this younger generation that prompted such flagrant disrespect? She hitched her bag higher on her shoulder. When she was his age, definitely north of thirty-five, she would never have sassed her elders. The notion that she was nearly a decade older than the ME was considerably depressing, but it was a reality she'd learned to deal with since whizzing past the dreaded milestone.

Whoever said that forty was the new thirty was so very full of crap.

Well, she pushed her glasses up on the bridge of her nose. There wasn't a thing she could do about getting older. The disrespect, however, she refused to stand for. Just because the still-wet-behind-the-ears ME was cute didn't mean she intended to ignore his attitude. "Excuse me..." He gazed up at her with egregious reluctance. She lifted her eyebrows in question. "Doctor...?"

"Schrader. Dr. Harlan Schrader."

"Well, Dr. Schrader, I understand you have steps, but if you would kindly just get your little thermometer out of your nifty bag and give me an approximate time of death I promise I'll be out of your way." She propped her lips into a smile she hoped wasn't too blatantly forged and added the perfunctory magic word. "Please."

"Okay." He held up his gloved hands in a show of dramatic surrender. "I'll do that right now."

"Thank you, Dr. Schrader."

Jess stepped to the door and surveyed the activity beyond the official vehicles cluttering the cobblestoned drive that encircled the massive fountain in front of the house. The historic mansion sat in the middle of six elegant and rare acres. With any luck the towering trees with their low-slung branches prevented street traffic from identifying the official vehicles ominously gathered. At the street, BPD uniforms blocked the entrance to the property in an effort to keep the curious and the newshounds at bay once word hit the airwaves. Having the press show up in droves, and in this posh neighborhood they definitely would, complicated any investigation. Frankly, she was surprised the impressive residence didn't come with its own private security team. Oddly, there was no security and no housekeeping staff—at least not today.

The crime scene techs had already documented the scene with photographs and video. Prints and trace materials were being collected now in hopes of discovering some sort of usable evidence. Sergeant Harper had gotten the call from the BPD's finest at 1:48 p.m. He and Lieutenant Prescott had rushed over without mentioning that as of today they were no longer assigned to Crimes Against Persons. Suited Jess just fine. Sitting on her laurels until a case was assigned to her new SPU—Special Problems Unit—wasn't how she'd wanted to start off her first week in the department.

Then again, foul play had not yet been established in this case. Jess considered the position of the body in the foyer next to the grand staircase. It appeared the victim, Darcy Chandler, had fallen over the upstairs railing to her death. Or she'd jumped. Either way, her death was, to their knowledge thus far, unaccompanied and obviously of a violent nature. An investigation was standard protocol.

When she first arrived Jess had followed the techs up the stairs and checked the landing. Her attention wandered there now. The hardwood floor was clear of debris and substances that might have posed a trip hazard or made it slippery. The railing didn't meet the height criteria for current building codes, but with historic homes, and this one dated back to the mid-1800s, features such as the railing were grandfathered in. A good thing for those who appreciated history, not so good for Ms. Chandler.

The only odd aspect of the scene Jess had noted so far

was the fact that Ms. Chandler's very expensive fuchsia-colored Gucci pumps, which exactly matched the elegant sheath she wore, sat next to the railing on the second floor. The careful placement gave the appearance that she had removed the shoes and positioned them just so, as if she feared scarring her favorite pair of designer shoes while taking her fatal dive. Judging by the meticulous organization of her closets as well as the pristine condition of the house in general, the victim was unquestionably a perfectionist to some degree. That could very well explain the decision to remove and set aside her shoes. Maybe. But in Jess's opinion the shoes merited a closer look.

"I would estimate time of death," Dr. Schrader announced, drawing Jess's attention back to him as he checked his wristwatch, "at between twelve noon and one."

Less than two hours before the arrival of the BPD. "Thank you, Dr. Schrader."

The glance he cast her way advised that her gratitude was not appreciated any more than her pushy approach had been. She'd have to find a way to get back in his good graces another time. Maybe a gift certificate from one of the trendy shops in the Galleria would do the trick since the polo, sports jacket, and stonewashed jeans he wore could have been stripped right off the mannequins adorning the storefronts of said shops.

Right now, however, a woman was dead and that was Jess's top priority. She could make nice with Dr. I'm-Too-Sexy-for-Manners later.

Armed with the vital piece of information she needed, she headed for the French doors at the end of the long hall that cut through the center of one of Birmingham's oldest and grandest homes. She squared her shoulders, cleared her throat, and exited to the terrace that flowed out into the gardens designed by a master gardener who hailed from England. And who, according to a bronze plaque that boasted the bragging rights, descended from a gardener to *the* royal family.

Only the rich and self-proclaimed fabulous would display the pedigree of the guy who cut the grass and watered the roses. Where Jess lived she was lucky if the guys who wielded the lawn mowers and weed whackers spoke English, much less shared their pedigrees. That information would likely get them deported.

Sergeant Chet Harper met Jess just outside the grand doors. "I don't know how much longer Lieutenant Prescott can keep the girls calm and their mothers compliant. One's already demanded to know if they're suspects."

"Wonderful. Thank you, Sergeant."

Prescott, the girls, and their mothers were seated in the butterfly garden. As soon as Harper had called, Jess had instructed him to see that the girls did not discuss the incident among themselves or with anyone else. Not an easy task. Particularly once the mothers had started to arrive and to demand to see their children. The girls all had cell phones and had called their mothers while the assistant teacher called 911.

Guess who showed up first? Not the police or EMS. Which guaranteed the scene had been contaminated repeatedly by little fingers and feet as well as by curious and horrified mothers.

God, she didn't want to think about it. Whether a murder had occurred or not, the scene should be handled with the same vigilant protocol.

"FYI," Harper added with a knowing glance above his stylish Ray-Bans, "Andrea insisted on calling the chief."

Jess groaned. Andrea Denton, Chief of Police Daniel Burnett's stepdaughter from his last failed marriage and a survivor from the first case Jess had worked on with the Birmingham Police Department scarcely two weeks ago. Funny, this was the third case Jess had supported since returning to her hometown, and Andrea had been a part of all three. The poor girl apparently had a knack for being in the wrong place at the wrong time.

"I suppose he's coming," Jess commented, trying valiantly not to show her disappointment. There was nothing like having the boss watching over her shoulder on her first official case as a deputy chief.

"He is."

Marvelous. "Any luck locating the husband?" Darcy Chandler was married to some famous Russian dancer, now retired and teaching ballet classes to the children of Birmingham's who's who. "What's his name again?"

"Alexander Mayakovsky," Harper reminded her. "Haven't located him yet. His cell still goes straight to voice mail."

"Since this is where he works, he's obviously not at work." Frustration and impatience wrinkled Jess's brow. She consciously forced the lines away. She had enough wrinkles, all of which had taken up residence in all the wrong places on her face. What she didn't have was the vic's husband. The worst part of working an unattended death, whether accidental, suicide, or homicide, was informing the next of kin.

"Go to the vic's parents. Maybe they'll have some idea where he is. Get as much information as you can before you give them the bad news." As coldhearted as that tactic sounded, it was the only way to glean coherent information in a timely manner. And when a person died some way other than from natural causes, he or she deserved a timely investigation. Since the parents hadn't shown up, there was reason to believe unofficial word hadn't reached them yet.

That would change very soon.

"Yes, ma'am."

Harper went on his way and Jess steeled herself for entering foreign territory. "You can do this," she murmured.

As she approached the mothers, their prepubescent daughters clinging to their bosoms, all six women started talking at once.

Jess had interviewed every manner of witness and person of interest, including more than her share of sociopaths and a handful of psychopaths, but somehow she'd never dreaded conducting an interview more than she did at this very moment.

Messages written in blood.
A murder scene straight out of a
Charles Manson playbook. Only one
special agent can get to the bottom of
Birmingham's latest nightmare...

Please turn this page
for a preview of

Rage

Five Points, 7:35 a.m.

Hello Jess.

The appearance of those two words on the screen of her cell phone should not have stolen her breath or weakened her knees, but they managed to do both in the space of a single heartbeat, forcing her to wilt down onto the toilet seat.

Jess Harris shoved a handful of damp hair behind her ear, then hugged her knees to her chest. It wasn't really the words that had her crouched on the toilet seat of the cramped bathroom. It was the identity of the sender.

Tormenter.

Eric Spears . . . the *Player.*

Jess curled her fingers into her sweaty palm to stop their trembling. She pressed her fist to her lips and fought the trepidation howling inside her. *Answer him!* This might be the last time he reached out to her if she didn't do something.

She touched the text box on the screen and prepared to enter a response. Before she tapped a single letter another bubble of words appeared.

I watched you on the news last night. Your ex has impeccable timing. I can't wait to see who wins this round.

Pulse fluttering wildly with an infusion of anger, she considered telling Spears that, as he was no doubt aware, his current location could be tracked via this connection and that she intended to promptly inform the bureau.

But that would be a lie. Worse, he would recognize the lie. Spears knew her far too well.

Using the pad of her thumb she tapped one letter at a time until she'd filled the text box with the message she wanted to send the sociopath who had murdered dozens of women, maybe a hell of a lot more, in his sadistic career as a serial torturer-murderer. Jess smiled as she reread the words she hoped would prompt his need to grow ever closer to her.

One thing's for sure, it won't be you. I'm the one who got away, Spears. Guess that makes you a loser and a coward.

After hitting send, she reveled in the idea that her words would burrow under his skin and fester like boils until he just had to claw at the itch. Eric Spears's malignant narcissistic side wouldn't deal well with failure. Not only did he not like to lose, he hated the idea of being wrong about anything or anyone. He'd made several mistakes of late. Skating so very close to getting caught was one of them. Allowing Jess to live was another.

Whatever it took, she would get him.

Her cell clanged that old-fashioned tone, announcing an incoming call. She jumped. Nearly dropped the damned thing. Spears wouldn't dare...

Harper calling appeared on the screen, banishing the stream of conversation between her and Spears.

"Jess, you are truly pathetic." She swallowed back the lump of undeniable fear that had risen into her throat and forced herself to breathe normally. "Harris."

"We have a homicide, Chief. Shady Creek Drive off Columbiana Road."

Jess dropped her feet to the floor and banished thoughts of Spears. "How many victims, Sergeant?"

"Just one... but..."

The silence that filled the air for several endless seconds had Jess's pulse revving with the surge of adrenaline charging through her veins.

"It's bad, Chief. Really bad. It's the wife of one of our own. Lieutenant Lawrence Grayson's wife, Gabrielle."

Oh damn. "Crimes Against Persons isn't working this one?" No need to start the week off like the last one, in a pissing contest with Deputy Chief Harold Black, bless his ornery heart. Today's staff meeting was supposed to clarify some ground rules and cement the team spirit to ensure better cohesion as they moved forward. That meeting likely wouldn't happen now. Couldn't be helped. Justice was the last thing the dead should have to wait for.

"I got the call since the first officers on the scene felt the murder might be connected to the Lopez situation," Sergeant Chet Harper explained. "The wife was decapitated and there's a message including some of the buzz words from this weekend's hit on your place."

"Jesus Christ." Jess scrubbed at her eyes with her free hand. Images from the destruction that had been her room at the Howard Johnson Inn flickered through her mind. They had to get a handle on this escalating gang situation.

It was turning into a blood bath and resurrecting the ugly memories of the city's violent, racially unjust past.

The MS-13 clique operating in Birmingham, once lorded over by Salvadore Lopez, was at war with a faction that had split off to follow his younger sister, Nina. The sister was currently in custody for kidnapping Jess, among other charges. Salvadore had gone into protective custody with the promise of rolling over on his infamous father, Leonardo. The elder Lopez was the messiah-like leader of the West Coast's rampant and ruthless MS-13 activities. Every three-letter agency in the country wanted him to go down, and now they had their chance.

Squaring her shoulders, Jess began the process of tuning out her personal frustrations with the whole damned Lopez family and the regret for the loss of life—particularly an innocent life—that would only get in the way. "Is Captain Allen on the scene?" Allen headed up Birmingham PD's Gang Task Force. His insights would be invaluable if a gang connection was substantiated.

"En route as we speak."

"I'll be there shortly, Sergeant. You know what to do."

Jess ended the call as she pushed to her feet and headed for the door. She caught her reflection in the mirror over the pedestal sink and paused mid-stride. Her damp hair would just have to dry on its own. She shoved her phone into her robe pocket so she could pile her blond locks into a manageable mass that was annoyingly curly when wet and snapped a claw clip in place. Makeup she could take care of en route. A flick of mascara and a dab of lip gloss would do.

She silently repeated the mantra she'd clung to for the past thirty-six hours or so. *I'll be okay.* It would take more than being kidnapped by some ditzy, power-hungry teenybopper and having her place and her things destroyed to knock Jess off her game.

The tone that accompanied an incoming text had her rummaging for her cell.

I'm deeply wounded, Jess. I thought by now you would miss me as much as I miss you. See you soon.

"The sooner, the better," she grumbled. Jess Harris was not afraid of anything. Except maybe the possibility of failing to get Spears before he added more victims to his heinous résumé.

With renewed purpose she deleted the conversation and emerged from the bathroom to find Lori, on her cell, probably getting the news about the murder. Jess grabbed the one suit that had survived last night's kill-the-deputy-chief's-stuff episode and ripped it free of the dry cleaner's plastic. She'd failed to pick it up from the dry cleaner on Friday, which was the only reason it had been spared from the carnage.

Since her Audi had been at the lab for processing related to her abduction—and still was, damn it—the car and this one suit were about all that remained of the belongings she'd rolled into Birmingham with. Well, except for the dress and the turquoise pumps she'd been wearing last night. The pumps would just have to do until she had time to shop.

"You need a cup of coffee to go?" Lori asked as she headed for the kitchen with her own mug. Her Five Points studio was one big room with a small bath and closet carved out of the already-tight floor space. Any level of privacy was basically impossible.

"That'd be great." Jess stepped into her pumps while

she picked through the bag of undergarments, cosmetics, and necessities she'd purchased at Walmart late last night. Living out of a plastic bag was no fun, and though Lori insisted she was happy to have her as a guest, Jess was anxious to get a place of her own. She liked Lori a lot, and was proud to have the detective on her team, but staying on Lori's couch was going to get old, fast. Maybe it had something to do with being in her forties and set in her ways, but having alone time felt immensely important, especially when she hadn't had any in about forty-eight hours. She needed her space. Along with a new wardrobe and almost everything else a woman required to operate on a day-to-day basis.

Unfortunately, all of that would have to wait.

She had a homicide to get to.

Shady Creek Drive, 8:30 a.m.

"Whoa." Lori surveyed the crowd gathered as she turned off Columbiana Road. "This is going to be complicated and"—she blew out a big breath—"messy."

News vans cluttered the intersection of Columbiana and Shady Creek. Birmingham Police Department cruisers lined the street on either side of where they needed to turn. This tragedy had befallen one of their own and a show of strength was expected. The gesture was heartfelt, but there was no place for crowds at a homicide scene. At least not until after complete scene documentation and thorough evidence collection. The potential for contamination and/or loss was far too great with every warm body that entered a crime scene.

"Do you know Lieutenant Grayson?" His name sounded familiar but Jess couldn't recall meeting him. She'd been introduced to so many of Birmingham's finest since her arrival scarcely three weeks ago that she couldn't say for sure whether she'd met him or not.

"I've seen him around but I don't really know him." Lori powered down her window and showed her badge to the uniform controlling access to the block. When he'd waved her through, she went on, "Grayson is with Field Operations, South Precinct."

Still didn't click for Jess.

"What kind of reputation does he have?" As wrong as it seemed, close family members were always the prime suspects in a case like this until evidence and alibies proved otherwise. Lawrence, aka Larry, Grayson was a cop, so the fundamental steps in a homicide investigation would be no surprise to him.

"A good one as far as I know. I've heard his name a few times when accommodations were handed out." She glanced at Jess. "If you're asking me if he would kill his wife, I don't know him that well, Chief."

"I guess that's something we'll need to learn." They were on duty now. Jess was the deputy chief of SPU, Special Problems Unit, and Lori Wells was one of her detectives. Their ability to be friends and step back from those rolls as needed fascinated Jess. After nearly two decades doing investigative work, this was her first time to have friends, in the true sense of the word, on the job. She'd certainly never been the houseguest of a coworker.

Maybe an old dog could learn a new trick.

The houses along Shady Creek were modest *Brady Bunch*–style ranches and split-levels, circa the seventies;

it was a typical blue-collar neighborhood. Good folks who were forever stuck on the low end of middle class while being overworked and underpaid.

Crime scene tape circled the yard, using trees and shrubs for support and announcing that bad things had happened to those who called this address home. Outside that gruesome yellow line a host of cops had surrounded an emotionally distraught man and were struggling to get him into the passenger seat of a sedan.

"That must be him." He looked vaguely familiar, but Jess still couldn't say for sure if she'd met him.

"Yeah. Damn." Lori shook her head. "Looks like he's lost it."

Jess grimaced at the emotionally charged scene. "Who wouldn't?" She steeled herself in preparation for what was to come. No matter how experienced the investigator, when murder hit this close to home—a fellow cop—it was difficult to take in stride.

"You see any sign of the coroner's wagon?" Between the cruisers and all the other vehicles crowding the street, not to mention what looked like a brigade of cops and no shortage of neighbors, it was difficult to see beyond the driveway.

Lori guided her Mustang as far to one side as possible considering the middle of the street was about all that was left in the way of unoccupied pavement and shut off the engine. "It's the van right behind that Camry riding my bumper."

Jess craned her neck to see. There appeared to be a male passenger but, with the sun glinting on the other side of the windshield, she couldn't see the driver. Opting to jerk to a stop in the middle of the street, whoever was at the wheel of the van didn't seem to care if more of a bottleneck was created.

Jess climbed out of the low-slung Mustang. Instantly the heat crushed around her. The humid air was as thick as molasses. Last night's storm had ensured a sweltering morning and that little or no viable evidence would be found outside the home.

With one more glance behind her, she checked to see if the ME had climbed out of the van yet. She probably wouldn't be lucky enough to get Schrader again. For all she knew Dr. Harlan Schrader could be on his way to the job offer at the Mayo Clinic by now. They'd worked a case together last week and not having to go through that awkward *first time* business again so soon would be nice.

The driver's side door of the van opened and a female emerged. Shoulder-length brown hair, pale complexion. No one Jess had met so far, that she recalled anyway. The woman wore a lavender wrap dress with matching strappy stilettoes. Her sophisticated—scratch that—arrogant body language confirmed they had not met. Jess was one hundred percent certain she would remember that cocky stride, not to mention the haughty tilt of the woman's chin.

"This should be interesting," Lori murmured as she moved up to the front of the Mustang, where Jess waited.

"What's that?" At the scene perimeter, Jess showed her badge to the uniform.

"That's the associate coroner, Dr. Sylvia Baron. She's the lieutenant's ex-wife." Lori ducked under the crime scene tape and Jess followed. "She's a little pushy. No one likes getting stuck on a case with her."

Pushy or not, sounded like a conflict of interest to Jess.

An older man had gotten out on the passenger side of

the van and joined the woman's purposeful movement toward the house as Jess and Lori made their way up the sidewalk. He looked vaguely familiar. Sixty maybe. Tall. Broad-shouldered. Blond and tanned. All he needed was a diamond stud in one ear and he'd have the whole Harrison Ford thing going on.

At the front door she and Lori stopped long enough to drag on shoe covers and gloves. "Who's the man with her?"

"That's Dr. Leeds."

That was Martin Leeds, the Jefferson County chief coroner? Jess really had to find some time to get to know the various chains of command in Birmingham. She was woefully uninformed. In her own defense, she'd held the position for only two weeks and she'd been embroiled in murder and mayhem all fourteen or so of those days. Well, maybe she'd had a small break here and there. The unbidden memory of steamy, stolen hours spent between the sheets with Daniel Burnett the weekend before last had butterflies taking flight in her belly.

Those frantic and breathless minutes in his fancy Mercedes just last night wouldn't exactly be dismissed any time soon either. Particularly since he was her boss.

"I don't want that bitch anywhere near my wife!"

Jess's attention snapped back to the street as Lieutenant Grayson's angrily shouted words reverberated in the impossibly thick air. Those closest to Grayson were trying to calm him, but he was having no part of it.

Jess decided that an introduction to Leeds and the former Mrs. Grayson could wait until they were inside and had surveyed the crime scene. The situation outside was a ticking bomb and it wasn't going to get any calmer until Lieutenant Grayson had been removed from the scene.

The man's wife had been murdered. The ability to think clearly or to reason was long gone.

Inside the house the atmosphere was somber and *cold.* Jess shivered. It was a sweltering dog day in August here in Alabama but she was wishing she had a sweater just now. Her nose twitched. Even the frosty temperature couldn't completely conceal the distinct odor of coagulated blood hanging in the air as if she'd stepped into a meat locker rather than a home where a family lived.

Techs were already on-site documenting the scene and gathering evidence. Jess's first step and top priority was to find the motive, in part based on what she observed here this morning. Had the wife been murdered during the commission of a robbery? Were drugs, money, or both the reason she was dead? There was always a slim chance the killing was a random act of violence. Slim because this was the home of a cop and the neighborhood was not exactly a prime target location for thieves. These weren't rich folks with a treasure trove of readily sellable goods for the taking.

In Jess's experience, when a cop or a cop's family was the target the motive was often vengeance. There was always jealousy, of course, if one or the other had a problem with fidelity. Whatever evidence Jess discovered here, final assessments and conclusions could not be reached until all witnesses or persons with knowledge were found and interviewed. Every hour that passed before all those steps happened lessened the likelihood of success in solving the case.

Harper spotted their arrival and made his way through the main living area and into the foyer. "Chief, the body's this way."

"Detective Wells"—Jess hesitated before following

Harper—"why don't you find the officers whose duty it is to protect the scene and explain how that concept works." She surveyed the number of warm bodies milling around inside the house and shook her head. "I want anyone who's not a witness or who doesn't belong to the Crime Scene Unit or the coroner's office out of here *now*."

"Yes, ma'am."

Lori headed in the opposite direction as Harper led Jess through the kitchen and down a few steps to a large room at the rear of the house. Jess stalled in the entryway of the room and gave herself a few moments to absorb the details of the scene.

There was so much blood.

Words were scrawled in blood around the walls.

Pig. Whore. Kill the bitch. Kill the pigs. One by one.

The chilly air seemed to freeze in Jess's lungs as she stared at the other word written in large, sweeping strokes.

Rage.

She blinked away the images from her motel room that attempted to transpose themselves over those currently burning her retinas. Shaking off the eerie sensation of déjà vu, she visually inventoried the rest of the room.

A massive flat panel television hung over the stacked-stone fireplace. A local morning talk show filled the screen but the sound had been muted. Beefy, well-worn leather sofas stood like sentinels on either side of the fireplace waiting for the family to gather. Windows, blinds tightly closed, spanned the walls. The only natural light breaching the space was from the broken sliding door, its two panels of glass lying in pieces on the tile floor. Beyond the broken door, a wood privacy fence surrounded the backyard and swimming pool.

Jess shivered again. "What's going on with the air-conditioning, Sergeant?"

"The thermostat was adjusted as low as it would go," he explained. "It's about sixty-two degrees in here."

"Seems our killer took the time to think things through before taking his leave." And he or she obviously knew a little something about skewing attempts at determining time of death. Just another reason to hate all those *CSI* shows.

"I believe the murder was carried out right here," Harper said as they moved across the room. "The child, a six-month-old boy, was left in his crib in a bedroom. Nothing in the house, as far as we can tell, was disturbed beyond the damaged patio doors. The standard grab-and-run items like laptops and jewelry are still here."

"Where's the child now?" Jess hoped he wasn't out there amid the chaos on the street. Grayson was in no condition to care for himself, much less a child.

"The lieutenant's partner, Sergeant Jack Riley, called his wife and she took the baby home with her as soon as a paramedic confirmed the child was unharmed."

After fishing for her glasses, Jess shoved them into place and moved closer to study the placement of the body. Dressed in a yellow spaghetti-strapped nightgown, the victim lay supine on the tile floor, a pool of coagulated blood around her, her head severed from her body but left right next to the stump of her neck. Tissue was torn in a jagged manner as if the perp had had a hard time getting started with a sawtooth-type tool. Multiple stab wounds along the torso had dotted the pale yellow gown with ugly rusty spots. Her arms were outstretched at her sides, crucifixion style. Legs were straight and together.

Across the victim's forehead, written in what appeared to be her own blood, were the words *PIG WHORE.*

Jess stepped nearer and eased into a crouch. She pointed to the victim's upper arms. "Looks like our killer had a good grip on her at some point." There was bruising on the chest, just above her breasts. Jess passed a gloved hand over the area. "He held her down while he committed this final atrocity. Judging by the bruise pattern I'd say he was right-handed."

Harper nodded. "I counted ten stabs to her torso. All postmortem, like the beheading. Didn't see any indication she had been sexually assaulted."

"I agree, Sergeant." The coroner's office would check for sexual assault, that was SOP. As for the rest, there wasn't nearly enough blood for the visible damage to have been inflicted while her heart was still beating. No arterial spray from the decapitation. A little castoff from the saw, but that was about it, other than the blood that gravity drained out of the body. In fact, seemed as if the killer waited until livor mortis was well under way before bothering to play psycho surgeon.

Harper pointed to the victim's hands. "No defensive wounds on her hands or forearms to indicate she fought her attacker. No ligature marks to indicate she was restrained."

Very strange. Lividity indicated she had been in this position since her death or very quickly thereafter. But why here and like this? Had the victim been watching television when her attacker crashed into the room? Had she fallen asleep on the sofa? Or did she hear the breaking glass and come to check it out? How had he disabled her?

"Could be damage to the back of the head," Jess suggested. There didn't appear to be any to the temple areas or the forehead.

"I don't see any blood matted in her hair close to the skull." Harper pointed to the long hair fanned around her head.

That was true. Jess rubbed at the wrinkle furrowing her brow with the back of a gloved hand. "Once he'd killed her, what distracted him for so long before he did the rest?" She glanced around the room. Had someone come to the door and interrupted his work? Had the baby started crying and thrown him off balance? The latter wasn't likely, since the baby was still alive.

"Reminds me of the Manson murders," Harper said. "I watched a documentary the other night. The anniversary is coming up this weekend."

Jess had noted that similarity, too, but she wasn't about to say it out loud. Not with so many ears around. All they needed was the media bringing that kind of connection into this. She scrutinized the tile floor around the victim. Not a single footprint. The perp had been exceptionally careful. "No blood anywhere else in the house?"

"Nothing we've found so far. Looks like someone showered recently in the hall bath. The shower floor is damp and so's the rug in front of it. There's a faint smell of shampoo, gardenias."

Surprised, Jess said, "The shampoo should be logged into evidence. We need to be sure the techs check the drain as well. What about a towel?"

Harper grunted a negative sound. "Not in the bathroom or laundry room. If the perp was the one who took the shower, he took the towel with him. Already took care of the rest."

Jess lifted the victim's arm. "We have full rigor. She's been dead nine or ten hours anyway. Maybe longer."

The manner of the decapitation was primitive. As if the perpetrator hadn't been able to get the job done on his first attempt, he'd started over a couple of times, mutilating tissue and making one heck of a mess. "No murder or mutilation weapon lying around?"

"No, ma'am. Whatever the perp used, he took that with him as well."

With no weapon and no ready signs the perp had been careless, the odds of nailing him were stacked against them. "Who discovered the body?"

"Johnny Trenton," Harper said. "The pool guy."

Jess made a face. "They have a pool guy?" She'd noticed the pool out back, but this wasn't exactly the kind of neighborhood where one expected to encounter a cabana boy.

"He arrived at six this morning, as scheduled, to clean the pool. He has a key to the garage and the door that leads out of the garage into the backyard." Harper gestured to the patio and sparkling pool beyond the broken sliding door. "He made the nine-one-one call. Says he didn't come inside for fear of stepping in the blood or otherwise damaging the scene. Since it was obvious Mrs. Grayson was dead, he figured there was nothing he could do anyway."

"He didn't come in the house to check on the child or the husband?" If he knew the family, he had to know there was a kid and a husband.

"He says the place was as quiet as a tomb when he arrived, so he assumed anyone else in the house was dead, too."

More likely he hadn't wanted to risk suspicion by entering the scene and leaving behind a footprint or fingerprint. "Where is this pool guy?"

"In the dining room. I didn't see any blood on him and his hair definitely doesn't smell like gardenias."

"Well, that certainly rules him out," Jess mused.

Harper cast a somber look at the victim and shook his head. "I don't think he did this, Chief. This involved some serious rage and a good chunk of time. Trenton doesn't seem like the type to invest that much emotion, if you know what I mean."

"Have him transported downtown. I'd like to question him in a more formal setting." Being driven downtown in the back of a police cruiser should have him eager to cooperate if he knew anything at all. And Jess did understand what Harper meant. Like a crop of choking crabgrass the I-don't-care-about-my-neighbors attitude had taken root among Southern folks, too. No one wanted to get involved anymore.

She pushed to her feet and walked to the now useless slider and stared across the yard. The lawn was thick and lush. No sign of mud, which meant no footprints out here either. Only the tops of neighboring homes were visible above the fence but one, at the farthest end of the yard, was a two-story like the Grayson home. A pair of side-by-side windows overlooked the Grayson's backyard.

"Have the neighbors been canvassed?" Jess strained to see any movement beyond the windows across the way. Anyone looking out those windows at just the right time would have had a clear view of the murder.

"Yes, ma'am." Harper pointed to the house with the windows that had captured Jess's attention. "We checked that one first. Looks abandoned. Yard's all grown up. The utility meter has been pulled. No answer and no vehicle in the drive."

"Damn." She turned her attention back to the victim, Gabrielle Grayson. Dark hair and olive skin. Thirty or thirty-two. "Latino?" she asked Harper.

"Mrs. Grayson was born in this country but her parents moved here from Spain. Lieutenant Grayson's partner told me she was a nurse until her son was born and she opted to become a full-time mother."

"We need to know if she has any connections whatsoever to the gang world." This was the fifth decapitation Jess had encountered in the last week. The other four ritual killings had been carried out by members of the MS-13 against those they deemed traitors. The major difference was those decapitations had been accomplished while the victims were still alive. This one looked wrong. The words scrawled on the walls were unfocused. The whole scene, including the possibility the perp had showered, was way off when compared to an MS-13 assassination scene.

"There's no connection that we know of, ma'am."

Another of those aggravating frowns tugged across her brow. "Where is Captain Allen? I thought he was en route."

Harper looked away and cleared his throat. "He... ah...dropped by. Took a quick look and said he'd let us know if he heard any rumblings about this. He knows Grayson. Said the lieutenant and his partner have been helping out with GTF but neither has been involved on a level that would ignite something like this. He doesn't think there's a connection."

"He couldn't hang around until I arrived?" Jess understood the guy had it in for her since she'd barged her way into the Lopez case and stolen the big takedown Allen had had planned, but this was a homicide for Christ's sake. A cop's wife.

Jess took a breath, brought her voice down an octave or two. "Stay on Allen, Sergeant, and find out from Grayson's division chief if he's worked a case, past or present, within the division that may have landed him on someone's hate list."

"Yes, ma'am."

Jess was as sure as anyone could be that this murder didn't have anything to do with the MS-13. It was way too neat and there were too many discrepancies. But she couldn't rule out that possibility just yet any more than Allen could. "We also need cause of death ASAP," she said, more to herself than to the detective next to her. "The media will have a field day with this. We need something to give them before they start making up stuff."

In the past forty-eight hours a Lopez hangout had been blown up and three clashes in the streets of downtown Birmingham had barely been defused without bloodshed. A couple of fires had been started in abandoned houses. No matter that the Lopez clique was falling apart all on its own, there were some in the community who were looking for an excuse to take matters into their own hands. The murder of a cop's wife—the mother of a small child—would fuel that fire into a raging inferno.

"There was another clash in Druid Hills just before daylight," Harper mentioned. "Another house burned after being hit by Molotov cocktails, but no one was injured."

Damn. Druid Hills was the neighborhood where this war had started. Jess had lived there for a while as a kid. Not much had changed in all this time. Harper's news just confirmed what she already knew. They needed damage control on this one. "What the devil is taking Leeds and his colleague so long?"

She hated waiting. Worse, Jess's attention settled on the victim; she hated for this woman to lie here like this any longer than necessary. She hoped Grayson and his ex hadn't gotten into a war outside.

"I'll check on that," Harper offered.

"Do that, Sergeant, and make sure—"

"If you'll get out of the way," a haughty female voice announced, "we'll try to make up the time we lost due to BPD's incompetence at securing the scene and preventing the flash mob outside."

Jess turned and came face-to-face with the tall brunette in the lavender dress who appeared determined to live up to her reputation of being pushy. *Sylvia Baron.*

"Somebody adjust that damned thermostat," she shouted at no one in particular. "Are we trying to turn this vic into a Popsicle or what?"

"I'll take care of that," Harper said as he made himself scarce.

Jess thrust out her hand. "I'm Deputy Chief Harris. I'll be investigating this case."

"Dr. Sylvia Baron, associate coroner and medical examiner. This is Dr. Martin Leeds, Jefferson County's chief coroner. As I said, if you will get out of the way, we'll attend to our responsibility in this matter."

As true as it was that the coroner had jurisdiction over the body, Jess was king of the hill when it came to the scene. "Dr. Baron, I'm certain this is an awkward and perhaps difficult time for you. Be that as it may, considering your ties to the victim's husband, I have strong reservations about your ability to maintain objectivity under the circumstances. Your being here obviously represents a conflict of interest."

Baron didn't look surprised that Jess had already heard about who she was. In fact, the ME laughed. "Like I care about your reservations. Now step aside or I'll call Chief Burnett and have you removed from this case."

A bad, bad feeling struck Jess. Was this woman another of Burnett's fancy private-school cronies? Or maybe Sylvia Baron was a former lover or another ex-wife? The man had at least two exes Jess hadn't met. Either way, she wasn't running this investigation. Jess was.

Big breath. Stay calm. She stepped around the body and moved closer to Baron. "I think that's a very good idea. Calling Chief Burnett, I mean." Jess kept her smile in place as she reached into her bag and retrieved her phone, then offered it to the other woman. "Why don't you use my phone? Burnett's at the top of my contact list."

The woman matched Jess's fake smile with one of her own. "No need." She whipped out her iPhone and made the call with scarcely more than a swipe and a tap. "He's at the top of mine as well."

THE DISH

Where authors give you the inside scoop!

♥ ♥ ♥ ♥ ♥ ♥ ♥ ♥ ♥ ♥ ♥ ♥ ♥ ♥ ♥

From the desk of Hope Ramsay

Dear Reader,

I have three brothers and no sisters. So when I was young, I read a lot of "boy" books—mostly having to do with space travel. When I reached the ripe age of thirteen, my aunt decided I needed to have my horizons broadened. She put three "girly" books in my hand: *Pride and Prejudice*, *Jane Eyre*, and *Little Women*. Need I say more?

I was hooked the moment I read the immortal line: "It is a truth universally acknowledged, that a single man in possession of a good fortune must be in want of a wife."

Holy moly, I had no idea what I was missing!

So it's not surprising that I turned to these favorite books when I decided to write a series featuring members of the Last Chance Book Club.

In the first book in this series, LAST CHANCE BOOK CLUB, the ladies of the club decide to read *Pride and Prejudice*. And before long some of them are finding some interesting similarities between the book and their lives.

In the beginning of my story, the hero and heroine dislike each other intensely. Like Darcy, Savannah White has come to Last Chance from the big city. She's there to renovate the old run-down theater. Dash Randall, like Lizzy Bennett, isn't at all pleased with this new arrival in town. Dash thinks Savannah is a stuck-up snob. And she thinks he's a no-account good ol' boy. My hero is the one with the snarky sense of humor, and my heroine the one with the preconceived notions that will have to soften. Even though my plot and setting are wildly different from Austen's, the underlying theme of pride and prejudice is what makes the love story of Dash and Savannah so much fun. I've also included a few other Austen-inspired complications, like a minister who is looking for a wife, a whole passel of matchmaking matrons, and a street dance that's surprisingly like the Netherfield Ball.

I had such a fun time writing this story. It allowed me to connect in a much deeper way with one of my old favorites. I'm sure Jane Austen fans will enjoy searching for the Easter eggs I've sprinkled through the book. But even if you aren't an Austen fan, you're still going to love this story about a couple who discover the hidden depths of character in each other as they grow from enemies to friends to lovers.

Hope Ramsay

♥ ♥ ♥ ♥ ♥ ♥

From the desk of Debra Webb

Dear Reader,

I am so thrilled to be sharing the Faces of Evil adventure with you! This series has lived for several years in my heart. I can't tell you how pleased I am to be working with the fabulous folks at Forever to bring these stories to you.

I grew up in Alabama with deep roots in Birmingham. While my husband served in the army, we traveled far and wide, but Alabama was still home and we were most happy to return. Many years would pass before I realized that Alabama was not only home for me but also a place with a rich past and a vibrant present perfect for the setting of suspense stories. I zeroed in on Birmingham, where much of Alabama's most volatile and notorious history has taken place. Being no stranger to the city, it was easy to settle in and have my characters experiencing all sorts of dilemmas in the Magic City.

Birmingham also holds a special place in my heart for its renowned Children's Hospital and incredible doctors. When my first child was born she was in serious trouble and in need of immediate surgery—a surgery that was her only hope for survival and at the same time a procedure she was unlikely to survive. The quick thinking of my small-town doctor, Dr. Louis Letson, got her straightaway to Birmingham in the hands of a revered pediatric surgeon. Dr. Letson's decisive action and the unparalleled skill of the folks at Birmingham's Children's Hospital saved my daughter's life. Eight weeks later the tiny girl who changed our lives proved to one and all that she had come into this world to live. And thirty-six years later she is still living life with immense passion. As you can see, Birmingham really is the Magic City!

Please watch for all twelve installments of the Faces of Evil series featuring Jess Harris and Dan Burnett and their journey through a maze of evils to find the love and happiness they both deserve.

Best,

Debra Webb